Skinned Alive

Skinned Alive

STORIES

Edmund White

Alfred A. Knopf
NEW YORK 1995

THIS IS A BORZOI BOOK
PUBLISHED BY ALFRED A. KNOPF, INC.

Some of the stories in this work were originally published in the following: "Running on Empty," "An Oracle," and "Palace Days" in *A Darker Proof*; "Reprise" in *Grand Street*; and "Skinned Alive" in *Granta*.

Library of Congress Cataloging-in-Publication Data

White, Edmund, [*date*]
    Skinned alive : stories / Edmund White.—1st ed.
        p.   cm.
    ISBN 0-679-43476-3
    I. Title.
PS3573.H463S58   1995
813'.54—dc20   95-2665
                                                        CIP

Manufactured in the United States of America
First American Edition

To my sister

Contents

Skinned Alive

Pyrography

Howard slid in beside Otis in Otis's old Lincoln four-door, and then they went to pick up Danny where he lived with his mother, not the best part of town. The morning was still cool but Howard knew the full heat of mid-August in Chicago wasn't far behind, like pain as soon as the anesthetic wears off. It was just six in the morning.

Before they got on the highway heading north they bought coffee and jelly-filled sugar donuts called Bismarcks. They rode with all four windows down and the radio blaring, but despite the noise they couldn't stop talking.

The way they were seated—Howard riding up front with Otis, and Danny in the rear—said it all. Otis and Howard were best friends, which dated way back, all the way back to eighth grade. Danny was just one of Otis's new friends.

Otis had brought along a carton of Parliaments, which he said was for all of them. He had a good summer job and was eager to spend some of the money he'd earned. Howard liked the taste of these cigarettes and the feel of the slightly recessed filter when he explored it with his tongue. Danny made a face and said, "Eeyou, it's like smoking something through Kotex." Otis's eyes went dead and a little laugh forced its way out of him.

Howard was worried by how handsome Danny was. Howard was afraid he'd start staring, lose the thread of the conversation, leave his tongue hanging out. Danny was lean and muscly with very black eyebrows, brown oily hair sun-bleached on top, suntanned skin glinting with gold hairs, and he had wonderfully white teeth and one gold tooth, far back in his mouth, not a whole tooth, just a gold crown glimpsed as a bar of brilliance between two sharp white teeth. He was good in all sports but a champion swimmer though he didn't get along with his teammates, they gave him a pain in the ass, he said. Otis had warned Howard that Danny didn't know how to control his moods and could become fighting mad over an imagined slight, yet he was a basically good guy. Howard liked Danny's eyebrows which almost met in the center and the intelligence—or was it wariness?—in his pale brown eyes flecked unevenly with gold, anyway not the sort of intelligence Howard understood or could easily play up to. Danny's eyes looked like old costume jewelry in which the gold backing is flaking off. Even when Howard looked straight ahead he could feel Danny seated behind him; not a restlessness but a pent-up energy like that of the crouched swimmer on the edge of the pool.

After they got out into the country they didn't talk so much, they just looked at the fences and barns and fields of corn soon to be harvested. They smoked their Parliaments and Howard touched the notched mouthpiece with his tongue, then licked one finger clean of raspberry jelly that had been inside his Bismarck. Every time Howard looked back at Danny, Danny smiled, which Howard was grateful for but puzzled by, since he didn't think he merited it. After all Howard wasn't really popular and not at all athletic, he was just Otis's best friend.

Danny's smile dazzled Howard. Was Danny eager to show right off the bat he was a terrifically friendly, open guy in order to dispel any rumors about his bad temper? After all, they were going to be spending the next ten days together in a canoe. Or was he just flashing that smile as an old angry dog automatically bares its teeth while concentrating on something else entirely, something hateful? Or here, in this car, did he think his athletic prowess counted for nothing and it was just as though he were starting out all over again in a new school, this was his first day, and he had to win new people over from scratch?

The radio blared and they patted the hot metal sides of the car in time to the music. For Howard, who'd lived in a strict boarding school for the last few years, riding in a car with two other fellows felt great, real free and independent. He knew Otis was used to tooling around in his car wherever and whenever he wanted and had probably even made out with dozens of girls on this very seat. He was the golden boy of his whole glamorous North Shore teen world, a world of picking up girls anywhere along the endless miles and miles of white beach beside Lake Michigan, of sharing a beer with some wild girl whose loud laugh was designed to attract a boy's attention, a girl who despite her laugh and vulgar way of chewing gum would turn out to live in a twenty-room mansion half-hidden from the street by old trees, the front door opened by a uniformed maid. On his vacations back in Evanston, Howard would catch glimpses of these kids, some with expensive sports cars, all of them with tennis-trained bodies, the same faded Bermuda shorts, penny loafers and no socks, the boys with dull, flat intonations, the girls with voices overflowing with worked-up excitement and forced hilarity.

Once the parents of some girl in Lake Forest had gone away and she had thrown a huge beer blast. It was a sultry August night and the dark lane outside her low-gabled fieldstone house was brilliant with gathering car lights and the night quaked with boys' loud voices and girls' shrieking laughter. There was even a threat of a rumble but nothing came of it. Howard was a bit in shock that all these kids knew each other, that they'd grown older and now had wheels and could buy kegs and they'd each had sex with three or four lovers or so Otis said. Boys in boarding school were complete innocents next to these womanizing, brawling Evanston guys. He and Otis stood outside in the dark. Howard looked in through the polished windows at all those boys and girls laughing or necking and felt he'd died and was looking down at the lights from the dark hilltop cemetery.

Howard had tried for years to be popular in Evanston, but his only achievement had been winning over Otis. Now Otis's popularity in Evanston was of no use to Howard, since Howard was no longer running in this particular race. What was left, however, was something that would endure forever, their marvelous friendship, which felt as old and tested as a good marriage.

It was a sacred thing, all the more so because it was so peculiar. Who would ever have guessed that Howard, a sissy, a brain, anything but a jock, someone other guys whispered acted like a pansy, would become best friends with someone so well liked that if he wasn't class president it was only because the Crowd thought public office was just for nerds? Otis's father was a locally famous judge and even he was too refined, come to think of it, to pass for a regular guy. Otis's parents had Welsh corgis, the small, bulky, short-legged dogs beloved by the Queen of England. The parents had commissioned oil portraits of their four children, which hung in the stairwell. Howard felt he could have advised the artist on how better to portray Otis's mouth and eyes, since he, Howard, had spent so many sleepless nights studying him. Otis had asked Howard to spend the night over once—oh, years back—and in the morning, reassured that Howard hadn't made a lunge for him, said, "Well, that went without a hitch. I don't see why you can't stay over whenever you want." It was the only time Otis ever said anything about all that; Otis seemed pleased that he'd been confirmed in his hunch that nothing weird would happen. Howard was shocked that Otis had set up that first night as a test. Howard thought friendship should not be submitted to tests. Also Howard hadn't quite believed until now that he had anything quite so solid as a reputation for being a fruit, the way bad girls have reputations for being sluts.

And yet Howard had taken Otis up on the invitation as often as possible, dozens of times over the years. Howard had gone on to have real sex with a few guys, including one guy at boarding school who was a lot cuter than even Otis.

But nothing could replace their love or friendship or whatever you wanted to call it. They liked to bullshit for hours about life and love and God and folk music. Sometimes Howard suspected Otis felt a little sorry for him because he, Howard, was screwed up sexually and probably would never get married or have kids or anything. Sometimes Howard thought Otis considered him a proof of how liberal he was, sort of like he was dating a Negro girl or something. But that didn't bother Howard. In a world where most people believed fruits were either sick sex fiends who should be deballed or pathetic clowns like Liberace, it was terrific someone as popular as Otis believed they should be pitied or tolerated.

But all that came up if at all only when other people were around. Otis and Howard spent most of their time—hours and hours—alone. If they had only one cigarette left they'd pass it back and forth in the dark from one twin bed to the other and talk and talk so late that getting up just three or four hours later on a winter morning when it was still dark and glitteringly cold outside seemed to run perversely against the life rhythms in their bodies. It was like an act of contrition or of spiritual devotion. But two or three nights later they'd be back at it, lying in T-shirts and underpants, sipping beer or pop and talking about ideas or friends or the future or hypothetical, farcical possibilities or just the dumb details of everyday life like how to get a term paper typed by next Monday. Usually Howard typed it, even wrote it, for Otis.

Howard was something of a seducer in the sense that he was in love and Otis wasn't. Howard wanted to become more and more intimate, that was an actual goal, whereas Otis probably didn't plan out their friendship at all. It was just like the air he breathed. But if they did get close he probably thought it was something that had just happened and he was probably pleased. They really did love each other. Otis was very strong and manly but when Howard would be heading back to his boarding school Otis would go down to the train station and shake his hand hard and look deep into his eyes. Silence gathered around them.

Otis wasn't good at school, in fact he was a terrible fuck-up, but he was good at everything else—playing tennis, talking to women, driving a car. He had a common touch and could work among working men on a summer job without riling them. But like a prince who passes time with wastrels and roisterers before being called to battle or the throne, he never forgot who he was going to be. His adolescence wasn't a preparation for later life but a vacation from it.

"How fast can this buggy go?" Danny asked, interrupting Howard's reverie.

"It can push one hundred and ten," Otis said.

"Oh, sure," Danny said skeptically.

Otis said nothing but eased the pedal to the floor. Soon the Burma Shave signs that spelled out humorous riddles clicked past too rapidly to be read. They overtook a farmer putt-putting along in an ancient Chevy pickup and Otis was forced to pass him even though he couldn't see around the curve. An oncoming car was suddenly on top of them and Otis slipped in front of the pickup just in time. Howard looked back: Danny's smile was radiant, his hands relaxed, tan, sinewy on the back of the seat.

They ate burgers at a greasy spoon and in the afternoon Howard took the back seat because he said he wanted to stretch out and catch some z's. In fact he was exhausted from feeling Danny's energy cooking just behind him. Howard also wanted to hear how regular guys talked to each other when alone. When Howard was with Otis he laughed at all of Otis's jokes, never interrupted, never supplied a word, nodded vigorously at every tentative assertion and elaborated with lavish resources of fantasy Otis's vaguest speculations.

[handwritten marginal note: We've all been here]

With Danny Otis was a lot more competitive. After all, Otis had lived in Evanston all his life and was the head of the Crowd, whereas Danny's mother had moved from Oak Park just two years ago. Otis had a position to protect—although that was probably just Howard's twisted way of looking at things. In fact Otis always said he didn't give a flying fuck about the Crowd and knew that high school wasn't exactly the alpha and omega of human achievement for Christ's sake.

But what frustrated Danny (or so Otis said) was that he was a champion swimmer and a grind who got straight A's in math and science and he'd burrowed into an exclusive relationship with a serious white-lipped girl he bullied and planned to marry—and yet no one much liked him, whereas Otis, this big fuck-up, awakened smiles wherever he went.

And yet there was nothing competitive about their conversation now as Howard, pretending to be asleep, eavesdropped. Danny and Otis let long comfortable silences fill up the spaces between them. Danny whistled softly along with the radio, not with puckered lips as girls do but rather in that tough-guy way of folding the lower lip back over the bottom teeth in order to create a sort of harmonica. They joked about something they saw along the highway ("Oh, terrific, that will come in real handy") but Howard couldn't figure out what it was. Howard felt that if he slept with his head on Danny's lap it would smell like piss and semen and wouldn't be very comfortable since Danny was so lean and muscly. He wasn't at all jealous of Danny and Otis's comfortable, palsy way of sitting together because he knew it didn't mean much to either of them. They'd never remember this calm, not even an hour later, because it was unattached to their self-discovery or ambitions. Howard had learned, exactly as though he were the big-sister not-too-swift-looking kind of girl, how to listen to guys and encourage them in their dopey, tentative way of talking about their future and inner feelings.

They crossed Wisconsin. Sometimes it seemed the only stores were beer takeouts and roadside bars, built like log cabins and dark and dank inside even by day. They ate thick beer pretzels while downing a couple of "brewskies," as girls called beer. No one asked to see their ID. They chewed on spicy thin bar sausages, each individually wrapped in cellophane.

"Hey, Otis, 'bout the size of your wiener, huh?" Danny said in a loud voice, laughing, holding up the skinny sausage. When Otis put his hands in his pockets, whistled and raised his eyes to the ceiling in mock exasperation, or as though to say, "Hey, who is this guy, could you get him off my back?" Danny laughed even louder. Howard had never seen Otis's dick except as a soft shape in the pocket of his underpants; he wondered if he'd see it on the canoe trip. Would they all go skinny-dipping? Howard guessed Otis's dick was small and Danny's was big.

Back in the car Danny took the wheel and Otis slid in the back seat. Howard studied Otis as he strummed his guitar. He had a small nose, straight dirty blond hair and a cowlick, perfect skin and eyelashes so pale they were visible only in this cross light. When he laughed—or concentrated, as he was doing now—a single line creased his forehead. His eyes were the blue of old lapis overexposed to the sun and his teeth slightly yellowed by some sulfa drug he'd been given as a kid. His body was nearly hairless except for a pale brown line just below his kneecap on the inner, upper side of his calf, as though the artist had wet his thumb and smudged the line there. His most distinctive mannerism was his laugh. He'd hold a sort of frozen smile while his eyes stayed enigmatic, and after a strange delay a tenor laugh, stabbing away at the same note, would come rattling out of him in volleys, a bit like the accelerating rhythm of a sewing machine before it stops to start a new seam.

Now he was wrapped around his guitar, one hand fretting, the other strumming, the top of his head with the shiny hair and the cowlick all that was visible, as though he were looking into the hole under the strings, as though the guitar were a woman's body he was looking into.

That night they ate in a diner and then got drunk at a roadside bar. Otis and Danny talked to the other men at the bar. Their voices became loud and their faces red. Howard didn't want to say anything or even move because he was afraid these men would catch on that he was a sissy and make Otis and Danny feel ashamed that they were traveling with him. Howard longed to be alone with his two friends. Only when they were all alone did Howard's brand of . . . *charm* take effect.

They slept in the country in their sleeping bags beside the car just off a dirt road. In the dark they talked about the possibility of a nuclear holocaust. Otis was willing to consider the option of living under Soviet rule. "I'd rather be Red than dead," he said. The next morning they didn't shave or bathe and they agreed they'd all grow their beards during the canoe trip.

They drove up through Minnesota and late in the afternoon reached the edge of the Quetico lake country, an immense park of lakes and waterways and islands that extended across the border up into Canada. Otis had done all this before and at the outfitter's, a good-sized store right next to the lake, he rented a canoe, a motor and a can of gas, a tent, backpacks, fishing rods, supplies. They paddled for about an hour, then felt lazy and motored deeper into the stillness.

"What's that weird cry?" Danny asked. He was at the back of the boat, next to the outboard.

"A loon," Otis said. "A bird. You'll see them—and hear them—everywhere. They have black heads and a silky black band around their black-and-white-striped necks."

The sound was heartbreaking, a nearly human cry—and utterly inhuman. Howard remembered his hours alone playing in the woods when he was a boy; back then he was what Mr. Redfern, the human sciences master, had called an "animist." He saw a spirit in every tree, worshiped a local deity at every clearing, ascribed human associations even to flowers—the four pure white petals of the bunchberry flower, worthy of a diplomatic sash, each petal mitered like a bishop's hat, the four composing a cross of Malta around the stigmas and anthers clustered at the center like tiny diamonds mounted at varying heights on slender stems.

But now the natural world no longer signified, or did so only intermittently. As they drifted in their canoe into a new lake, for a moment he could see the black trunk of a fire-scarred red pine as a demon's beard carbonized with heat, but a moment later he lapsed into seeing it as an unconscious plant decomposing faster than usual.

As the evening gradually intensified, Howard didn't know if he was sad because the pines and their reflections were black as a backbone in an X ray and the big, rounded cloud above and its rippled double below as pink and luminous as a pair of lungs, one damaged—or was he sad because they weren't human at all, just light, atmosphere and an accelerating loss of heat? Nature was either a cathedral, the walls of quartz and feldspar, the columns soaring jack pines and paper birches, the altar one of those massive stones shoved by a glacier into an improbable place and called an "erratic" by geologists—or it was empty, desolate, even nauseatingly empty.

They put up their tent at the top of a hill softly carpeted with moss and lichens, so that if it rained the water wouldn't collect under their sleeping bags. Howard liked the musty or was it moldy smell of the canvas—a smell of armies and attics, of World War II uniforms stored away under the eaves. Whereas Otis and Howard were lethargic and had to sit and think a moment before moving, Danny was always crackling with energy; you could almost hear the electricity singing in his body. Danny gathered wood and had soon constructed a tidy little fire. They drank the cold, clear water directly from the lake; it was so cold it hurt Howard's teeth. Once the sun went down a chill rose up out of the very earth. They gathered close to the fire and ate powdered mashed potatoes and the walleye Danny had caught and cleaned. After dinner they went one after another into the woods to piss; Danny called back that he was being embraced by a horny she-bear.

The lake lapped at itself like a sleeping dog. When Howard looked up at the stars—he'd never seen so many—he thought of them as the jewels powering God's Bulova watch. There was a sudden quaking of light at the horizon that Otis called "the Northern Lights." An owl, far away, hooted. Sometimes the water would be slapped by fin or paw—Howard preferred not to guess which. The fire died down and Danny banked it, hoping the coals would last till morning.

They slipped out of their blue jeans in the dark and into their sleeping bags. Howard was in the middle, between Otis and Danny, who lay closest to the tent flaps. A single mosquito did diploma-level flying lessons around Howard's ear.

"Hey, guys," Otis said, "it looks like I'm going to let a fart."

"Oh, gross," Danny said. Howard groaned too. He sniffed for the odor but caught no whiff of it.

"You know, guys," Otis went on, "did you notice there weren't any blueberries this year?"

"So what?" Danny asked. "Anyway, I've seen plenty."

Howard liked the vibrant hum of their voices, Otis's higher in his left ear and Danny's lower and hoarser in his right.

"There are no berries. That means the bears are hungry and aren't above eating a white boy or two, especially those closest to the tent flaps."

"Shi-i-it . . ." Danny exhaled, "you sure like to make your pals feel good. Frankly I think a bear would prefer a nice soft North Shore tennis player to a stringy old swimmer like me."

The silence condensed like fog on the darkening glass of Howard's mind. He turned on his right side toward Danny and imagined he glimpsed a glint of his gold tooth—was he smiling?

The next morning a heavy mist dematerialized the other side of the lake, fudging the line between water and the horizon of black spruce. That farther shoreline was already invaded by light—the lower, paler band of fog, the little, violet line of trees painting the upper, shell-pink sky with thousands of dark fingers. The foreground was still dark blue, almost black, the pine sapling near them silhouetted against the illuminated mist.

After a breakfast of pancakes, the batter made from lake water added to a mix, they packed up while smoking a Parliament. Danny decided not to smoke anymore—he needed his lung power for swimming—and he razzed them for smoking women's Kotex cigarettes. That remark, added to last night's gibe about a soft tennis player's body, must have rubbed Otis the wrong way because soon he was griping about Danny's littering.

"Look, guys," he said, "I don't want to sound like a fucking Eagle Scout, but you've gotta bury your litter at least a foot

deep and rake your fire out and drown it with some lake water."
Little smile. "Remember Smokey the Bear."

"Yeah, right," Danny said. "And what about your fuckin'
Parliament filters? Those fuckin' babies are indestructible,
they're eternal."

"Can it," Otis said. Danny did shut up, but Howard doubted
he'd really canned it.

The sun rose and the day turned hot. They took off their
rain slickers, their sweaters, finally their shirts. Otis taught
Howard how to paddle, to reach far forward, to dig a deep
stroke and push through with it, to turn the blade sideways
at the end and lift it just high enough not to skim the surface
of the water. Howard kept slapping the water on the upstroke
or plowing off to one side instead of straight down and each
time Otis shook his head, fatherly and defeated.

"Let up on him, for crying out loud," Danny said, irritated.
"He's doing fine." Howard felt like a kid fought over by his
parents.

In the midday heat they breasted their way through a shallow
lake of reeds. They could touch bottom with their paddles.
The reeds dragged against the bottom of the boat and in their
wake sprang back in place.

Howard paddled in the bow and Danny in the stern, guiding
them, while Otis hunched over his guitar. He was composing
a song, words and music, about their trip: "We're pulling up
the river, boys, / just as far as we can go. . . ." He'd piece
together two or three notes with the appropriate chords, then
play them quickly together to get the effect, strangely synco-
pated by the reeds dragging across the hull, brushes on drums
and cymbals, and by the tragic laugh of a loon, the one drunk
in the audience.

At last they were out of the marshlands and into open water
again. The lake hung before them tremblingly like tears that
won't fall. Otis pointed out moose tracks—two deep toe marks

separated by a delicate ridge—trotting across the sandy beach beside them.

A sudden shot rang out above their heads. Otis and Howard looked back to see Danny, grinning broadly, with a smoking pistol in his hand. Otis lunged toward him, they wrestled, the boat rocked wildly and Howard, still in front, couldn't see past Otis's back to figure out what he was doing. "What the *hell*, what the *hell*," Otis was shouting.

"Let-go-fucker, you hear me, I said, let-go-*now*," Danny was saying in a steady, hate-filled voice.

Finally Otis gave up. He returned to his seat and took up his guitar. Danny was still smiling, though his eyes looked small and startled. He lowered the motor in place and started it on the second try. The canoe headed out until they were alongside the dead loon, floating in the water, a crimson-and-black hole blasted out of its body.

That night Danny plucked and cleaned his bird and skewered it with a stick and roasted it over the fire. No one said anything. Otis refused to touch it and rustled up some bacon and powdered scrambled eggs for Howard and himself. When Danny poked the plate of cooked and cut-up loon toward them, Howard refused it with a smile, rolling his eyes to indicate Otis, who'd turned his back on them. Danny's jaw muscle kept working with exasperation. He tried to eat it but couldn't. Was it too tough? It stunk of oil, a fishy oil. All of a sudden he jumped up and went off into the woods and a few minutes later they could hear gunshots ringing out. Howard figured he was shooting at squirrels in the last dying light.

"If I'd known he was carrying a gun, I'd never have let him come along," Otis said. Suddenly he hit the ground with his fist. "Damn! My instincts told me not to let that yo-yo loose on the wilderness. You know shooting a loon is strictly against the law. For the Canadians shooting a loon would be like shooting a bald eagle in America."

Otis and Howard smoked their Parliaments. Howard liked the dry, strangulated taste of the heavily filtered smoke, as though this neat white cylinder and its mild emissions were the necessary link to civilization. But they were careful to push the butts with their long filters deep into the sand beside the untroubled lake in which reflected stars were taking shape like obsessions in a gloomy mind. Otis played the two lines of the song he'd pieced together today, then sang through a blues song about a New Orleans bordello, "The House of the Rising Sun." Danny had come back but was sitting by himself on a log, cleaning his pistol. Finally Otis got up and walked over to Danny and held out his hand, which Danny shook. "Sorry if I got too bossy today," Otis said. "You took me by surprise with shots suddenly whizzing over my head." Danny didn't say anything but smiled.

"Shall we turn in and catch some z's?" Howard asked, hoping to break the tension. Otis's strange little mirthless laugh came rattling out of him on its single tinny note, the sound of coins falling into a piggy bank.

They talked about their beards. Danny's beard was coming in thick in proper gold, whereas Otis's was just a smudge of mustache and goatee and then a beardless jaw and a wisp of fuzz along his neck. Howard couldn't see his own beard but Danny, standing just a foot away from him now and studying his face by the dying firelight, said he thought it was coming in brown and ginger with an empty whorl just to the left of his mouth.

Danny said his underpants were getting grungy. He turned his back to them and slipped out of them, then put his jeans back on over his bare ass and washed out his Jockey shorts in the lake with a bar of soap and hung them to dry on a bough of balsam fir. Howard caught a glimpse of Danny's very narrow hips, as brown as his torso, and he realized he must have lain in the sun entirely naked, but where? "Those underpants are

Bear there too!

going to attract some horny she-bear," Howard said, tactfully alluding to a creature Danny had already invented.

"Do you really think there are bears in these woods?" Danny asked.

"Sho' nuff—black bear. There is plenty black bear," Otis said with a hint of hillbilly twang. Suddenly for no reason they all three started rocking with laughter.

When they went into the tent, took off their jeans and slipped into the sleeping bags, Howard was almost unbearably excited by the idea Danny was naked from the waist down inside his sack. Otis tried to scare them by saying he heard a hungry bear crashing through the underbrush but soon he was asleep, his breath rasping softly like an emery board drawn back and forth across a fingernail. Howard turned on his right side toward Danny at the same moment Danny turned toward him and they were looking wide-eyed at each other in the dark.

"Do you hear that dog barking?" Howard whispered. "Where did he come from?"

Danny replied in his low rasping voice, "Otis said a ranger lives on this lake in his cabin—it must be his dog."

"Oh," Howard said. He wanted to reach out and touch Danny's arm, which he'd folded back behind his head. It was just a few inches away. A few hairs showed in his armpit which Howard remembered was intricate with rigged and anchored muscles. Howard's erection was so hard it hurt.

"Good night," Danny said and smiled. Soon he turned away and dropped into serene sleep. Slowly, slowly, Howard eased his underpants down around his thighs and then masturbated as quickly and silently as possible. When he came he smoothed the semen over his stomach. He almost resented Otis's presence.

The next day they lay in bed yawning and talking. The tent was translucent and Howard said he felt they were living inside a lime wedge. Otis sang, "I'm in the nude for love."

They paddled down a river through whitewater and then arrived at a portage where they had to empty their supplies and carry the inverted canoe on their heads like a hat. They walked through the woods. Both Otis and Danny were quietly solicitous of Howard, as though afraid of tiring him. They followed the path. The soil to each side was damp and covered with dark green mosses, light green ferns and young maple trees the height of a man crowding around the soaring corrugated trunks of jack pines often spotted with pale lichens. The path itself was thick with brown pine needles and scattered pinecones; the needles covered but didn't conceal the long roots of trees and the boulders that had been fractured by frost in winter, the cracks invaded by orange lichen.

Howard stumbled on a rock and Danny, who was just behind him, patted him lightly on the butt as football players do to reassure one another, as though to say, "I'm here, we're in this together." Howard could feel the touch of Danny's hand for a long time afterward on his ass and he became conscious of his own hips moving inside his jeans.

That night they were worn out from their trek and said little. Danny took off all his clothes and swam with perfect form far out into the lake. Otis caught Howard looking at Danny's retreating head, arcing arms and rapidly churning feet and seemed to frown, but Howard wasn't sure why or even if Otis was really frowning. Was it because Danny was taking a risk by swimming out so far? Or was Otis pissed off because Howard was looking at Danny so hungrily? Otis kept hoping Howard would outgrow this twisted sex thing and settle down with some nice girl; that was probably one reason Otis had invited him along, to toughen him up, give him some confidence or at least a taste for the company of normal guys doing normal-guy things close to nature. And yet Howard felt that if the great outdoors was for normal men then he didn't belong in it; for him it was the church of an alien cult and he tiptoed through it warily.

Howard forced himself to open the map and study it so that he wouldn't be looking at Danny when he came naked out of the water. "I really love all these names," Howard said. "Little Saganaga Lake. Granite River. Gunflint Lake." But here was Danny naked and trembling, hugging himself beside the camp-fire. No way to tell if his penis was big, it had shrunk with the cold.

"Cold as a witch's tit," he said, laughing, his teeth chattering.

If Otis hadn't been there Howard would have rubbed Danny down to warm him up, get the blood flowing. Danny's body was hard and brown and virile even if he looked like a boy. His wet hair hung in bangs on his forehead and his long, muscled arms were hugging his lean torso. Without clothes he looked smaller than when he was dressed. It was hard to reconcile this small body with the force it unleashed when he swam. His stomach was hard and forked muscles ran up it.

Later it began to rain and water seeped up through the comfortable moss bed they'd staked the tent out over. They were all wet and miserable, especially Danny who was down-hill, so Howard and Danny squeezed uphill closer to Otis. Howard kept his back to Otis. He was looking at Danny's tan neck and could smell the clean smell of lake water on Danny's skin.

The next morning it was too wet to get a fire going so they just drank some powdered milk and ate the last of their sliced white bread, which was getting moldy. In the boat they huddled under their rain slickers, ran the motor and didn't even bother to paddle. They had only half a gallon of gasoline left. When it ran out the sky turned blue-black and a cold wind drilled them with fine, stinging rain. The lake turned rough and they had a hard time reaching the shore, where they had to pitch tent in the rain. They couldn't find a dry campsite but at least this time they avoided moss and lichen and staked out their pegs and cords on high ground. A gray jay kept fussing at them from a high branch. A saprophyte, repulsively colorless Indian pipe, had sprung out of a rotting stump; there was something frightful about it, like fetuses in jars of formaldehyde, their bodies similarly silvery and translucent.

Danny went into the woods and started shooting. Otis laughed his laugh and said, "That crazy motherfucker. I really want to apologize to you, Howard. I just didn't know." Howard shrugged benevolently, ashamed that he was so attracted to Danny. "We could get into real trouble with the law," Otis continued. "We could be dragged out of these woods in chains. Not to mention that crazy guy could gun us down."

"What's up with him, anyway?" Howard asked. "Do you think he's jealous of our friendship?" Howard wanted Otis to recognize that their friendship was sufficiently admirable as to be enviable.

"Could be," Otis said. "Or maybe the wilderness has made him go buggy. It can have that effect." He strummed his guitar, then played a loud dissonant chord and threw the instrument aside. "I keep feeling he hates my guts. But why? He didn't before. Do you think I did anything to provoke him?"

So sad

Howard was always ready to take the blame for irritating other people, especially men, but he couldn't imagine what Otis had said or done.

"Maybe he doesn't like it that you're the self-appointed leader," Howard ventured. "Maybe you should play the goof-off and force him to make all the decisions."

"Good idea."

They began to talk as they had always talked when alone. It was a bit like floating in a pool on a rubber raft and pushing off again and again when the raft softly bumped against one side or the other. They were both dreamers, idlers, and Danny's harrowing, scarcely hidden violence had drained all the water out of the pool.

Danny came back with two small red squirrels he'd shot. Cleaning them was grizzly and all that was left were two tiny, bug-eyed skinless monsters. Danny splayed them on sticks but even he couldn't eat them after they were cooked and Otis shared with him some of the delicious lake trout he'd fished that evening off the campsite. They talked about steaks and how they'd eat big T-bones as soon as they were back to civilization.

In Evanston Danny was a hardworking, well-spoken student preparing himself for an education in engineering. When he wasn't studying at his girlfriend's house he was swimming laps or running errands for his mother, who was the school nurse and worked long hours. He went to the Lutheran church every Sunday with his mother and girlfriend and he was active at the YMCA in the Eisenhower Club (Otis belonged to the more prestigious Jefferson Club). Every second of his time was accounted for and all his demonic energy was fully harnessed. Howard thought he probably wasn't fucking his girlfriend but that he'd convinced her to give him a handjob on Saturday nights.

Out here, though, Danny wouldn't talk about any of their favorite subjects—life after death, the existence of God, the terrors of totalitarianism, the pros and cons of premarital sex. The language had become coarser, as though they were all in boot camp. Was he trying to intimidate them by proving how tough he was under the model-citizen veneer he'd assumed in Evanston? Or was he spooked by the woods and finding it necessary to act tough in order to survive? Or was he just free at last to unleash the animal that had been crouching inside him all the while?

The next morning they laughed and said they were living inside a lime wedge and Otis warbled again, "I'm in the nude for love." He had added more verses to his song, which included the place-names of the lakes and rivers they had visited; he sang it out now in his bawling, unsupported voice, a comic voice different from the hillbilly crooning voice he used for his ballads and blues.

Although the sun came out, a steady breeze made it tiring to paddle. Light sparkled on the faceted waves and more than once Howard discovered he'd been hypnotized for a minute or was it ten by the dazzle and the constant rhythm of their paddles. The aspens danced in the wind, bending and flipping their small leaves from the silver to the pale green side, whereas the evergreens stood as tall and motionless as crack soldiers. They passed through a narrows from one lake to the next and Howard saw the trunk of a paper birch in full sunlight, slowly unscrolling its bark, watermarked by small horizontal dashes in the filigrain. Each layer cast an undulating shadow on the bark beneath; these superimposed layers were the color and form of wind-sculpted dunes in the desert. Danny said nothing but "shit" and "horseshit," called every object a "mother-fucker" and attributed to every noun the adjective "fuckin'."

That night the wind died down and the weather turned airless, hot, sweaty hot. They tied the tent flaps back, then finally Howard and Danny moved their sleeping bags outside. Otis thought the tent offered more protection against the mosquitoes. He was right. The mosquitoes were tireless in their attentions to Howard's face, neck, arms.

Danny was entirely naked and at first retracted even his head into the sleeping bag to stop being bitten but then he was driven out by the heat. He ended up lying naked and sweating on top of his sleeping bag slapping at the bugs. He'd lost weight on the trip and his eyes looked hollow and sunken in the moonlight. His beard was coming in thick and was made up of brass wires as straight as pine needles or pins. Howard, too, was lying on top of his sleeping bag but in his underpants.

Danny turned toward Howard and smiled, then lay on his back with his legs apart and one arm thrown back over his eyes.

Howard suddenly understood everything. Danny hated Otis and was jealous of everything he possessed, including Howard's devotion. Danny had figured out that Howard was completely under his spell. He was competing with Otis for Howard's love. Not because Danny wanted it—no, he wanted perversely to show that his power over Howard was stronger even than Otis's. But if Howard ever responded—if Howard ever reached out and touched this body—then Danny would crow triumphantly, reject Howard brutally and demand of Otis if he and Howard were lovers and pansy playmates. Danny would tell everyone at Evanston High that they were fruits and Otis would be forced to give up Howard's friendship.

Howard was afraid he was going crazy. Danny hadn't made a single sign that he was attempting to seduce Howard in order to denounce him and destroy his friendship with Otis. Danny might have his problems with Otis and he might naturally welcome an ally, but where was the slightest piece of evidence that he had any darker or more devious schemes? Perhaps Danny would welcome a handjob or blowjob, but that didn't seem likely. After all, Howard was the one with the hard-on, not Danny. Danny's penis (it was big) lay there peacefully beside a scrotum made large and shiny by the heat, like a serpent dozing and curled around its two eggs.

When they returned the canoe and tent to the outfitter's there were still a few hours left before dark and they drove into Ely, Minnesota, and took a motel room, then cruised the streets and smoked cigarettes—Luckies this time since they'd finished the carton of Parliaments, and Luckies went better with their beards and tans. Howard looked forward to being alone again soon with Otis; together they could push off from the shore of reality and float on their dreams even if in separate boats, twin beds. In the motel bathroom Howard had been gratified to see how golden tan he was and how his beard, scrappy though it might be, still made him look older and more manly. But he wondered if looking more virile wouldn't actually make him less attractive to Danny.

Otis said he was horny for some pussy and told Danny to drive slowly to the curb while he trolled for it. He asked two really young girls who were maybe in junior high school if they wanted a ride home and they just giggled and ran. One older woman scowled and said nothing and Howard was afraid she'd report them to the cops.

Danny was laughing like a banshee and drumming the steering wheel with pleasure. Maybe Otis was following Howard's advice to play the fuck-up and cast Danny in the more responsible role, even if it was too late for that. Anyway, since they'd turned in the canoe Danny had reverted to his old personality, become nicer, more reasonable and well spoken. For a second Howard considered the possibility that Danny had felt an attraction for him and had been fending it off by playing dumb and dirty.

Otis changed his technique with the next girl. He said, "We're nice guys. You can see that, can't you, miss? We're just lonely backwoodsmen. You've heard of the voyageurs?"

She laughed and said, "You're not even from around here. You have Illinois license plates."

"That doesn't mean we're not lonely. Ride with us for a few blocks, miss. We'll buy you a beer. No harm being nice to three lonely guys, is there?"

Howard braced himself for her outrage but suddenly she smiled and said, "OK," and slipped in beside him in the back seat.

They all introduced themselves. Her name was Sue. "Sue Helen, if you must know," she said. She was wearing an adult beehive hairdo perched imposingly over a small heart-shaped face with tiny features. On the street, in her heels and tight skirt and beehive she'd looked like an adult in her early twenties, even a young mother, but now Howard could see it was all just pretense and she was only sixteen or seventeen, like them.

Soon they were in a bar, peering into a jukebox bubbling warmly and brilliantly under their red hands as they studied its magic charts and made their choices. Sue Helen sat with them in the highbacked booth and told them her sad story, how her mother had remarried and her stepdad was an Adventist who thought she was a sinner and a slut and how she had a job as a door-to-door cosmetics saleswoman but she couldn't sell anything, the women in Ely were all too poor and overworked and they wore cheap housedresses and curlers and had big butts and didn't even use any makeup. Sue Helen said, "You guys are so . . . different. You're so kind and speak so educated. I'd love to go to Chicago. People say it's different."

Soon Otis was dancing with Sue Helen to a slow tune sung by Brenda Lee. Danny had shrunk back inside himself. His smile had faded. He'd looked at Otis with admiration. Maybe Danny had been attracted to Otis but had been afraid to show it, so he'd turned to Howard instead, as a substitute. Of course Howard had no evidence to go on; he continued building these castles with matchsticks but they kept tottering and collapsing.

Howard already missed the sweet hot pulp of blueberries the day they'd found a patch and eaten them just as fast as they could pick them. He knew the woods would start filling up with snow in just six or seven weeks. Soon there'd be no paradise to regain. He could hear the lonely laughter of the loons. He could picture Danny's naked body twisting and turning that one hot night as he moaned in his sleep, goaded by mosquitoes.

After all that time in the wilderness the lights almost hurt and people's voices seemed unbearably loud. Sue Helen looked minuscule in Otis's arms. His eyes were closed as they slow danced but when he turned her around Howard could see hers were wide open.

Running on Empty

On the charter flight from Paris to New York Luke sat on the aisle. Next to him, in the center seat, was a man in his mid-twenties from the French Alps, where his parents owned a small hotel for skiers. He said he cooked all winter in the hotel and then took quite a long vacation every spring. This year it was the States, since the dollar was so low.

"Not *that* low," Luke said when Sylvain mentioned he had only a hundred dollars with him for a five-week stay.

They were speaking French, since Sylvain confessed he couldn't get through even one sentence in English. Sylvain smiled and Luke envied him his looks, his health, even his youth, although that was absurd, since Luke himself was barely twenty-nine.

Next to Sylvain, by the window, sat a nun with an eager, intelligent face. Soon she had joined in the conversation. She was Sister Julia, an American, though a member of a French convent for a reason she never explained, despite their nonstop chatter for the seven and a half hours they were in the air. Her French was excellent, much better than Luke's. He noticed that Sylvain talked to her with all the grace notes kept in, whereas with Luke he simplified down to the main melody.

It turned out Luke and Sister Julia had both been in France for four years. Of course a convent was a "total immersion," undreamed of even by Berlitz. Nevertheless Luke was embarrassed to admit to his seat partners that he was a translator. From French to English, to be sure. It was pointless to explain to this handsome, confident Sylvain that a translator must be better in the "into language" than in the "out-of language," that a translator must be a stylist in his own tongue.

Sylvain was, in any event, more intrigued by Sister Julia's vows than by Luke's linguistic competence. He asked her right off how a pretty girl like her could give up sex.

"But I'm not a girl," she said. "I'm forty-six. This wimple is very handy," she said with a trace of coquetry, "for covering up gray hair."

She was not at all like the stern, bushy-eyebrowed, downy-chinned nuns who'd taught Luke all the way through high school. When Sylvain asked her if she didn't regret having never known a man—and here he even raised his muscular arms, smiled and stretched—she said quite simply, "But I was married. I know all about men."

She told them her father had been a composer, she'd grown up an Episcopalian in Providence, Rhode Island, she'd taught music theory at Brown and built harpsichords. Her religious vocation had descended on her swiftly, but she didn't provide them with the conversion scene; she had little sense of the dramatic possibilities her life provided, or perhaps flattening out her own narrative was a penance for her. Nor was her theology orthodox. She believed in reincarnation. "Do you?" she asked them.

"I'm an atheist," Luke said. He'd never said that to a nun

before, and he enjoyed saying it, even though Sister Julia wasn't the sort to be shocked or even saddened by someone else's lack of faith—she was blessed by the convert's egotism. There was nothing dogmatic about her clear, fresh face, her pretty gray eyes, her way of leaning into the conversation and drinking it up nor her quick nods, sometimes at variance with the crease of doubt across her forehead. When she nodded and frowned at the same time, he felt she was disagreeing with his opinions but affirming him as a person.

Love it

Sylvain appeared to be enjoying his two Americans. Luke and Sister Julia kept giving him the names and addresses of friends in the States to look up. "If you're ever in Martha's Vineyard, you must stay with Lucy. She's just lost a lot of weight and hasn't realized yet she's become very beautiful," the nun said. Luke gave him the names of two gay friends without mentioning they were gay—one in Boston, another in San Francisco. Of course Sylvain was heterosexual, that was obvious, but Luke knew his friends would get a kick out of putting up a handsome foreigner, the sort of blond who's always slightly tan, the sort of man who looks at his own crotch when he's listening and frames it with his hands when he's replying. Certainly both Luke and the nun couldn't resist overresponding even to Sylvain's most casual remarks.

When the flight attendant served them lunch, Sylvain asked her in his funny English where she was from. Then he asked, "Are all zee womens in Floride as charming like you?"

She pursed her lips in smiling mock reproach as though he were being a naughty darling and said, "It's a real nice state. France is nice, too. I'm going to learn French next. I studied Latin in high school."

Sister Julia said to Sylvain, "If you can speak English like that you won't need more than a hundred dollars."

When they all said good-bye at the airport Luke was disappointed. He'd expected something more. Well, he had Sylvain's address, and if someday Luke returned to France he'd look him up. Ill as he was, Luke couldn't bear the thought of never seeing France again, which suddenly seemed synonymous with some future rendezvous with Sylvain.

Luke changed money and planes—this time for Dallas. He was getting pretty ill. He could feel it in the heaviness of his bones, in his extreme tiredness, and he almost asked a porter to carry his bags. He had just two hundred dollars with him—he was half as optimistic as Sylvain. He'd never had enough money, and now he worried he'd end up a charity case or, even worse, dependent on his family. He was terrified of having to call on the mercy of his family.

He'd grown up as the eighth of ten children, all of them small if wiry and agile. His mother was a Chicana, but no one ever took her for Mexican—she didn't appear to have much Indian blood and her mother prided herself on being "Castilian." His father was a mean little man with a tweezered mustache who'd worked his whole life as the janitor in a Lubbock, Texas, high school. He'd converted to Catholicism to please his wife and enrage his Baptist kin (Lubbock proudly called itself "the buckle on the Bible Belt"). Luke's father and brothers and sisters all shared a glee he'd learned to name only years later—Schadenfreude, the taking of malicious pleasure in someone else's pain. Spite and envy were their ruling sentiments. If someone fell and hurt himself, they'd howl with glee. Their father would regale them with hissing, venomous accounts of the misfortunes of superiors at school. The one sure way to win the family's attention was to act out the humiliation that had befallen Mrs. Rodriguez after mass last Sunday or Mr. Brown, the principal, during the last PTA meeting. Luke's father grumbled at the TV, mocked the commercials, challenged the newscasters, jeered at the politicians. "Look at him, he thinks he's so great, but he'll look like he's smelled a fart when he sees the final vote." Everyone would

Damn

laugh except Luke's mother, who went about her work gravely, like a paid employee eager to finish up and leave.

In high school—not the public high school where his father worked, but the much smaller parochial school—Luke had emerged as the nuns' favorite. He'd been a brilliant student. Now that his brain was usually fuzzy—becoming like over-cooked minestrone during the toxoplasmosis crisis, all swimming and steamy with shreds and lumps rising only to sink again—he regarded his former intelligence with respect. He'd once known how to use the ablative absolute. He'd once read the *Symposium* in Greek without understanding the references to love between men.

Glimpses of my clan

Perhaps because of his miserable, mocking family, Luke had always felt unsure of himself. Nevertheless he'd done everything expected of him, everything. He'd been a cross-country champ, he'd stayed entirely virginal, avoiding even masturbation except for rare lapses, he'd won the statewide *Prix d'honneur* in French, he'd once correctly and even humorously translated on the spot an entire *Time* magazine article into Latin, though the page had been handed to him only seconds before by the judge of the Cicero Club contest.

In another era he would have grown up to be one of those priests who play basketball in a soutane and whose students complain when he beats them at arm wrestling ("Jeez, Father Luke . . .").

He'd only narrowly escaped that fate. He'd found a job in a liberal, primarily Jewish private school just outside New York, and though he'd grown a beard and spouted Saint-Simonism, he hadn't been able to resist becoming the best beloved, most energetic teacher in the history of Dempster Country Day. The kids worshiped him, called him Luke, and phoned him in the middle of the night to discuss their abortions, college-entrance exams and parents' pending divorces. Several of them had invited him to their mansions, where Luke, the gung-ho jock and brain—nose always burned from the soccer field and tweed-jacket pocket always misshapen from carrying around Horace's *Odes*—had had to study his own students to discover how to wield an escargot clamp and use a finger bowl.

What was harder was to keep up that ceaseless, bouncy energy that is always the hallmark of rich people who are also "social." Whereas Luke's father had beguiled his brutal brood with tales of other people's folly and chagrin, the Lords of Long Island looked at you with distrust the instant you criticized anyone—especially a superior. Envy proved your own inferiority. Since the parents of Luke's students were usually at the top of their profession or industry, they interpreted carping and quibbles as envy. They usually sided with the object of any attack. With them generosity—like stoicism and pep—had become signs of good breeding.

Luke learned generosity, too, as easily as he'd mastered snails. The ingredient he added to the package, the personal ingredient, was gratitude. He was grateful to rich people. He was grateful to almost everyone. The gratitude was the humble reverse side of the family's taste for Schadenfreude. Luke could express his gratitude in such an earnest, simple way, in his caressing tenor voice with the baritone beginnings and endings of sentences, that no one took it for cringing—no one except Luke himself, who kept seeing his father, hat in hand, talking to the district supervisor.

Luke had left the abjection and exaltation of Dempster and found work as a translator. Working alone was less engrossing than playing Father Luke, but the thrill of wielding power or submitting to it at school had finally sickened him. As a kid he'd managed to escape from his family through studies; he'd stayed in school to consolidate that gain, but now he wanted to be alone, wanted to work alone into the night, listening to the radio, fine-tuning English sentences. Luckily he'd had a rent-controlled apartment on Cornelia Street in Manhattan, and luckily an older gay man, the king of the translators, had taken him under his wing. He became a translator, joining an honest if underpaid profession.

By subletting this apartment for four times what he paid, Luke had had enough money to live in Paris in a Montmartre hotel on a steep street near Picasso's old studio, a hotel of just eighteen rooms where the proprietor, a hearty woman from the Périgord, watched them as they ate the meals she prepared and urged them to pour wine into their emptied soup bowls and knock it back. *"Chabrol! Chabrol!"* she'd say, which was both an order and a toast. She'd point at them unsmilingly if they weren't drinking. She liked it when everyone was slightly tipsy and making conversation from table to table.

He'd never enjoyed gay life as such. At least New York clones had never struck him as sexy. In turn they hadn't liked his look—wire-rim glasses, baggy tweeds, shiny policeman's shoes—or his looks. He was small, his eyes mocking or hostilely attentive or wet and grateful, his nose a red beak, his slim body featureless under the loose pants and outsize jackets but smooth and well-built when stripped, the pale, sweated body of a featherweight high school wrestler, but clones had had to work to get to see it.

Luke had sought out sex with working men, straight men or close approximations of that ideal. He'd haunted building sites, suburban weightlifting gyms, the bar next to the fire-house, the bowling alley across from the police station, the run-down Queens theater that specialized in kung-fu movies. He liked guys who didn't kiss, who had beer bellies, who wore T-shirts that showed through their Dacron short-sleeved shirts, who watched football games, who shook their heads in frustration and muttered "Women!" He liked becoming pals with guys who, because they were too boring or too rough or not romantic or cultured enough, had lost their girlfriends.

In Paris he'd befriended a Moroccan boxer down on his

luck. But very little of his time was devoted to Ali. He spent his mornings alone in bed, surrounded by his dictionaries, and listened to the rain and translated. He ate the same *salade Auvergnate* every lunch at the same neighborhood café. In the afternoons he often went to the Cluny museum. Luke liked medieval culture. He knew everything about Romanesque fortified churches and dreamed of meeting someone with a car who could take him on a tour of them.

At night he'd haunt the run-down movie palaces near Barbès-Rochechouart, the Arab quarter, or in good weather cruise the steps below Sacré-Coeur—that was where you met his type: men-without-women, chumps too broke or too dumb to get chicks, guys with girlie calendars tacked on the inner side of the closet doors, guys who practiced karate chops as they talked on the telephone to their mothers.

He didn't want to impersonate that missing girlfriend for them. No, Luke wanted to be a pal, a sidekick, and more than once he'd lain in the arms of a CRS (a French cop) who'd drawn on his Gitane *blonde* and told Luke he was *un vrai copain,* a real pal.

That was why he'd been surprised when he of all people had become ill. It was a gay disease and he scarcely thought of himself as gay. In fact, earlier on he'd once talked it over with an Irish teacher of English who lived in his hotel, a pedophile who couldn't get it up for anyone over sixteen. They'd agreed that neither of them counted as gay.

For him, the worst immediate effect of the disease was that it sapped his confidence. He felt he'd always lived on nerve. He should have lived the dim life of his brothers and sisters—one a welfare mother, another a secretary in a lumberyard, two brothers in the air-conditioning business, another one an exterminator, two unemployed boys, another (the family success) an army officer who'd taken early retirement to run a sporting-goods store with an ex–football star. He had another brother, Jeff, an iron worker who'd dropped out of the union, who lived in Milwaukee with his girl and traveled as far away as New York State to bend steel and put up the frames of buildings. Jeff was a guy who grew his hair long and partied with women executives in their early forties fed up with (or neglected by) their white-collar male contemporaries. The last thing Luke had heard, Jeff had broken up with his girl because she'd spent fifty of his bucks hiring a limo to ferry her and two of her girlfriends around Milwaukee just for the fun of it.

Luke had sprung the family trap. He'd eaten oysters with rich socialists, worried over the right slang equivalents in English to French obscenities—he'd even resisted the temptation to strive to become the headmaster of Dempster Country Day. As the runt of his family, he'd always had to fight when he was a kid to get enough to eat, but even so as an adult he'd chosen freelance insecurity over a dull future with a future.

But all that had taken confidence and now he didn't have any. The translation he was working on would be his last. Translating required a hundred small dares per page in the constant trade-off between fidelity and fluency, and Luke couldn't find the necessary authority.

He never stopped worrying about money. He'd lie in bed working up imaginary budgets. When he returned to New York, Dempster Country Day might refer students to him for coaching in French, but would the parents worry that their children would be infected? He'd read of the hysteria in America. If his doctor decided he should go on AZT, how would he ever find the twelve thousand dollars a year to pay for it?

When he landed in Dallas his favorite cousin, Beth, was there. Growing up he'd called her Elizabeth. Now he was training himself to call her Beth, as she preferred. She hadn't been told he was ill and he looked for a sign that his appearance shocked her, but all she said was "My goodness, you'll have to go to Weight Watchers with me before long." If she'd known how hard he'd worked for every ounce on his bones, she wouldn't joke about it; his paunch, however, he knew, was bloated from the cytomegalovirus in his gut and the bottle of Pepto-Bismol he had to swallow every morning to control his diarrhea.

Beth's husband, Greg, had just died of an early heart attack. She'd mailed Luke a cassette of the funeral, but he'd never listened to it because he hadn't been able to lay his hands on a tape recorder—not a problem that would have occurred to her, she who had a ranch house stocked with self-cleaning ovens, a microwave, two Dustbusters, three TVs, dishwasher, washer and dryer and Lord knew what else. So he just patted her back and said, "It was a beautiful service. I hope you're surviving."

"I'm doing fine, Luke, just fine." There was something hard and determined about her that he admired. Beth's bright Texas smile came as a comfort. He told her he'd never seen her in such pretty dark shades of blue.

"Well, thank you, Luke. I had my colors done. It was one of the last presents Greg gave me. Have you had yours done yet?"

"No, what is it?"

"You go to this lady, she measures you in all sorts of scientific ways, skin tones and all, and then she gives you your fan. I have mine here in my purse, I always carry it, 'cause don't you know I'll see a pretty blouse and pick it up but when I get home with it it doesn't look right at *all* and when I check it out it won't be one of my hues. It will be *close* but not exact."

Beth snapped open a paper fan. Each segment was painted a different shade. "Now the dark blue is my strong color. If I wear it, I always get compliments. You complimented me, you see!"

And she laughed and let her smiling blue eyes dazzle him, as they always had. Her face made him think of Hollywood starlets of the past, as did her slight chubbiness and smile, which looked as though it were shot through gauze.

Her little speech about colors had been an act of courage, at once a pledge she was going to be cheerful as well as a subtle blend of flirting with him (as she would have flirted with any man) and giving him a beauty tip (as she might have done with another woman). She didn't know any other gay men; she wanted to be nice; she'd found this way to welcome him.

He'd been the ring-bearer at her wedding to Greg. They'd been the ideal couple, she a Texas Bluebonnet, he a football star, she small and blond, he dark and massive. Now she was just forty-five and already a widow with two sons nearly out of college, both eager to be cattlemen.

"For a while Houston was planning to be a missionary," Beth was saying, "but now he thinks he can serve the Lord just by leading a Christian life, and we know there's nothing wrong with that, don't we?" She added an emphatic "No sirree Bob," so he wouldn't have to reply.

Since Luke belonged to the disgraced Catholic side of the family, Beth was careful usually not to mention religion. Texans were brought up not to discuss religion or politics, the cause of so many gunfights just two generations ago, but Baptists were encouraged to proselytize. Beth was even about to set off on a Baptist mission to England, she said, and she asked Luke for tips about getting along with what she called "the locals." Luke tried to picture her with her carefully streaked permanent, fan-selected colors from Neiman-Marcus, black-leather shoulder-strap Chanel bag and diamond earrings ringing the bell of a lady in a twinset and pearls in a twee village in the Cotswolds: "Howdy, are you ready to take the Lord into your heart?" Today she was holding her urge to convert in check. She didn't want to alienate him. She loved family, and he was family, even if he was a sinner—lost, indeed damned, for he'd told her ten years ago about his vice.

The program was they were to visit relatives in East Texas and then drive over to Lubbock, where Luke would stay with his parents for a week before flying home to New York. He was worried he might become critically ill while in Lubbock and have to remain there. He felt very uprooted, but New York—scary, expensive—was the closest thing to home. He was eager to consult the doctor awaiting him in New York.

Unlike some of his friends, who'd become resigned and either philosophical or depressed, Luke had taken his own case on and put himself in charge of finding a cure. In Paris he'd worked as a volunteer for the hot line, answering anxious questions and in return finding out the latest information and meeting the best specialists. He had a contact in Sweden who was keeping him abreast of an experiment going on there; through the French he knew the latest results in Zaire. He'd memorized the list of drugs and their side effects; he knew that the side effects of trimethoprim for the pneumonia were kidney damage, depression, loss of appetite, abdominal pain, hepatitis, diarrhea, headache, neuritis, insomnia, apathy, fever chills, anemia, rash, light sensitivity, mouth pain, nausea and vomiting—and those were just the results of a treatment.

The father of one of his former students at Dempster had promised to pay Luke's bills "until he got better." Luke felt getting well was a full-time job; he'd even seen all the quacks, swallowed tiny white homeopathic doses, meditated and "imaged" healthy cells engulfing foul ones, been massaged on mystic pressure points, done yoga, eaten nothing but brown rice and slimy or pickled vegetables arranged on the plate according to wind and rain principles. The one thing he couldn't bring himself to do was meet in a group with other people who were ill.

They drove in Beth's new beige Cadillac on the beltway

skirting Fort Worth and Dallas and headed the hundred miles south to Hershell, where Beth had just buried Greg and where their great-aunts Ruby and Pearl were waiting for them. Once they were out of the city and onto a two-lane road, the Texas he remembered came drifting back—the wildflowers, especially the Indian blanket and bluebells covering the grassy slopes, the men with the thick tan necks and off-white straw cowboy hats driving the pickup trucks, the smell of heat and dampness lifting off the fields.

Hershell was just a flyspeck on the road. There were two churches, one Baptist and one Church of Christ, a hardware store where they still sold kerosene lamps and barbed-wire stretchers, a saddle shop where a cousin of theirs by marriage worked the leather as he sipped cold coffee and smoked Luckies, a post office, a grocery store with nearly empty shelves and the "new" grade school built of red brick in the 1950s.

Ruby's house was a yellow-brick single story with a double garage and a ceiling fan that shook the whole house when it was turned on, as though preparing for liftoff. The paintings—flowers, fruits, fields—had been done long ago by one of her aunts. Luke was given a bedroom with a double bed covered with a handsome thick white chenille bedspread— "chenille" was a word he'd always said as a child, but only now did he connect it with the French word for "caterpillar." Beth was given a room across the street with Pearl.

Pearl's house had been her parents'. The house was nothing but additions. Her folks had built a one-room cabin and then added rooms on each side as they had the money and inclination to do so. She showed them pictures of their great-grandparents and their twelve children—one of the pale-eyed, square-jawed boys, named Culley, was handsome enough to step out toward them away from his plump, crazed-looking siblings. Pearl's Hershell high school diploma was on the wall. When Luke asked her what the musical notes on it meant, she said, "Be sharp, be natural but never be flat."

Pearl said it right out. She was intelligent enough to recognize how funny it was, but as the local chair of the Texas Historical Society, she took pride in every detail of their heritage. The miles and miles of brand-new housing developments Luke had seen on the Dallas–Fort Worth Beltway, all with purely arbitrary names such as Mount Vernon or Versailles, had spooked him, made him grateful for these sun-bleached lean-tos, for the irises growing in the crick, for the tabernacle, that open-sided, roofed-over meeting place above the town.

He and Beth sat for hours and hours with their great-aunts, "visiting" after their supper of fried chicken and succotash. They drank their sweetened iced tea and traded stories. There were solemn moments, as when the old ladies hugged Beth and told her how courageous she was being.

"That Greg was a fine man," Ruby said, her eyes defiant and sharp as though someone might challenge her judgment. Her enunciation had always been clear—she'd taught elocution for years in high schools all over the state—but she hadn't weeded the country out of her voice.

Then there were the cheerful moments, as when Luke recounted the latest follies of folks in Paris. "Well, I declare," the ladies would exclaim, their voices dipping from pretended excitement down into real indifference. He was careful not to go on too long about a world they didn't know or care about or to shock them. He noticed they didn't ask him this time when he was going to get hitched up: perhaps he'd gone over that invisible line in their minds and become a "confirmed" bachelor. They did tease him about his "bay window," which he patted as though he hadn't noticed it before, which made them laugh.

Beth and he went on a long walk before the light died. They

had a look at the folks on the corner they'd heard about who lived like pigs; the old man had gone and shot someone dead and now he was in the pokey for life, and the old woman— didn't it beat all—had a garden sale going on every day, but who would want that old junk? He and Beth walked fast, with light hearts. He appreciated their shared views—they both loved and respected their aunts and they were both glad to slip away from them.

They walked down to see the old metal swing bridge; earlier Ruby had shown them a photo of Billy Andrews, in their class of 1917, swinging from the bridge as a stunt, big grin on his face, fairly popping out of his graduation suit with the celluloid collar, his strong calves squeezed into the knickers.

Oh, Luke ached for sex. He thought that if he could just lie next to a man one more time, feel once more that someone wanted him, he could die in peace. All his life he'd been on the prowl, once he'd broken his vows of virginity—in French he'd learned there were two words for boy virgins, neither comical: *un puceau* and *un rosier,* as though the boy were a rose bush, blossoms guarded by thorns. He'd lived so fast, cherished so little, but now he lingered over sexy memories he'd never even summoned up before, like that time he'd followed a Cuban night watchman into a Park Avenue office building and they'd fucked in the service elevator and stopped, just for the hell of it, on every one of the forty-two floors. Or he remembered sex that hadn't happened, like that summer when he was twelve, a caddie, and he'd sat next to one of the older caddies on the bench waiting for a job in the airless, cricket-shrill heat. He'd molded his leg so perfectly to the guy's thigh that finally he'd stood up and said to Luke, real pissed off, "What are you, some sort of fuckin' Liberace?" And he thought of the cop who'd handcuffed him to the bedstead.

As he and Beth were walking out past a field of cows standing in the fading light, he started picking a bouquet of wildflowers for Ruby—he got up to twenty-nine flowers without repeating a single variety. Beth walked with vigor, her whole body alert with curiosity. She'd always struck him as a healthy, sexy woman. He wondered if she'd remarry. With her religion and all she couldn't just pick up a man in a bar. She'd have to marry again to get laid. But would she want to? How did she keep her appetite in check?

The next day was hot enough to make them all worry what the summer would bring. They were going to what was called the "graveyard working," ten miles east of Hershell. Once a year the ten or so families who had kin buried there came together to set the tombstones upright, hoe and rake, stick silk or plastic flowers in the soil—real ones burned up right away—and then eat. Ruby and Pearl had both been up for hours cooking, since after the graveyard working everyone shared in a big potluck lunch.

They drove out in Beth's Cadillac. Ruby was wearing a bonnet, one she'd made herself for gardening. The cemetery, which was also named after Hershell since he'd donated the land, was on top of a hill looking over green, rolling farmland. There were ten or eleven cars and pickup trucks already parked outside the metal palings that guarded the front but not the sides of the cemetery. Big women with lots of kids were already setting up for the lunch, unfolding card tables and stacking them with coolers of iced tea and plates of chicken fried in broken-potato-chip batter, potato salad, pickled watermelon rind, whole hams, black-eyed peas, loaves of Wonder Bread, baked beans served right out of the can and pecan pies and apple pies. There weren't more than a hundred graves altogether and all of them had already been decently looked after, thanks to the contributions solicited every year by Ruby, who hired a part-time caretaker.

Luke felt a strange contentment hoeing his grandfather's grave. Pearl had to show him how to hoe, but she didn't tease him about being a city slicker. He realized he could do no wrong in her eyes, since he was kin. Everyone here was kin. Several of the men had Luke's beaky red nose. He kept seeing his own small, well-knit body on other men—the same narrow shoulders and short legs, hairless forearms, the thinning, shiny hair gone to baldness here and there. Because of the rift in the family he'd met few of these people before and he had little enough in common with them, except he did share the same body type, possibly the same temperament.

His grandfather had been a Woodsman of the World, whatever that was, and his tomb marker was a stone tree trunk. His wife was buried under a tablet that read "She Did the Best She Could."

So relatable

Beth was standing in front of Greg's grave, which was still fresh. Luke worried that her mission to England might shake her faith. Wouldn't she see how flimsy, how recent and, well, how corny her religion was once she was in that gray and unpleasant land? They were planning, the Southern Baptists, to fan out over the English countryside. Wouldn't Beth be awed, or at least dismayed, by Gloucester Cathedral, by the polished intricacy of its cloisters? Wouldn't she see how raw, raw as this fresh grave, her beliefs were beside the civilized ironies of the Church of England? It was as though she were trying to introduce Pop-Tarts into the land of scones.

During the picnic Beth told Luke that her one worry about her son Houston was that he always seemed so serious and distracted these days, as though dipped and twirled in darkness. "I tell him, 'Son, you must be *happy* in the Lord. The Bible tells us to be happy in our faith.' "

Luke couldn't resist tweaking Beth for a moment. He asked her what she thought about the scandals—adultery, group-sex

parties, embezzled church funds—surrounding a popular television evangelist and his wife.

"I expected it."

"You did?"

"Yes, it's good. It's a good sign. It shows that Satan is establishing his rule, which means that we'll live to see the Final
Days, the Rapture of the Church." She spoke faster and with
more assurance than usual. Luke realized she probably saw
his disease as another proof of Satan's reign or God's punishment. He knew the Texas legislature was considering impris-
oning diseased homosexuals who continued having sex.

Ruby came up to them, energized by the event, and asked
him if he'd marked off a plot for himself. "You can, you know.
Doesn't cost a penny"—she pronounced it "pinny." "You just
put stones around where you want to be. Up here it's all filling
up but out yonder we've got lots to go."

"No," Luke said. "I want to be cremated and put in the
Columbarium at Père Lachaise. In Paris."

"I declare," Ruby said, "but you've got years and *years* to
reconsider," and she laughed.

That night, as the ladies visited and told family stories, Luke
felt trapped and isolated. Beth sat there nodding and smiling
and saying, "Auntie Pearl, now you just sit and let me." But
he knew she was lonely, too, and maybe a bit frightened.
Other old ladies, all widows, stopped in to visit, and Luke
wondered if Beth was ready to join grief's hen club. Girls
started out clinging together, whispering secrets and flouncing
past boys. Then there was the longish interlude of marriage,
followed by the second sorority of widowhood; all these humped
necks, bleary eyes, false teeth, the wide-legged sitting posture
of country women sipping weak coffee and complaining about

one another. "She wanted to know what I paid for this place and I said, 'Well, Jessie, it is so *good* of you to worry about my finances, but I already have Mr. Hopkins at Farmers First to look after that for me,' and don't you know but that shut her up fast?" On and on into the night, not really vicious but complaining, naturally good but studiously petty, often feisty, sometimes coquettish, these women talked on and on. Those who couldn't hear nodded while their eyes timidly wandered, like children dismissed from the table but forbidden to play in their Sunday best.

Luke imagined he and Beth were both longing for a man—she for Greg, he for one of his men, one of these divorced cowboys, the sort of heartbroken man Randy Travis or George Strait sings about. . . . They'd met a man like that during their walk past the old bridge yesterday—a sunburned man whose torso sat comfortably on his hips as though in a big, roomy saddle. This sunburned rancher had known who they were; the whole town had been alerted to their visit. He didn't exactly doff his hat to Beth but he took it off slowly and stared into it as he spoke in a deep, nearly inaudible Texas voice. Without his hat on he looked kinder, which, for Luke, made him less sexy. When he left he swung up into his truck and pulled it into gear all in one motion. He hadn't been at the graveyard working, although Luke had looked for him.

The next morning they drove a hundred miles west to Henderson, where Beth's mother, Aunt Olna, still lived. Her husband, now dead, had been a brother of Luke's dad—estranged because Luke's dad had married a Mex and become an "old" Catholic (for some reason people hereabouts always smiled sourly, lifted one eyebrow and said in one breath, as though it were a bound form, "old-Catholic"). Beth's mother had grown up Church of Christ but had converted to her husband's religion years after their marriage. One day she'd simply read a pamphlet about what Baptists believed and she'd said to herself, "Well, that's what I believe, too," and had crossed over on the spot.

Aunt Olna was always harsh to Beth, ordering her around: "Not that one, Elizabeth." "That one which, Mother?" Beth would wail. Beth's mother was too "nervous" to specify her demands. "Turn here," she'd say in the car. "Turn right or left, Mother? Mother? Right or left?" Olna was also too nervous to cook. She didn't tremble, as other nervous people did. Luke figured the nervousness must be a confusion hidden deep in a body made fat from medication. Because she couldn't cook she'd taken three hundred dollars out of the bank to entertain them. She named the sum over and over again. She was proud her husband had left her "well fixed." When Beth drove to the store, Olna said, "Greg left Beth very well fixed. House all bought and paid for. A big *in*-surance policy. She need never worry."

Aunt Olna liked Luke. She'd always told everyone Luke was about as good as a person could get. Of course she knew almost nothing about his life, but she'd clung to her enthusiasm over the years and he'd always felt comfortable with her. And she wasn't given to gushing. When he'd praised her house, she'd said, "Everything in it is from the dime store. Always was." She told him how she'd inherited a dining-room "suit" but had had to sell it because it was too fine for her house.

Even so he liked the shiny maple furniture in the front parlor, the flimsy metal TV dinner trays on legs used as side tables, the knubby milk-glass candy dishes filled with Hershey's kisses. He liked the reproduction of the troubadour serenading the white-wigged girl, a sort of East Texas take on Watteau. He liked the fact there was no shower, just a big womanly tub, and that the four-poster bed in his room was so tall you had to climb up to get into it. Best of all he liked leaving his door open onto the night.

The rain steamed the sweetness up out of the mown grass

and the leaves of the big old shade trees kept up a frying sound; when the rain died down it sounded as though someone had lowered the flame under the skillet. He was surrounded by women and death and yet the rain dripping over an old Texas town of darkened houses made him feel like a boy in his early teens again, a boy dying to slip away to find men. These days, of course, desire entailed hopelessness—he'd learned to match every pant of longing with a sigh of regret.

The next day the heat turned the sweet smell sour, as though spring peas had been replaced with rancid collard greens. Olna took them to lunch at a barbecue place where they ate ribs and hot biscuits. In the afternoon they drove to a nursing home to visit Olna's sister. That woman remembered having baby-sat Luke once twenty-five years ago. "My, you were a cute little boy. I wish I could see you, honey. I'd give anything to see you again. My little house just sits empty and I'd love to go back to it, but I can't, I can't see to mind it. I don't know why the good Lord won't gather me in. Not no use to *no* one."

The waiting room had a Coke machine and a snack dispenser. One of the machines was making a nasty whine. The woman's hand looked as pale as if it'd been floured through a sifter.

"My husband left me," she was saying, "and after that I sold tickets at the movie the-ay-tur for nine dollars a week, six days a week, on Saturdays from ten till midnight, and when I asked for a raise after ten years, Mr. Monroe said no." She smiled. "But I had my house and cat and I could see."

In the past, when Luke had paid these calls on relatives in nursing homes he'd felt he was on a field trip to some new and strange kind of slum, but today there was no distance between him and this woman. In a month or a week he could be as blind, less cogent, whiter.

He went for a walk with Beth through the big park the town of Henderson had recently laid out, a good fifty acres of jogging paths, tennis courts, a sports arena, a playground and just open fields gone to weeds and wildflowers. On the way they passed a swimming pool that had been there over twenty years ago, that time Luke had served as Beth's ring-bearer. Now the pool was filled, clean, sparkling, but for some reason without a single swimmer, an unheeded invitation. "Didn't they used to have a big slide that curved halfway down and that was kept slick with water always pouring down it?" Luke asked.

"Now I believe you are one hundred percent correct," Beth said with the slightly prissy agreeableness of southern ladies. "What a wonderful memory you have!" She'd been trained to find fascinating even the most banal remarks if a man made them. Luke wasn't used to receiving all the respect due his gender and kept looking for a mote of mockery in Beth's eye, but it wasn't there. Or perhaps she had mockery as much under control as grief or desire.

They walked at the vigorous pace Beth set and went along the cindered jogging path under the big mesquite trees; their tiny leaves, immobile, set lacy shadows on the ground.

That sparkling pool, painted an inviting blue-green, and the memory of the flowing water slide and the smell of chlorine kept coming to mind. He'd played for hours and hours during an endless, cloudless summer day. Play had been rare enough for him, who'd always had early-morning newspaper-delivery jobs, afternoon hardware jobs, weekend lawn-mowing jobs, summer caddying jobs as well as the chores around the house and the hours and hours of homework, those hours his family had ridiculed and tried to put a stop to. But he'd persisted and won. He'd won.

When he and Beth reached the end of the park, they turned to the left, mounted a slight hill and saw a parked pickup truck under a tree. Two teenage boys with red caps were sitting inside and a third was standing unsteadily on the back of the truck, shirtless, jeans down, taking a leak. "Oh, my goodness,"

Beth said, "just don't look at them, Luke, and let's keep on walking."

The guys were laughing at Luke and Beth, playing loud music, probably drunk, and of course Luke looked. The guy taking a leak was methodically spraying a dark brown circle in the pale dust. He was a redhead, freckled, tall, skinny, and his long body was hairless except where tufted blond. He looked like a streak of summer lightning.

"But they're not doing any harm," Luke said with a smile.

"You think not?" Beth spat out. "Some folks here might think—!" But she interrupted herself, mastered herself, smiled her big missionary smile.

Luke felt rage go coursing through his tired body and tears—what sort of tears?—sting his eyes.

Tears of humiliation: he was offended that a virus had been permitted to win an argument. He'd been the one to learn, to leave home, break free. He'd cast aside all the old sins, lived freely—but soon Beth could imagine he was having to pay for his follies with his life. It offended him that he would be exposed to her self-righteousness.

Aunt Olna invited them out to a good steak dinner in a fast-food place near the new shopping mall. The girls ordered medium-size T-bones and Luke went for a big one. But then he suffered a terrifying attack of diarrhea halfway through his meal and had to spend a sweaty, bowel-scorching thirty minutes in the toilet, listening to the piped-in music and the scrapings and flushings of other men. Aunt Olna appeared fussed when he finally returned to the table, his shirt drenched and his face pale, until he explained to her he'd caught a nasty bug drinking the polluted Paris water. Then she relaxed and smiled, reassured.

When they left the restaurant Olna told the young woman cashier, "My guests tonight have come here all the way from Paris, France."

He berated himself for having lapsed from his regime of healthy food, frequent naps, jogging and aerobics, no stress. He was stifling from frustration and anger. When they returned to Olna's it was already dark, but Luke insisted he was going jogging. Olna and Beth didn't offer the slightest objection and he realized that in their eyes he was no longer a boy but a man, a lawgiver. Or maybe they were just indifferent. People could accept anything as long as they weren't directly affected.

A sad truth

He ran through the streets over the railroad tracks, past Olna's new Baptist church, down dark streets past houses built on GI loans just after the war for six or seven thousand dollars. Their screened-in porches were dimly lit by yellow, mosquito-repellent bulbs. He smelled something improbably rich and spicy, then remembered Olna had told him people were taking in well-behaved, industrious Vietnamese lodgers studying at the local college—their only fault, apparently, being that they cooked up smelly food at all hours.

The Vietnamese were the only change in this town during the last twenty-five years. Otherwise it was the same houses, the same lawns, the same people playing Ping-Pong in their garages, voices ricocheting off the cement, the same leashless dogs running out to inspect him, then walking dully away.

There was the big house where Beth had married Greg so many years ago in the backyard among her mother's bushes of huge yellow roses. And there—he could feel his bowels turning over, his breath tightening, his body exuding cold sweat— there was the house where, when he was fifteen, Luke had met a handsome young man, a doctor's son, five years older and five hundred times richer, a man with black hair on his pale knuckles, a thin nose and blue eyes, a gentle man Luke would never have picked for sex but whom he'd felt he could love, someone he'd always meant to look up again: the front doorbell glowed softly, lit from within. The house was white clapboard with green shutters, which appeared nearly black in the dim streetlight.

On and on he ran, past the cow palace where he'd watched a rodeo as a kid. Now he was entering the same park where he and Beth had walked today. He could feel his energy going, his legs so weak he could imagine losing control over them and turning an ankle or falling. He knew how quickly a life could be reduced. He dreaded becoming critically ill here in Texas; he didn't want to give his family the satisfaction.

He ran past the unlit swimming pool and again he remembered that one wonderful day of fun and leisure so many years ago. On that single day he'd felt like a normal kid. He'd even struck up a friendship with another boy and they'd gone down the water slide a hundred times, one behind the other, tobogganing.

Now he was thudding heavily past the spotlit tennis court. No one was playing, it was too hot and still, but two girls in white shorts were sitting on folding chairs at the far end, talking. Then he was on the gravel path under low, over-hanging trees. The crickets chanted slower than his pulse and from time to time seemed to skip a beat. He passed a girl walking her dog and he gasped, "Howdy," and she smiled. The smell of honeysuckle was so strong and he thought he'd never really gotten the guys he'd wanted, the big high school jocks, the blonds with loud tenor voices, beer breath, cruel smiles, lean hips, steady, insolent eyes, the guys impossible to befriend if you weren't exactly like them. He thought that with so many millions of people in the world the odds should have been that at least one guy like that would have gone for him, but things hadn't turned out that way. Of course, even when you had someone, what did you have?

But then what did anyone ever have—the impermanence of sexual possession was a better school than most for the way life would flow through your hands.

In the distance, through the mesquite trees, he could see the lights of occasional cars nosing the dark. Then he remembered that right around here the redhead had pissed a brown circle and Luke looked for traces of that stain under the tree. He even touched the dust, feeling for moisture. He wondered if just entertaining the outrageous thought weren't sufficient for his purposes, but, no, he preferred the ceremony of doing something actual.

He found the spot—or thought he did—and touched the dirt to his lips. He started running again, chewing the grit as though it might help him to recuperate his past if not his health. The transfusion of wet dirt even gave him a new burst of energy.

Skinned Alive

I first saw him at a reading in Paris. An American writer, whom everyone had supposed dead, had come to France to launch a new translation of his classic book, originally published twenty-five years earlier. The young man in the crowd who caught my eye had short red-blond hair and broad shoulders (bodyguard broad, commando broad) and an unsmiling gravity. When he spoke English, he was very serious; when he spoke French, he looked amused.

He was seated on the other side of the semicircle surrounding the author, who was slowly, sweetly, suicidally disappointing the young members of his audience. They had come expecting to meet Satan, for hadn't he summoned up in his pages a brutish vision of gang rape in burned-out lots, of drug betrayals and teenage murders? But what they were meeting now was a reformed drunk given to optimism, offering us brief recipes for recovery and serenity—not at all what the spiky-haired kids had had in mind.

I was charmed by the writer's hearty laugh and pleased that he'd been able to trade in his large bacchanalian genius for a bit of happiness. But his new writings were painful to listen to and my eyes wandered restlessly over the bookshelves. I was searching out interesting new titles, saluting familiar ones, reproaching a few.

And then I had the young man to look at. He had on black trousers full in the calf and narrow in the thighs, his compact waist cinched in by a thick black belt and a gold buckle. His torso was concealed by an extremely ample, long-sleeved black shirt, but despite its fullness I could still see the broad, powerful chest, the massive shoulders and biceps—the body of a professional killer. His neck was thick, like cambered marble.

My French friend Hélène nudged me and whispered, "There's one for you." Maybe she said that later, during the discussion period after the young man had asked a question that revealed his complete familiarity with the text. He had a tenor voice I was sure that he'd worked to lower or perhaps his voice sounded strangled because he was just shy—a voice, in any event, that made me think of those low notes a cellist draws out of his instrument by slowly sawing the bow back and forth while fingering a tremolo with the other hand.

From his accent I couldn't be certain he was American; he might be German, a nationality that seemed to accommodate his contradictions better—young but dignified, athletic but intellectual. There was nothing about him of the brash American college kid, the joker who has been encouraged to express all his opinions, including those that have just popped into his head. The young man respected the author's classic novel so much that he made me want to take it more seriously. I liked the way he referred to specific scenes as though they were literary sites known to everyone. This grave young man was probably right, the scandalous books always turn out to be the good ones.

Yes, Hélène must have nudged me after his question, because she's attracted to men only if they're intelligent. If they're literary, all the better, since, when she's not reading, she's talking about books. I'll phone her toward noon and she'll say, "I'm in China" or "Today, it's the Palais-Royal" or "Another unhappy American childhood," depending on whether the book is a guide, a memoir or a novel. She worries about me and wants me to find someone, preferably a Parisian, so I won't get any funny ideas about moving back to New York. She and I always speak in English. If I trick her into continuing in French after an evening with friends, she'll suddenly catch herself and say indignantly, "But why in earth are we speaking French!" She claims to be bilingual, but she speaks French to her cats. People dream in the language they use on their cats.

She is too discreet, even with me, her closest friend, to solicit any details about my intimate life. Once, when she could sense Jean-Loup was making me unhappy, I said to her, "But you know I do have two other . . . people I see from time to time," and she smiled, patted my hand and said, "Good. Very good. I'm delighted." Another time she shocked me. I asked her what I should say to a jealous lover, and she replied, "The answer to the question, 'Are you faithful, *chéri?*' is always 'Yes.'" She made vague efforts to meet and even charm the different men who passed through my life (her Japanese clothes, low voice and blue-tinted glasses impressed them all). But I could tell she disapproved of most of them. "It's Saturday," she would say. "Jean-Loup must be rounding you up for your afternoon shopping spree." If ever I said anything against him, she would dramatically bite her lip, look me in the eye and nod.

But I liked to please Jean-Loup. And if I bought him his clothes every Saturday morning, that afternoon he would let me take them off again, piece by piece, to expose his boyish body, a lean-hipped and priapic body. On one hip, the color of wedding-gown satin, he had a mole, which the French more accurately call a *grain de beauté*.

Since Jean-Loup came from a solid middle-class family but had climbed a social rung, he had the most rigid code of etiquette, and I owe him the slight improvements I've made in my impressionistic American table manners, learned thirty years ago among boarding-school savages. Whereas Americans are taught to keep their unused hand in their lap at the table, the French are so filthy minded they assume hidden hands are the devil's workshop. Whereas Americans clear each plate as soon as it's finished, the French wait for everyone to complete the course. That's the sort of thing he taught me. To light a match after one has smelled up a toilet. To greet the most bizarre story with the comment, "But that's perfectly normal." To be careful to serve oneself from the cheese tray no more than once ("Cheese is the only course a guest has the right to refuse," he told me, "and the only dish that should never be passed twice").

Also not to ask so many questions or volunteer so many answers. After a two-hour train ride he'd ask me if I had had enough time to confide to the stranger at my side all the details of my unhappy American childhood. Like most Frenchmen who have affairs with Americans, he was attracted by my "niceness" and "simplicity" (ambiguous compliments at best), but had set out to reform those very qualities, which became weaknesses once I was granted the high status of honorary Frenchman. "Not Frenchman," he would say. "You'll never be French. But you are a Parisian. No one can deny that." Then to flatter me he would add, *"Plus parisien tu meurs,"* though just then I felt I'd die if I were less, not more, Parisian.

But if Jean-Loup was always "correct" in the salon, he was "vicious" and "perverse" (high compliments in France) in the *chambre*. The problem was that he didn't like to see me very often. He loved me but wasn't in love with me, that depressing (and all too translatable) distinction (*"Je t'aime mais je ne suis pas amoureux d'amour"*). He was always on the train to Bordeaux, where his parents lived and where he'd been admitted to several châteaux, including some familiar even to me because they were on wine labels. He'd come back with stories of weekend country parties at which the boys got drunk and tore off the girls' designer dresses and then everyone went riding bareback at dawn. He had a set of phrases for describing these routs (*"On s'éclatait"; "On se marrait"; "On était fou, mais vraiment fou et on a bien rigolé"*), which all meant they had behaved disreputably with the right people within decorous limits. After all they were in their own "milieu." He slept with a few of the girls and was looking to marry one who would be intelligent, not ugly, distinguished, a good sport and a slut in bed. He even asked me to help him. "You go everywhere, you meet everyone," he said, "you've fixed up so many of your friends, find me someone like Brigitte but better groomed, a good slut who likes men. Of course, even if I married that would never affect our relationship." Recently he'd decided that he would inform his bride-to-be that he was homosexual; he just knew she'd be worldly about it.

With friends Jean-Loup was jolly and impertinent, quick to trot out his "horrors," as he called them, things that would make the girls scream and the boys blush. Twice he showed his penis at mixed dinner parties. Even so, his horrors were, while shocking, kindhearted and astute. He never asked about money or class, questions that might really embarrass a Frenchman. He would sooner ask about blowjobs than job prospects, cock size than the size of a raise. In our funny makeshift circle—which I had cobbled together to amuse him and which fell apart when he left me—the girls were witty, uncomplicated and heterosexual, and the boys handsome and homo. We were resolutely silly and made enormous occasions out of each other's birthdays and saint's days. Our serious, intimate conversations took place only between two people, usually over the phone.

I neglected friends my own age. I never spoke English or talked about books except with Hélène. A friend from New York said, after staying with me for a week, that I was living in a fool's paradise, a gilded playpen filled with enchanting, radiant nymphs and satyrs who offered me "no challenge." He disapproved of the way I was willing to take just crumbs from Jean-Loup.

Brioche crumbs, I thought.

I didn't know how to explain that now that so many of my old friends in New York had died—my best friend, and also my editor, who was a real friend as well—I preferred my playpen, where I could be twenty-five again but French this time. When reminded of my real age and nationality, I then played at being older and American. Youth and age seemed equally theatrical. Maybe the unreality was the effect of living in another language, of worrying about how many slices of *chèvre* one could take and of buying pretty clothes for a bisexual Bordelais. At about this time a punk interviewed me on television and asked, "You are known as a homosexual, a writer and an American. When did you first realize you were an American?"

"When I moved to France," I said.

That Jean-Loup was elusive could not be held against him. He warned me from the first he was in full flight. What I didn't grasp was that he was running toward someone even he couldn't name yet. Despite his lucid way of making distinctions about other people ("She's not a liar but a mythomaniac; her lying serves no purpose") he was indecisive about everything in his own future: Would he marry or become completely gay? Would he stay in business or develop his talent, drawing adult comic strips? Would he remain in Paris or continue shuttling between it and Bordeaux? I teased him, calling him Monsieur Charnière (Mr. Hinge).

Where he could be decisive was in bed. He had precise and highly colored fantasies, which I deduced from his paces and those he put me through. He never talked about his desires until the last few times we had sex, just before the end of our "story," as the French call an affair; his new talkativeness I took as a sign that he'd lost interest in me or at least respect for me, and I was right. Earlier he had never talked about his desire, but hurled it against me: he needed me here not there, like this not that. I felt desired for the first time in years.

My friends, especially Hélène, but even the other children in the playpen, assumed Jean-Loup was genteelly fleecing me with my worldly, cheerful complicity, but I knew I had too little money to warrant such a speculation. He'd even told me that if it was money he was after he could find a man far richer than me. In fact I knew I excited him. That's why I had to find him a distinguished slut for a wife. I had corrupted him, he told me, by habituating him to sex that was "hard," which the French pronounce "ard" as in "ardent" and, out of a certain deference, never elide with the preceding word.

He didn't mind if I talked during sex, telling him who he was, where we were and why I had to do all this to him. I was used to sex raps from the drug-taking 1970s. Now, of course, there were no drugs and I had to find French words for my obsessions, and when I sometimes made a mistake in gender or verb form Jean-Loup would wince. He wouldn't mention it later; he didn't want to talk anything over later. Only once, after he'd done something very strange to me, he asked, laughing as he emerged from the shower, "Are you the crazy one or am I? I think we're both crazy." He seemed very pleased.

For the first year we'd struggled to be "lovers" officially, but he devoted more of his energy to warding me off than embracing me. He had a rule that he could never stay on after a dinner at my place; he would always leave with the other members of the playpen. To stay behind would look too domestic, he thought, too queer, too *pédé*. After a year of such partial intimacy I got fed up. More likely I became frightened that Jean-Loup, who was growing increasingly remote, would suddenly drop me. I broke up with him over dinner in a restaurant. He seemed relieved and said, "I would never have dared to take the first step." He was shaken for two or three days, then recovered nicely. As he put it, he "supported celibacy" quite effortlessly. It felt natural to him, it was his natural condition.

I went to New York for a week. By chance he went there after I returned. When we saw each other again in Paris we were as awkward as adolescents. His allergies were acting up; American food had made him put on two kilos; a New York barber had thrown his meaty ears into high relief. "It's terrible," Jean-Loup said, "I wanted my independence, but now that I have it. . . . Undress me." I did so, triumphant while registering his admission that he was the one after all who had wanted to be free.

After that we saw each other seldom but when we did it was always passionate. The more people we told that we were no longer lovers, the more violent our desire for each other became. I found his heavy balls, which he liked me to hold in my mouth while I looked up at him. I found the mole on his smooth haunch. Because of his allergies he couldn't tolerate colognes or deodorants; I was left with his natural kid-brother smell. We had long since passed through the stage of smoking marijuana together or using sex toys or dressing each other up in bits of finery. Other couples I knew became kinkier and kinkier over the years if they continued having sex or else resigned themselves to the most routine, suburban relief. We were devouring each other with a desire that was ever purer and sharper. Of course such a desire is seldom linked to love. It can be powerful when solicited but quickly forgotten when absent.

Perhaps the threat of ending things altogether, which we'd just averted, had made us keener. More likely, Jean-Loup, now that he thought he'd become less homosexual by shedding a male lover, me, felt freer to indulge drives that had become more urgent precisely because they were less well defined. Or perhaps I'm exaggerating my importance in his eyes; as he once said, he didn't like to wank his head over things like that (*"Je ne me branle pas trop la tête"*).

I was in love with him and, during sex, thought of that love, but I tried to conceal it from him.

I tried to expect nothing, see him when I saw him, pursue other men, as though I were strictly alone in the world. For the first time when he asked me if I had other lovers I said I did and even discussed them with him. He said he was relieved, explaining that my adventures exonerated him from feeling responsible for me and my happiness. He was a lousy lover, he said, famous for being elusive; even his girlfriends complained about his slipperiness. That elusiveness, I would discover, was his protest against his own passivity, his longing to be owned.

———

Things changed day by day between us. He said he wasn't searching for other sexual partners; he preferred to wait until he fell in love, revealing that he didn't imagine that we'd become lovers again. Nor was he in such a hurry to find a distinguished and sympathetic slut for a wife. When I asked him about his marital plans, he said that he was still looking forward to settling down with a wife and children someday but that now he recognized that when he thought of rough sex, of *la baise harde,* he thought of men. And again he flatteringly blamed me for having corrupted him even while he admitted he was looking for someone else, another man, to love.

Once in a very great while he referred to me playfully as his "husband," despite his revulsion against camp. I think he was trying to come up with a way that would let our friendship continue while giving each of us permission to pursue other people. Once he somberly spoke of me as his *mécène* (or "patron") but I winced and he quickly withdrew the description. I wouldn't have minded playing his father, but that never occurred to him.

I'm afraid I'm making him sound too cold. He had that sweet kid-brother charm, especially around women. All those former debutantes from Bordeaux living in Paris felt free to ask him to run an errand or install a bookcase, which he did with unreflecting devotion. He was careful (far more careful than any American would have been) to distinguish between a pal and a friend, but the true friends exercised an almost limitless power over him. Jean-Loup was quite proud of his capacity for friendship. When he would say that he was a rotten lover— elusive, unsure of his direction—he'd also assure me that he'd always remain my faithful friend, and I believed him. I knew that he was, in fact, waiting for our passion to wear itself out so that a more decent friendship could declare itself.

He wasn't a friend during sex or just afterward; he'd always shower, dress and leave as quickly as possible. Once, when he glanced back at the rubble we had made of the bedroom, he said all that evidence of our bestiality disgusted him. Nor was he especially kind to me around our playmates. To them, paradoxically, he enjoyed demonstrating how thoroughly he was at home in my apartment. He was the little lord of the manor. Yet he'd compliment me on how well I "received" people and assure me I could always open a restaurant in New York someday if my career as a writer petered out. He didn't take my writing too seriously. It had shocked him the few times he'd dipped into it. He preferred the lucidity and humanism of Milan Kundera, his favorite writer. In fact none of our playmates read me, and their indifference pleased me. It left me alone with my wet sand.

He took a reserved interest in my health. He was relieved that my blood tests every six months suggested the virus was still dormant. He was pleased I no longer smoked or drank (though like most French people he didn't consider champagne alcoholic). During one of our sex games he poured half a bottle of red Sancerre down my throat; the etiquette of the situation forbade my refusal, but it was the only time I had tasted alcohol in nearly ten years. We were convinced that the sort of sex we practiced might be demented but was surely safe; in fact we had made it demented since it had to stay safe.

He was negative. While he waited for his results, he said that if they turned out positive his greatest regret would be that he wouldn't be able to father children. A future without a family seemed unbearable. As long as his boy's body with its beautifully shaped man's penis remained unmarked, without a sign of its past or a curse over its future, he was happy to lend himself to our games.

———

Sometimes his laugh was like a shout—boyish, the sound, but the significance, knowing and Parisian. He laughed to show that he hadn't been taken in or that he had caught the wicked allusion. When I was in the kitchen preparing the next course, I'd smile if I heard his whoop. I liked it that he was my husband, so at home, so sociable, so lighthearted, but our marriage was just a poor invention of my fancy.

It reassured me that his sexuality was profoundly, not modishly, violent. He told me that when he had been a child, just seven or eight, he had built a little town out of cardboard and plywood, painted every shutter and peopled every house and then set the whole construction afire and watched the conflagration with a bone-hard, inch-long erection. Is that why just touching me made him hard now (bone-hard, foot-long)? Could he see I was ablaze with ardor for him (ardor with a silent *h*)?

The violence showed up again in the comic strips he was always drawing. He had invented a sort of Frankenstein monster in good French clothes, a creature disturbed by his own half-human sentiments in a world otherwise populated by robots. When I related his comics to the history of art, he'd smile a gay, humiliated smile, the premonitory form of his whooping, disabused Parisian laugh. He was ashamed I made so much of his talent, though his talent was real enough.

He didn't know what to do with his life. He was living as ambitious, healthy young men live who have long vistas of time before them: despairingly. I, who had already outlived my friends and had fulfilled some of my hopes but few of my desires (desire won't stay satisfied), lived each day with joy and anguish. Jean-Loup expected his life to be perfect: there was apparently going to be so much of it.

Have I mentioned that Jean-Loup had such high arches that walking hurt him? He had one of his feet broken, lowered and screwed shut in metal vices that were removed six months later. His main reason for the operation was to take a break from the bank for a few weeks. His clinic room was soon snowed under with comic strip adventures. After that he walked with a bit of a Chaplinesque limp when he was tired.

I often wondered what his life was like with the other young Bordelais counts and countesses at Saint-Jean-de-Luz every August. I was excluded from that world—the chance of my being introduced to his childhood friends had never even once entered his head—which made me feel like a demimondaine listening avidly to her titled young lover's accounts of his exploits in the great world. Although I presented Jean-Loup to my literary friends in London, he had few opinions about them beyond his admiration for the men's clothes and the women's beauty and apparent intelligence. "It was all so fast and brilliant," he said, "I scarcely understood a word." He blamed me for not helping him with his English, though he hated the sounds I made when I spoke my native language. "You don't have an accent in French—oh, you have your little accent, but it's nothing, very charming. But in American you sound like a duck, it's frightful!"

I suppose my English friends thought it was a sentimental autumn-and-spring affair. One friend, who lent us her London house for a few days, said, "Don't let the char see you and Jean-Loup nude." The warning seemed bizarre until I understood it as an acknowledgment of our potential for sensual mischief. Perhaps she was particularly alive to sensual possibilities, since she was so proud of her own handsome, artistic husband.

After I returned to Paris, I spent my days alone reading and writing, and in fair weather I'd eat a sandwich on the quay. That January the Seine overflowed and flooded the highway on the Right Bank. Sea gulls flew upstream and wheeled above the turbulent river, crying, as though mistaking Notre Dame for Mont Saint-Michel. The floodlights trained on the church's

façade projected ghostly shadows of the two square towers up
into the foggy night sky, as though spirits were doing axono-
metric drawings of a cathedral I had always thought of as
malign. The gargoyles were supposed to ward off evil, but to
me they looked like dogs straining to leap away from the devil
comfortably lodged within.

I went to Australia and New Zealand for five weeks. I wrote
Jean-Loup many letters, in French, believing that the French
language tolerated love better than English, but when I returned to Paris Jean-Loup complained of my style. He found
it *mièvre*, "wimpy" or "wet."

He said I should write about his ass one day, but in a style
that was neither pornographic nor wimpy. He wanted me to
describe his ass as Francis Ponge describes soap: an objective,
exhaustive, whimsical catalog of its properties.

I wanted someone else, but I distrusted that impulse, because it seemed, if I looked back, I could see that I had never
been happy in love and that with Jean-Loup I was happier
than usual. As he pointed out, we were still having sex after
two years, and he ascribed the intensity to the very infrequency
that I deplored. Even so, I thought there was something all
wrong, fundamentally wrong, with me: I set up a lover as a
god, then burned with rage when he proved mortal. I lay
awake, next to one lover after another, in a rage, dreaming of
someone who'd appreciate me, give me the simple affection I
imagined I wanted.

When I broke off with Jean-Loup over dinner he said, "You
deserve someone better, someone who will love you completely." Yet the few times I had been loved "completely" I'd
felt suffocated. Nor could I imagine a less aristocratic lover,
one who'd sit beside me on the couch, hand in hand, and
discuss the loft bed, the "mezzanine," we should buy with the
cunning little chair and matching desk underneath.

But when I was alone night after night, I resented Jean-

Loup's independence. He said I deserved something better, and I knew I merited less but needed more.

It was then I saw the redhead at the reading. Although I stared holes through him, he never looked at me once. It occurred to me that he might not be homosexual, except that his grave military bearing was something only homosexuals could (or would bother to) contrive if they weren't actually soldiers. His whole look and manner were studied. Let's say he was the sort of homosexual other homosexuals recognize but that hetero-sexuals never suspect.

The next day I asked the owner of the bookstore if she knew the redhead. "He comes into the shop every so often," she said, with a quick laugh to acknowledge the character of my curiosity, "but I don't know his name. He bought one of your books. Perhaps he'll come to your reading next week."

I told her to be sure to get his name if he returned. "You were a diplomat once," I reminded her. She promised but when I phoned a few days later she said he hadn't been in. Then on the night of my reading I saw him sitting in the same chair as before and I went up to him with absolute confidence and said, "I'm so glad you came tonight. I saw you at the last reading, and my *copine* and I thought you looked so interesting we wished we knew you." He looked so blank that I was afraid he hadn't understood and I almost started again in French. I introduced myself and shook his hand. He went white and said, "I'm sorry for not standing up," and then stood up and shook my hand, and I was afraid he'd address me as "sir."

Now that I could look at his hair closely I noticed that it was blond, if shavings of gold are blond, only on the closely cropped sides but that it was red on top—the reverse of the sun-bleached strawberry blond. He gave me his phone number, and I thought this was someone I could spend the rest of my life with, however brief that might be. His name was Paul.

I phoned him the next day to invite him to dinner, and he said that he had a rather strange schedule, since he worked four nights a week at a disco.

"What do you do?" I asked.

"I'm the physiognomist. The person who recognizes the regulars and the celebrities. I have to know what Brigitte Bardot looks like *now*. I decide who comes in, who stays out, who pays, who doesn't. We have a house rule to let all models in free." He told me people called him Cerberus.

"But how do you recognize everyone?"

"I've been on the door since the club opened seven years ago. So I have ten thousand faces stored in my memory." He laughed. "That's why I could never move back to America. I'd never find a job that paid so well for just twenty hours' work a week. And in America I couldn't do the same job, since I don't know any faces there."

We arranged an evening and he arrived dressed in clothes by one of the designers he knew from the club. Not even my reactionary father, however, would have considered him a popinjay. He did nothing that would risk his considerable dignity. He had white tulips in his surprisingly small, elegant hand.

All evening we talked literature, and, as two good Americans, we also exchanged confidences. Sometimes his shyness brought all the laughter and words to a queasy halt, and it made me think of that becalmed moment when a sailboat comes around and the mainsail luffs before it catches the wind again. I watched the silence play over his features.

He was from a small town in Georgia. His older brother and he had each achieved the highest score in the statewide scholastic aptitude test. They had not pulled down good grades, however; they read Plato and *Naked Lunch*, staged *No Exit* and brawls with the boys in the next town, experimented with hallucinogens and conceptual art. Paul's brother made an "artwork" out of his plans to assassinate President Ford and was arrested by the FBI.

"I just received the invitation to my tenth high school reunion," Paul said.

"I'll go with you," I said. "I'll go as your spouse."

He looked at me and breathed a laugh, save it was voiced just at the end, the moving bow finally touching the bass string and waking sound in it.

Paul's older brother had started a rock band, gone off to New York where he died of AIDS—another musician punished. He had been one of the first heterosexual male victims, dead already in 1981. He contracted the disease from a shared needle. Their mother, a Scottish immigrant, preferred to think he had been infected by another man. Love seemed a nobler cause of death than drugs.

"Then I came to Paris," Paul said. He sighed and looked out of my open window at the roofs of the Ile Saint-Louis. Like other brilliant young men and women he dissolved every solid in a solvent of irony, but even he had certain articles of faith, and the first was Paris. He liked French manners, French clothes, French food, French education. He said things like "France still maintains cultural hegemony over the whole world," and pronounced "hegemony" as *hégémonie*. He had done all his studies as an adult in France and French. He asked me what the name of Platon's *Le Banquet* was in English (that's what they call *The Symposium*, for some reason). He had a lively, but somewhat vain, sense of what made him interesting, which struck me only because he seemed so worthy of respect that any attempt he made to serve himself up appeared irrelevant.

He was wearing a white shirt and dark tie and military shoes and a beautiful dark jacket that was cut to his Herculean chest and shoulders. He had clear eyes, pale blue eyes. The white tulips he brought were waxen and pulsing like lit candles, and his skin, that rich hairless skin, was tawny-colored. His manners were formal and French, a nice Georgia boy but Europeanized, someone who'd let me lazily finish my sentences in French (*"Quand même,"* we'd say, *"rien à voir avec . . ."*). His teeth were so chalky white that the red wine stained them a faint blue. His face was at once open and unreadable, as imposing as the globe. He nodded slowly as he thought out what I said, so slowly that I doubted the truth or seriousness of what I was saying. He hesitated and his gaze was noncommittal, making me wonder if he was pondering his own response or simply panicking. I wouldn't have thought of him panicking except he mentioned it. He said he was always on the edge of panic (the sort of thing Americans say to each other with big grins). Points of sweat danced on the bridge of his nose, and I thought I saw in his eye something frightened, even unpleasant and unreachable. I kept thinking we were too much alike, as though at any moment our American heartiness and our French *politesse* would break down and we'd look at each other with the sour familiarity of brothers. Did he sense it, too? Is that why our formality was so important to him? I was sure he hadn't liked himself in America.

Speaking French so long had made me simplify my thoughts—whether expressed in French or English—and I was pleased I could say now what I felt, since the intelligence I was imputing to him would never have tolerated my old vagueness. Whereas Jean-Loup had insisted I use the right fork, I felt Paul would insist on the correct emotion.

Sometimes before he spoke Paul made a faint humming sound—perhaps only voiced shyness—but it gave the impression of muted deference. It made me think of a student half raising his hand to speak in a seminar too small and egalitarian to require the teacher's recognition. But I also found myself imagining that his thought was so varied, occurring on so many levels at once, that the hum was a strictly mechanical downshift into the compromise (and invention) of speech. After a while the hum disappeared, and I fancied he felt more at ease with me, although the danger is always to read too much into what handsome men say and do. Although he was twenty years younger, he seemed much older than I.

"Would you like to go to Morocco with me?" I asked him suddenly. "For a week? A magazine will pay our fares. It's the south of Morocco. It should be amusing. I don't know it at all, but I think it's better to go somewhere brand new—" ("with a lover" were the words I suppressed).

"Sure."

He said he hadn't traveled anywhere in Europe or Africa except for two trips to Italy.

Although I knew things can't be rushed, that intimacy follows its own sequence, I found myself saying, "We should be lovers—you have everything, beauty and intelligence." Then I added: "And we get on so well." My reasoning was absurd: his beauty and intelligence were precisely what made him unavailable.

I scarcely wanted him to reply. As long as he didn't I could nurse my illusions. "That would depend," he said, "on our being compatible sexually, don't you think?" Then he asked, with his unblinking gravity, "What's your sexuality like?" For the first time I could hear a faint Georgia accent in the way the syllables of "sexuality" got stretched out.

"It depends on the person," I said, stalling. Then, finding my answer lamentable, I pushed all my chips forward on one number: "I like pain."

"So do I," he said. "And my penis has never—no man has ever touched it."

He had had only three lovers and they had all been heterosexuals or fancied they were. In any event they had had his sort of *pudeur* about uttering endearments to another man. He had a lover now, Thierry, someone he met two years before at the club. The first time they saw each other, Paul had been tanked up on booze, smack and steroids, a murderous cocktail, and they had a fistfight which had dissolved into a night of violent passion.

Every moment must have been haloed in his memory, for he remembered key phrases Thierry had used. For the last two years they had eaten every meal together. Thierry dressed him in the evening before Paul left for work and corrected his French and table manners. These interventions were often nasty, sometimes violent. "What language are you speaking now?" he would demand if Paul made the slightest error. When Paul asked for a little tenderness in bed, Thierry would say, "Oh-ho, like Mama and Papa now, is it?" and then leave the room. Paul fought back—he broke his hand once because he hit Thierry so hard. "Of course he'd say that it was all my fault," Paul said, "that all he wants is peace, blue skies." He smiled. "Thierry is a businessman, very dignified. He has never owned a piece of leather in his life. I despise leather. It robs violence of all the"—his smile now radiant, the mainsail creaking as it comes around—"the *sacramental*." He laughed, shaking, and emitted a strange chortle that I didn't really understand. It came out of a sensibility I hadn't glimpsed in him before.

Paul longed for us to reach the desert; he had never seen it before.

We started out at Agadir and took a taxi to the mud-walled town of Taroudant. There we hired a car and drove to Ouarzazate, which had been spoiled by organized tourism: it had become Anywhere Sunny. Then we drove south to Zagora. It was just twenty kilometers beyond Zagora, people said, that the desert started. I warned Paul the desert could be disappointing: "You're never alone. There's always someone spying on you from over the next dune. And it rains. I saw the rain pour over Syria."

Paul loved maps. Sometimes I could see in him the solitary Georgia genius in love with his best friend's father, the sheriff, a kid lurking around home in the hot, shuttered afternoons, daydreaming over the globe that his head so resembled, his mind racing on homemade LSD. He knew how to refold maps, but when they were open he would press his palms over their creases as though opening his own eyes wider and wider.

I did all the driving, through adobe cities built along narrow, palm-lined roads. In every town boys wanted to be our guides, sell us trinkets or carpets or their own bodies. They hissed at us at night from the shadows of town walls: lean and finely muscled adolescents hissing to attract our attention, their brown hands massaging a lump beneath the flowing blue acrylic jellabas mass-produced in China. To pass them up with a smile was a new experience for me. I had Paul beside me, this noble pacing lion. I remembered a Paris friend calling me just before we left for Morocco, saying he had written a letter to a friend, "telling him I'd seen you walking down the boulevard Saint-Germain beside the young Hercules with hair the color of copper." In Morocco there was no one big enough, powerful enough or cruel enough to interest Paul.

Perhaps it was due to the clear, memorable way Paul had defined his sexual nature, but during our cold nights together I lay in his great arms and never once felt excited, just an immense surge of peace and gratitude. Our predicament, we felt, was like a Greek myth. "Two people love each other," I said, "but the gods have cursed them by giving them the identical passions." I was being presumptuous sneaking in the phrase "Two people love each other," because it wasn't at all clear that he loved me.

One night we went to the movies and saw an Italian adventure film starring American weightlifters and dubbed in
French, a story set in a back-lot castle with a perfunctory
princess in hot pants. There was an evil prince whose handsome face melted to reveal the devil's underneath. His victim
("All heroes are masochists," Paul declared) was an awkward
bodybuilder not yet comfortable in his newly acquired bulk,
who had challenged the evil prince's supremacy and now had
to be flayed alive. Paul clapped and chortled and, during the
tense scenes, physically braced himself. This was the Paul
who had explained what Derrida had said of Heidegger's inter-
pretation of Trakl's last poems, who claimed that literature
could be studied only through rhetoric, grammar and genre
and who considered Ronsard a greater poet than Shakespeare
(because of Ronsard's combination of passion and logic, satyr
and god, in place of the mere conversational fluency which
Paul regarded as the flaw and genius of English): this was the
same Paul who booed and cheered as the villain smote the hero
before a respectful audience, the air thick with smoke and the
flickers of flashlights. It was a movie in which big men were
hurting each other.

Jean-Loup would have snorted, his worst prejudices about
Americans confirmed, for as we traveled, drawing closer and
closer to the desert, we confided more and more in each other.
As we drove through the "valley of a thousand Casbahs," Paul
told me about threats to his life. "When someone at the club
pulls a gun on me, and it's happened three times, I say, 'I'm
sorry but guns are not permitted on the premises,' and it
works, they go away, but mine is a suicidal response." Paul
was someone on whom nothing was wasted; nevertheless he
was not always alive to all possibilities, at least not instantly.
I told him I was positive, but he didn't react. Behind the

extremely dark sunglasses, there was this presence, breathing and thinking but not reacting.

Our hotel, the Hesperides, had been built into the sun-baked mud ramparts in the ruins of the pasha's palace. We stared into an octagonal, palm-shaded pool glistening with black rocks that then slid and clicked—ah, tortoises! There couldn't have been more than five guests, and the porters, bored and curious, tripped over themselves serving us. We slept in each other's arms night after night and I stroked his great body as though he were a prize animal, *la belle bête*. My own sense of who I was in this story was highly unstable. I flickered back and forth, wanting to be the blond warrior's fleshy, pale concubine or then the bearded pasha himself, feeding drugged sherbets to the beautiful Circassian slave I had bought. I thought seriously that I wouldn't mind buying and owning another human being—if it was Paul.

The next day we picked up some hitchhikers, who, when we reached their destination, asked us in for mint tea, which we sipped barefoot in a richly carpeted room. A baby and a chicken watched us through the doorway from the sun-white courtyard. Every one of our encounters seemed to end with a carpet, usually one we were supposed to buy. In a village called Wodz, I remember both of us smiling as we observed how long and devious the path to the carpet could become: there was first a tourist excursion through miles of Casbahs, nearly abandoned except for an old veiled woman poking a fire in a now roofless harem; then we took a stroll through an irrigated palm plantation, where a woman leading a donkey took off her turban, a blue bath towel, and filled it with dates, which she gave us with a golden grin; and finally we paid a "surprise visit" to the guide's "brother," the carpet merchant who happened to have just returned from the desert with exotic Tuareg rugs. Their prices, to emphasize their exoticism, he pretended to translate from Tuareg dollars into dirham.

We laughed, bargained, bought, happy anytime our shoulders touched or eyes met. We told everyone we were Danes, since Danish was the one language even the most resourceful carpet merchants didn't know. ("But wait, I have a cousin in the next village who once lived in Copenhagen.")

Later, when I returned to Paris, I would discover that Jean-Loup had left me for Régis, one of the richest men in France. For the first time in his life he was in love, he would say. He would be wearing Régis's wedding ring, my Jean-Loup who had refused to stay behind at my apartment after the other guests had left lest he appear too *pédé*. People would suspect him of being interested in the limousine, the town house, the château, but Jean-Loup would insist it was all love.

When he told me, on my return, that he would never sleep with me again—that he had found the man with whom he wanted to spend the rest of his life—my response surprised him. *"Ça tombe bien,"* I said ("That suits me fine").

Jean-Loup blurted out: "But you're supposed to be furious." It wasn't that he wanted me to fight to get him back, though he might have enjoyed it, but that his vanity demanded that I protest; my own vanity made me concede him with a smile. Feverishly I filled him in on my recent passion for Paul and the strategies I had devised for unloading him, Jean-Loup. It's true I had thought of fixing him up with a well-heeled handsome young American.

Jean-Loup's eyes widened. "I had no idea," he said, "that things had gone so far." Perhaps in revenge he told me how he had met Régis. It seems that, while I was away, a dear friend of mine had fixed them up.

I was suddenly furious and couldn't drop the subject. I railed and railed against the dear friend: "When I think he ate my food, drank my drink, all the while plotting to marry you off to a millionaire in order to advance his own miserable little interests. . . ."

"Let me remind you that Régis's money means nothing to me. No, what I like is his good humor, his sincerity, his discretion. It was hard for me to be known as your lover— your homosexuality is too evident. Régis is very discreet."

"What rubbish," I would say a few days later when Jean-Loup repeated the remark about Régis's discretion. "He's famous for surrounding himself with aunties who discuss the price of lace the livelong day."

"Ah," Jean-Loup replied, reassured, "you've been filled in, I see" (*"Tu t'en renseignes"*).

All sparkling and droll, except a terrible sickness, like an infection caused by the prick of a diamond brooch, had set in. When I realized that I would never be able to abandon myself again to Jean-Loup's perverse needs, when I thought that Régis was enjoying the marriage with him I'd reconciled myself never to know, when I saw the serenity with which Jean-Loup now "assumed" his homosexuality, I felt myself sinking, but genuinely sinking, as though I really were falling, and my face had a permanently hot blush. I described this feeling of falling and heat to Paul. "That's jealousy," he said. "You're jealous." That must be it, I thought, I who had never been jealous before. If I had behaved so generously with earlier loves lost it was because I had never before been consumed by a passion this feverish.

Jealousy, yes, it was jealousy, and never before had I so wanted to hurt someone I loved, and that humiliated me further. A member of the playpen dined at Régis's *hôtel particulier*. "They hold hands all the time," she said. "I was agreeably surprised by Régis, a charming man. The house is more a museum than a house. Jean-Loup kept calling the butler for more champagne, and we almost burst out laughing. It was like a dream."

Every detail fed my rancor—Régis's charm, wealth, looks ("Not handsome but attractive").
Everything.

Paul had a photographic memory, and, during the hours spent together in the car in Morocco, he recited page after page of Racine or Ronsard or Sir Philip Sidney. He also continued the story of his life. I wanted to know every detail—the bloody scenes on the steps of the disco, the recourse to dangerous drugs, so despised by the clenched-jaw cocaine set. I wanted to hear that he credited his lover with saving him from being a junkie, a drunk and a thug. "He was the one who got me back into school."

"A master, I see," I thought. "*School* master."

"Now I study Cicéron and prepare my *maîtrise*, but then I was just an animal, a disoriented bull—I'd even gotten into beating up fags down by the Seine at dawn when I was really drunk."

He gave me a story he had written. It was Hellenistic in tone, precious and edgy, flirting with the diffuse lushness of a Pre-Raphaelite prose, rich but bleached, like a tapestry left out in the sun. I suppose he must have had in mind Mallarmé's "Afternoon of a Faun," but Paul's story was more touching, less cold, more comprehensible. That such a story could never be published in the minimalist, plain-speaking 1980s seemed never to have occurred to him. Could it be that housed in such a massive body he had no need for indirect proofs of power and accomplishment? Or was he so sure of his taste that recognition scarcely interested him at all?

The story is slow to name its characters, but begins with a woman who turns out to be Athena. She discovers a flute and how to get music out of it, but her sisters, seeing her puffing away, laugh at the face she's making. Athena throws the flute down and in a rage places a curse on it: "Whoever would make use of it next must die." Her humiliation would cost a life.

The next user is a cheerful satyr named Marsyas. He cleverly learns how to imitate people with his tunes: "Prancing along behind them he could do their walk, fast or slow, lurching or clipped, just as he could render their tics or trace their contours: a low swell for a belly, shrill fifing for fluttering hands, held high notes for the adagio of soft speech. At first no one understood. But once they caught on they slapped their thighs: his songs were sketches."

Apollo is furious, since he's the god of music and his own art is pure and abstract. He challenges Marsyas to a musical duel:

Marsyas cringed before him like a dog when it walks through a ghost, bares its teeth and pulls back its ears. Anguished, he had slept in the hot breath of his flock; his animals had pressed up against him, holding him between their woolly flanks, as though to warm him. The ribbon his jolly and jiggling woman had tied around one horn flapped listlessly against his low, hairy brow, like a royal banner flown by a worker's barge.

To the gods, as young as the morning, Marsyas seemed a twilight creature; he smelled of leaf mold and wolf-lair. His glance was as serious as a deer's when it emerges from the forest at dusk to drink at the calm pool collecting below a steaming cataract.

And to Marsyas his rival was cold and regular as cambered marble.

Since Marsyas knew to play only what was in front of him, he "rendered" Apollo—not the god's thoughts but the faults he wedged into the air around him. The sisters watched the goatman breathe into the reeds, saw him draw and lose breath, saw his eyes bulge, brown and brilliant as honey, and that made them laugh. What they heard, however, was music that copied sacred lines, for Marsyas could imitate a god as easily as a bawd. The only trick was to have his model there, in front of him. If Marsyas gave them the god's form, the god himself revealed the contents of his mind. His broad hand swept the lyre, and immediately the air was tuned and the planets tempered. Everything sympathetic trembled in response to a song that took no one into account, that moved without moving, that polished crystal with its breath alone, clouding then cleansing every transparency without touching it. Marsyas shuddered when he came to and realized that the god's hand was now motionless but that the music continued to devolve, creaking like a finger turning and tracing the fragile rim of the spheres.

The satyr was astonished that the muses didn't decide instantly in their brother's favor but shrugged and smiled and said they found each contestant appealing in different ways. The sun brightened a fraction with Apollo's anger, but then the god suggested they each play their music backwards. The universe shuddered as it stopped and reversed its rotations; the sun started to descend toward dawn as Apollo unstrung the planets. Cocks re-crowed and bats re-awakened, the frightened shepherd guided his flock backward down the hill as the dew fell again.

Even the muses were frightened. It was night and stormy when Marsyas began to play. He had improvised his music strophe by strophe as a portrait; now he couldn't remember it all. The descending figures, so languishing when played correctly the first time, made him queasy when he inverted them. Nor could he see his subject.

The muses decided in the god's favor. Apollo told Marsyas he'd be flayed alive. There was no tenderness but great solicitude in the way the god tied the rope around the satyr's withers, cast the slack over a high branch of a pine and then hoisted his kill high, upside down, inverted as the winning melody. Marsyas saw that he'd won the god's full attention by becoming his victim.

The blood ran to Marsyas's head, then spurted over his chest as Apollo sliced into his belly and neatly peeled back the flesh and fat and hair. The light shone in rays from Apollo's sapphire eyes and locked with Marsyas's eyes, which were wavering, losing grip—he could feel his eyes lose grip, just as a child falling asleep will finally relax its hold on its father's finger. A little dog beside his head was lapping up the fresh blood. Now the god knelt to continue his task. Marsyas could hear the quick sharp breaths, for killing him was hard work. The god's white skin glowed and the satyr believed he was inspiring the very breath Apollo expired.

As I read his story I stupidly wondered which character Paul was—the Apollo he so resembled and whose abstract ideal of art appeared to be his own, or the satyr who embodies the vital principle of mimesis and who, after all, submitted to the god's cruel, concentrated attention. The usual motive for the story, Apollo's jealousy, was left out altogether. His story was dedicated to me, and for a moment I wondered if it was also addressed to me—as a reproach for having abandoned the Apollonian abstractness of my first two novels or, on the contrary, as an endorsement for undertaking my later satires and sketches. It was unsettling dealing with this young man so brilliant and handsome, so violent and so reflective.

At night Paul let me into his bed and held me in his arms, just as he sometimes rested his hand on my leg as I drove the car. He told me that although Thierry often petted him, Paul was never allowed to stroke him. "We've never once kissed each other on the lips."

We talked skittishly about the curse the gods had put on us. I pathetically attempted to persuade Paul he was really a sadist. "Your invariable rage after sex with your lover," I declared melodramatically, "your indignation, your disgusting excursions into fag bashing, your primitive, literalist belief that only the biggest man with the biggest penis has the right to dominate all the others, whereas the sole glory of sadism is its strictly cerebral capacity for imposing new values, your obvious attraction to my fundamentally docile nature—" and at that point my charlatanism would make me burst out laughing, even as I glanced sideways to see how I was doing.

In fact my masochism sickened him. It reminded him of his own longing to recapture Thierry's love. "He's leaving me," he would say. "When calls come in he turns the sound off on the answering machine and he never replays his messages when I'm around. His pockets bulge with condoms. He spends every weekend with purely fictive 'German businessmen' in Normandy; he pretends he's going to visit a factory in Nice, but he's back in Paris four hours later; he stood me up for the Mr. Europe Bodybuilding contest at the Parc de Vincennes, then was seen there with a famous Brazilian model. . . . He says I should see a psychiatrist, and you know how loony you have to be before someone French will suggest that."

When a thoughtful silence had reestablished itself in the car I added, "That's why you want to reach the desert. Only its vast sterility can calm your violent soul."

"If you could be in my head," he said, not smiling, "you'd see I'm in a constant panic."

To be companionable I said, "Me too."

Paul quickly contradicted me: "But you're the calmest person I know."

Then I understood that was how he wanted me to be—masterful, confident, smiling, sure. Even if he would someday dominate, even hurt me, as I wished, he would never give me permission to suffer in any way except heroically.

I drove a few miles in silence through the lunar valley, mountains on both sides, not yet the desert but a coarse-grained prelude to it—dry, gently rolling, the boulders the color of eggplants. "You're right, except so many of the people I've known have died. I used to talk this way with my best friend, but that was in America and now he is dead." That night, in Paul's arms, I said, "It's sacrilegious to say it, especially for an atheist, but I feel God sent you not to replace my friend, since he's irreplaceable, but . . ."

A carpet salesman assured us the desert was about to begin. We had been following a river through the valley and at last it had run dry, and the date palms had vanished, and the mountains knelt like camels just before setting out on a long journey. In Zagora we saw the famous sign, "Timbuctoo: 54 days." In a village we stopped to visit the seventeenth-century library of a saint, Abu Abdallah Mohammed Bennacer, a small room of varnished wood cases beside a walled-in herbal garden. The old guide in his white robes opened for us—his hands were wood-hard—some of the illustrated volumes, including a Koran written on gazelle skin. Paul's red hair and massive body made him rarer than a gazelle in this dusty village. That night a village boy asked me if I had a "gazelle" back in Paris, and I figured out he meant a girlfriend and nodded because that was the most efficient way to stanch a carpet-tending spiel.

Paul continued with his stories. The one about the French woman he had loved and married off to the paratrooper, who had already become his lover. The one about the Los Angeles sadist he ridiculed and who then committed suicide. About his second date with Thierry, when he'd been gagged and chained upside down in a dungeon after being stuffed with acid, then made to face a huge poster of the dead L.A. lover. The one about the paratrooper scaling the mountain at the French-Italian border while cops in circling helicopters ordered him to descend immediately—"and applauded in spite of themselves when he reached the top barehanded," Paul exulted, "without a rope or pick or anything to scale the sheer rock face but balls and brawn."

We're too alike, I thought again, despairing, to love each other, and Paul is different only in his attraction to cartoon images of male violence and aggression. Unlike him, I couldn't submit to a psychopath; what I want is Paul, with all his tenderness and quizzical, hesitating intelligence, his delicacy, to hit me. To be hurt by an enraged bull on steroids doesn't excite me. What I want is to belong to this grave, divided, philosophical man.

It occurred to me that if I thought only now, at this moment in my life, of belonging to someone, it was because my hold on life itself was endangered. Did I want him to tattoo his initials on a body I might soon have to give up? Did I want to become his slave just before I embraced that lasting solitude?

The beginning of the desert was a dune that had drifted through the pass between two mountains and had started to fill up the scrubland. A camel with bald spots on its elbows and starlet eyelashes was tethered to a dark felt tent in which a dirty man was sprawling, half-asleep. Another man, beaming and freshly shaved, bustled out of a cement bunker. With a flourish he invited us in for a glass of mint tea. His house turned out to be a major carpet showroom, buzzing with air-conditioning and neon lamps. "English?"

"No. Danish."

That was the last night of our holiday. The hotel served us a feast of sugared pigeon pie and mutton couscous, and Paul had a lot to drink. We sat in the dark beside the pool, which was lit from within like a philosopher's stone. He told me he thought of me as gay in the Nietzschean, not the West Hollywood, sense, but since I insisted that I needed him, he would love me and protect me and spend his life with me. Later in bed he pounded me in the face with his fists, shouting at me in a stuttering, broken explosion of French and English, the alternatively choked and released patois of scalding indignation.

If the great pleasure of the poor is, as they say, making love, then the great suffering of the rich is loving in vain. The troubadours, who spoke for their rich masters, are constantly reminding us that only men of refinement recognize the nobility of hopeless love; the vulgar crowd jeers at them for wasting their time. Only the idle and free can afford the luxury (the anguish) of making an absence into the very rose-heart of their lives. Only they have the extravagance of time to languish, shed tears, exalt their pain into poetry. For others time is too regulated; every day repeats itself.

I wasn't rich, but I was free and idle enough to ornament my liberty with the melancholy pleasure of having lost a Bordeaux boy with a claret-red mouth. All the while I'd been with Jean-Loup I'd admitted how ill suited we were and I sought or dreamed of seeking someone else either tepidly or hotly, depending on the intensity of my dissatisfaction.

Now that Jean-Loup had left me for Régis, I could glorify their love and despise them and hate myself while sifting through my old memories to show myself that Jean-Loup had been slowly, if unconsciously, preparing this decampment for a long time.

When I am being wicked I tell people, "Our little Jean-Loup has landed in clover. He'll soon be installed in the château for the summer and he can fill the moat with his *bandes des-*

sinées. The only pity is that Jean-Loup is apparently at Régis's mercy and Régis is cunning. He holds all the cards. If he tires of Jean-Loup, the poor boy will be dismissed without a centime, for that wedding ring doesn't represent a claim, only a—"

But at this point bored, shocked friends laugh and hiss, "Jealous, jealous, this way lies madness." Jealousy may be new to me but not to them. My condition is as banal as it is baneful.

And then I realize that the opposite is probably true: that Jean-Loup had always dealt with me openly, even at the end, and had never resorted to subterfuge. As soon as he knew of his deep, innocent love for Régis he told me. I am the one who attributes scheming to him.

He always wanted me to describe his ass, so I'll conclude with an attempt not to sound too wet.

I should admit right off that by all ocular evidence there was nothing extraordinary about it. It wasn't a soccer player's muscled bum or a swimmer's sun-molded twin *charlottes.* It was a kid brother's ass, a perfunctory transition between spine and legs, a simple cushion for a small body. Its color was the low-wattage white of a winter half-moon. It served as the neutral support (as an anonymous glove supports a puppet's bobbing, expressive head) for his big, grown-up penis, always so ready to poke up through his flies and take center stage. But let's not hastily turn him around to reveal Régis's Daily Magic Baguette, as I now call it. No, let's keep his back to us, even though he's deliciously braced his knees to compensate for the sudden new weight he's cantilevered in his excitement, a heavy divining rod that makes his buttocks tense. Concave, each cheek looks glossy, like costly white satin that, having been stuffed in a drawer, has just been smoothed, though it is still crazed with fine, whiter, silkier lines. If he spreads his cheeks—which feel cool, firm and plump—for the kneeling admirer, he reveals an anus that makes one think of a Leica lens, shut now but with many possible f-stops. An expensive aperture, but also a closed morning-glory bud. There's that *grain de beauté* on his hip, the single drop of espresso on the wedding gown. And there are the few silky hairs in the crack of his ass, wet now for some reason and plastered down at odd angles as though his fur had been greedily licked in all directions at once. If he spreads his legs and thinks about nothing—his fitting with the tailor, the castle drawbridge, the debs whose calls he can no longer return—his erection may melt and you might see it drooping lazily into view, just beyond his loosely bagged testicles. He told me that his mother would never let him sleep in his *slip* when he was growing up. She was afraid underpants might stunt his virile growth. These Bordeaux women know to let a young wine breathe.

His Biographer

He had traveled so much that, paradoxically, the few authentic places left in the world looked especially fake to him, as though where Nantucket had once been, a real whaling village built by hardworking Quakers, now there was only a theme park that contained or embalmed it, as a ceramic crown reproduces in a dead material the still-living but whittled-down tooth it sheathes. In the same way the Ile Saint-Louis was no longer a place where people lived, shopped for food and worked but rather an ensemble of stately, empty investment flats that stood dark and untenanted eleven months out of twelve, the seventeenth-century façades concealing luxury twentieth-century interiors rarely visited by their owners, who were groups of American or Saudi—well, not even people but corporations. Key West—famous for its decrepitude, Cuban cigar makers, shrimpers and destitute artists—was now glistening with hasty but radical restorations perpetrated by retired tax accountants growing their gray hair long.

No, all that was real in the world was its despised, inter-changeable platitudes, the suburban shopping malls, the millions of vernacular miles of California strip architecture or, on a lower level still, the sprawling concrete apartment buildings outside Cairo or Istanbul fissuring and rusting even before completed, open sewers between them seeping through the red mud.

From an airplane that's all you could see no matter where you flew over the globe and anything that could be described as charming or picturesque—the snow-topped red barn in Vermont, the historic heart of Basel—was either a guest house or a neighborhood of psychiatrists' offices, a self-conscious reference to itself, words between quotation marks, a boutique or about to become one. From an airplane Greenwich Village wasn't visible, just miles and miles of Lefrak City. From a plane you couldn't see Bourges, which in any event was composed of polyurethane half-timbering out of a kit tacked onto fresh stucco and new car-free cobblestones reflecting like fish scales the lights bouncing off the cathedral *son et lumière;* no, all that was visible from a plane was industrialized wheat farms and drizzle-flecked 1960s public housing, regular as tombstones in a military cemetery.

Worse, he had the same bleak view of himself, the feeling that the only parts that were genuine were those that had never been remarked on precisely because they were unremarkable. For a long time he'd told himself he was tough and unsentimental, but for the last two years he'd admitted he was simply numb and empty of sentiments, a hive that looked normal and functioning until closer inspection revealed it had long ago been burned out and abandoned. Two years ago his nephew had said to him, "There was a study in which all these women complained their husbands were incapable of showing their feelings, and then after lots of therapy it turned out the men just didn't have any feelings."

Charles said to his nephew, "I'm like that. I don't feel anything." He wanted to see if his nephew would protest or if some inner bell would start clanging to warn him he was plunging into deep nonsense. But nothing happened. His nephew flickered into a half smile. The words just hung there in the air, like the devastating truth a stand-up comic tells about himself, funny exactly to the degree that no one before had ever admitted so simply and with such chipper panache to something so sordid.

That's why Charles could tolerate only the malls and council flats of his soul, the parts that functioned routinely, that were no better than or even different from comparable parts in everyone else. He doggedly admired the part that could watch four hours of CNN at a stretch or eat heavily sugared cornflakes at midnight as he stood half-nude and half-awake by the cryptic light of the fridge or talk about the weather to the grocer. Even those actions were too "typical," too "revealing." The person who filled out a registration form when checking into a hotel, who poked a hemorrhoid back into his arse after a shit, who ironed a shirt, that person was perhaps possible.

Perhaps that was also why he wobbled on the balance between equal weights of vanity and irritation at the idea of someone writing his biography. Charles "was the author of" (i.e., had somehow stumbled, both panicked and exhausted, to the end of) biographies of three twentieth-century French writers (Cocteau, Jouhandeau and Stuart Merrill) and he knew that no matter how diligent a biographer might be in sorting out the chronology and uncovering unpublished manuscripts and letters, no matter how skeptical in discounting the special claims the living might have on their dead subject, no matter how subtle he might be in tracing out the indirect, even reciprocal, links between the life and the work, what readers expected and publishers demanded was, quite simply, the *key*, or at least a *scoop*. The key was almost always sexual and inserted into the nursery door; Virginia Woolf's incestuous brush with her older half brother had been a capital moment in the locksmith's art. Ideally the scoop, also sexual, would be the discovery of a previously hidden document that would confirm that Cocteau's father had indeed committed suicide because he was a homosexual or that Jouhandeau's wife had denounced her ex-lovers as Jews to the Gestapo or that Stuart Merrill had contracted syphilis during his brief return to the United States to attend a university (his American parents, long settled in Paris, had been horrified to discover that their son, who at seventeen was one of the original Symbolist poets, could scarcely speak English, but their plans to educate this exquisite dandy in the rough and tumble of Columbia University resulted only in his publishing a single slim volume in English, *Pastels in Prose*, before he sailed back to France, despite the pleas of America's most eminent novelist, William Dean Howells, to stay in the New World, where his talent was much more needed than in a France already surfeited with genius).

But what would this Mr. Tremble dig up on him, Charles? What keys would he insert, one after another, into the frozen lock? Perhaps the most obvious theme to develop would be how he, Charles, who'd written about two homosexuals and one aesthete, was, in spite of his small stature, soft voice and diplomatic ways, an insatiable and improbably successful womanizer. (But he hoped Mr. Tremble wouldn't dwell on that too much; after all, his wife, Catherine, even after thirty years of marriage, was still jealous and, above all, *pudique* about what strangers might say and think).

Or Mr. Tremble might build up the paradox that Charles, a Jew from Lebanon born to an Egyptian father and Turkish mother, had moved to France after the fall of Beirut and devoted himself entirely to—well, to what? Here the lines of the design became tangled, since Cocteau (the plural of "cocktail") had played host to modernism, whereas Jouhandeau, that dreadful little clown who couldn't stop writing and had penned almost a hundred books, had ignored the present entirely and harnessed the pure language of Racine to his own petit bourgeois mixture of Catholicism and sexual slumming (*Don Juan's Breviary*, the subtitle of one of his books, said it all). If Cocteau and Jouhandeau were major writers, Merrill was just a curiosity, although the late poems he wrote in Versailles about the Great War achieved a certain marmoreal (the English would say "Georgian") grandeur. No, one could always propose that Charles the eternal outsider had a fine psychological take on Cocteau, who was at once the very heart of Paris *frivole* for five decades and almost carelessly despised by all the men who mattered most to him (Gide, Picasso, Stravinsky). Or Mr. Tremble could play up, rather crudely, Charles's heterosexual Don Juanism as the basis of his grasp of Jouhandeau's "abjection" amongst butcher boys (this prospect made Charles bristle). Or Merrill the Marginal—but then, who didn't consider himself to be marginal? In France, every *vieux con* conservative government minister, born in Saint-Germain-en-Laye and graduated from Sciences Po, dressed in Sulka suits and Weston shoes, would smile, show his palms and declare during a long television interview that he was something of a "dreamer" and "misfit," despite his rich wife and his own aristocratic parents and his teenage daughter off riding to hounds in Ireland. Oh, no, everyone was "marginal," just as everyone was "passionate" about his work. It was all part of the aristocratization of everyday French life; no one could dare admit he worked to get rich or out of habit or just to eat. No, work had to be a "passion." . . .

He'd have to pretend, no doubt, to Mr. Tremble that passion had driven him to write his autobiography and his three biographies, though in fact he'd become a writer to escape the drudgery of door-to-door canvassing for an electronics firm, the job he'd landed when he was washed up on the coast of Brittany after he'd escaped from Beirut. He'd never been a good worker or student. In fact he'd never been a good adult. He'd been happiest as a boy when he'd lived amongst his mother and sisters and girl cousins, something like the pasha's son in the harem, the only other intact male. He despised work and if he were a millionaire he'd never write another line.

What he did like—what he was passionate about, if to be passionate meant you couldn't stop doing it—was research. He wanted to know everything, not because he was vain of his knowledge. No, he'd never been after honors or even passing admiration and had nearly flunked out of school, though he did like it when a woman would smile at him because he'd murmured the name or word or title all the big, important men had been vainly seeking. No, his research was linked to his sexuality, though to say so sounded like biographical key-rattling. He wanted to see the insides of dossiers, bedrooms, bodies, he wanted access to archives and intimate secrets, and the first "No," far from discouraging him, only made his eventual conquest more piquant. Difficult people, even impossible people, fascinated him.

His very success in all domains made the going harder now, since in the past, before he was known to be a Don Juan, each woman had thought she must be the first to take pity on him, so uncomely was he with his gap teeth, frail body, balding head, just as each doddering French book collector had thought there could be no harm in showing an *inédit* to such a diplomatic little Lebanese Jew who skirted so cleverly all Parisian literary feuds and belonged to no *chapelle*.

Now things were closing in on him, at least in Paris, precisely because of his all-too-conspicuous literary and amorous successes. To be sure, now that he was infamous certain women wanted to know what all the fuss was about, just as certain collectors were charmed to be seduced by the man who'd already deflowered libraries long thought to be beyond approach. *The Seducer in Letters and Love*—would that be the subtitle of Mr. Tremble's clumsy little effort?

He'd been delighted to accept this yearlong appointment in New England, because he thought it would give him a breather. To tell the truth, he wasn't the least bit like Don Juan, since he, Charles, never dropped anyone, loved everyone and remained true to them all after his fashion. *Tant pis,* since that meant he had to listen to a lot of weeping and had to run frantically from one rendezvous to another all day every day. Now his women would have a year to cool off.

Although Catherine, as tiny as he, was stunning and always elegant, in his extracurricular romances he specialized in women who were a bit . . . "homely," to use the cozy, domestic American word, as well as those who were just a bit "over the hill" (his English was improving; he kept long lists of expressions that amused him or "caught his fancy" and he eschewed any more diligent approach to the language). Cocteau and Jouhandeau worshiped their lovers (Cocteau thought of them as gods, Jouhandeau as God) and needed them to be beautiful (for Cocteau they were gleaming, well-carved chessmen the Poet advanced in his brilliant but losing game with Death; for Jouhandeau they were altars before which he knelt, at once defiled and exalted by these boys). Charles didn't worship his women. He made them laugh. He was tender with them. He liked knowing where a woman was vulnerable. In Beirut he'd once even made love to a woman with a wooden leg and he'd finally convinced her to let him unharness her.

One of his women now was Jade, a Chinese stockbroker in her fifties who'd not been touched once in the last ten years by her handsome, scholarly husband, head of a now-discredited cultural organization founded by the Chinese Nationalists that had attempted to "regild its coat of arms" (*redorer son blason*) by offering courses in computer science to unemployed Chinese hooligans in the fifteenth arrondissement. Jade had clearly given up on love and had been astonished when Charles, whom she'd met at a dinner given by the grandson of Stuart Merrill's best childhood friend, had invited her to lunch. She'd assured him she wasn't that kind of broker, she only handled corporate portfolios, but he'd persisted. By the end of the lunch she'd already told him she'd long ago been a tennis champion as a teenager in Singapore—and she'd given him her private number at the office. At the Bibliothèque Doucet he'd met other women, young and old, intelligent and not. As he'd grown more successful with each biography, he'd become more handsome—better dressed, better coiffed, more confident.

But he resented the way Catherine had slowly domesticated him. They'd lived together a long time before they married. That had been the exhilarating time when they'd met in Beirut where she, a proper Breton girl, had come in search of adventure. His father was still rich then with his Renault dealership and Charles had worked freelance in advertising only very occasionally. He'd sometimes gone to his family's seaside house for weeks on end with Catherine, each of them outfitted with a suitcase full of books. Hers were English comic novels in French translation (Austen, Waugh, Lodge) and his were detective stories in any language at all. But then after his father had lost his money (the bit that he hadn't gambled away at the Beirut casino just days before they'd been forced to evacuate the city) Charles had had to work full-time in Brittany, where they'd taken refuge with Catherine's parents. His idle, bohemian existence had come to an end. In the Breton drizzle he'd had to go from apartment building to building in Rennes ringing doorbells and subjecting those who responded to questionnaires that took an hour to fill out. Fortunately, the French were complacent, pedantic and bored—a combination that made them wonderfully susceptible to such imbecile bureaucratic exercises. Whereas they would have bridled if they'd

been asked personal questions, their vanity tweaked to a prob-
ing of their least significant habits. Far from brushing him
aside or rushing through the form, his respondents made a
substantial meal out of the absurdly detailed interviews. One
of his first respondents had been Milan Kundera, newly arrived
from Czechoslovakia to teach literature at Rennes. He assumed
the questionnaire must have been issued by a government
agency and accordingly answered each question with dogged
application. Later Charles liked to joke that he had in his
possession a long interview of Kundera that had never been
published and that showed him in an unusual light.

His spies had told him Tremble already had three hours
of interviews with Charles's estranged Mexican-Jewish re-
searcher, Tom Smith, as he blithely called himself, though
his real name was Tomăs Weingarten Smith, the appropriated
"Smith," in accordance with Spanish custom, indicating his
English mother's surname, whereas his real "last name" in the
Anglo-Saxon sense was Weingarten, the family name of his
father, a Russian-Jewish immigrant. Tomăs, a Paris acquain-
tance who'd worked fitfully on the Cocteau research (he'd
mainly dined out on his expense account with Jean Marais,
Cocteau's actor-lover), was a balding, self-hating, overweight
homosexual; he systematically turned on everyone who'd ever
helped him and following his system was now filling in missing
mischievous misinformation about Charles in interviews
granted to the American press. Tom Smith had undoubtedly
told Tremble all about Catherine, Jade, the Bibliothèque Doucet harem and so on.

Tremble was due to arrive in half an hour on the train from
Boston. Charles could walk to the station from his office, in
the French Department's luxurious quarters, in just fifteen
minutes. He had time to give a few more teasing instructions
to the department secretary, a *sympathique* roly-poly widow in
her sixties from the intriguingly named town of Tallahassee—

an Indian name, she'd explained. He was going to ask her if she had some Seminole blood. Could that explain why her white hair had taken on such a mysterious blue tint? Would she let him look at her palm just a moment? He knew something about how to read the palms of Occidentals and Orientals, but he had no experience at all with *les Peaux Rouges,* not that her skin could possibly be whiter—or softer, he might add.

He hurried down the hill past the white wooden church everyone here swooned over but that he'd found most unappealing at first, though now he could just begin to understand the frozen spiritual yearning the steeple expressed—or was it a finger accusing heaven of not conforming to the strictest political correctness? The fruit trees were all in flower, which made Charles gasp and wheeze. A bed of daffodils wavered in the cool breeze. It was a late April day, the sun's warmth was concealing a treacherously cold *fond de l'air.* After the bleak winter the students with their small features and big bottoms were all lolling on the grass in shorts. The "women" (i.e., *filles*) sometimes wore sweatpants over their immense *po-pos.* The pock-pock of a distant tennis ball sounded at irregular intervals, then disconcertingly stopped altogether. Two jocks (or was that word "Jacques"?) trudged toward each other like moonwalkers, their baseball caps turned front to back. They said in loud, uninflected voices, "Hey, dude." Luckily these robots wrote "personal essays" in French class, which revealed cultured, ironic minds dartingly at work, completely at odds with their inflated spacesuit bodies and idiotic conversation.

Charles had scrupulously left his door open during private conferences with "female" students (he had a hard time making Americans understand that in French *femelle* could apply only to an animal). Eventually Charles became wary even with boys, since intergenerational sodomy was also much on everyone's mind. He gave everyone A's, partly because he had been hostile to grades ever since his own student days, when he'd sounded such low notes, and partly because he'd learned that in the States a B could provoke accusations of rape. It appeared some old professorial "goats" actually did flunk those "kids" who wouldn't "put out" (these infernal English prepositions—was it "put *in*"?). Students considered an A (*vingt sur vingt*) to be their birthright and Charles was delighted to cooperate in this amusing fantasy. Never in history had there been a culture less coquettish, less seductive. On the streets no one looked at anyone. On a date there was no teasing, no flirting, no courting. Apparently one passed directly from indifference to safe sex or from copious yawns to rape.

The university was feeling him out to see if he might like a full-time appointment in the French Department. Charles doubted if he could stay away so long from Paris, but he did like the option and he was sure Tremble's meddling wouldn't help, not on a campus where feminism, two decades after it had died out in France, was still in full cry ("A lesbian is the condensed rage of all women" announced a poster Charles had put up in his bathroom. "Be the bomb you throw").

So far Charles had not had the least problem, since he'd remained studiously neutral, even neutered, on every "gender-related issue" and had won a few extra points by proposing a course on Luce Irigary, Hélène Cixous and Monique Wittig, three forgotten Frog frauds whom only American feminists still mentioned. No, but if Biographer Tremble used Don Juanism as a *key*, then Charles would never receive tenure (Charles pictured Tremble as a matronly *châtelaine* with a heavy bunch of cumbersome keys dangling from his waist).

Of course Tremble would probably not deliver the bio (*Lebanese Lothario*) until five years from now. Tremble was forty and had never published a book. He was an itinerant instructor in the Chinese language who had never received tenure anywhere because he'd never produced a book. Charles had done a bit of counter-research and discovered Tremble had been married once. Despite his unusual surname (French for "aspen") apparently it was just an open fan, a flickering subterfuge, masking a German-Jewish visage and a long name of all consonants like a bad Scrabble hand. Even though his paternal grandparents had been German, Tremble had been raised in Toronto.

What would a Canadian Jew make of his family's complex heritage? Charles wondered as he traversed a bridge that had recently been flung across the dirty, rusty river, paved over for decades but liberated in the last six months as part of a hopeless program to "beautify" the center city, a melancholy ensemble of baby skyscrapers from the 1920s, boarded-up storefronts and a vast windswept, deserted square. The only center of animation was an all-night diner frequented by bikers and "home boys" (one word or two?) who would surround a car waiting at a stoplight and beat drunkenly on its roof with their fists, even start to rock it and threaten to overturn it. Charles and Catherine had been subjected to this initiation on their very first night in town.

The question about Charles's Jewish heritage wasn't an idle one, since he knew perfectly well that if Doubleday had commissioned this biography it was to follow up the sweet, windfall success of Charles's own memoirs, *Passports*, which had become a bestseller against all odds. Apparently the only people who bought books in America were Jews, or rather Jewish women, and these *âmes soeurs* had been intrigued by the English translation of his book (a nonevent in France). *Passports* had delightfully jumbled all their preconceptions.

Charles's mother's ancestors had been Spanish Jews who'd been welcomed by the Ottoman Sultan at the time of the Spanish Inquisition. In fact Charles's mother spoke Ladino, an ancient Romance language that had been preserved from the fifteenth century down to the present. His maternal great-grandfather, a Turkish merchant, had happened to be traveling in Algeria at the very moment when the French government was offering French citizenship to Algerian Jews. He wasn't an Algerian, but he fudged his papers and obtained the citizenship anyway. After that, every generation of his family was duly registered at the French consulate in Istanbul and attended the French *lycée* there, though not one person in the family ever lived in France or had even visited it. When Charles's mother met and married his father, an Egyptian Jew, the only language they had in common was French; their children, raised in Beirut, were duly registered in the French embassy, attended a French Jesuit school and spoke French (and of course Arabic).

Charles's father's passport was Egyptian until Farouk fell. He then bought an Iranian passport—valid until the Shah was driven out. Next he purchased a Panamanian passport, but a new dictator canceled all his predecessor's deals. When Beirut went up in flames and down in rubble, Charles and his brother and mother had no problem finding refuge in France, since they were all French citizens, but Charles's father was still stateless and was allowed to settle in Paris provisionally only because the other members of his family were French. For the first time this "French" family saw France.

The story didn't end there. Charles's older brother, while growing up, had always played with Muslim children and had despised Maronite Christians and Zionists—and in France he'd become a professor of Arabic, converted to Islam and had even married a woman of North African heritage who did not herself speak Arabic, so it was he who had to teach their children the language. His parents were distraught and flare-ups occurred at every family reunion. As though to compensate for his brother's apostasy, Charles was studying Ladino (so that the language would not die out in their family with his mother) and he and Catherine spent their holidays in Turkey in the Istanbul Jewish summer colony of Büyükada. Catherine had never been happier than during her four years in Beirut, and Charles missed it too. They both found Istanbul to be the closest approximation to Beirut, though Istanbul was dirtier and poorer, more dour and more majestic with its palaces and mosques stepping away from the Golden Horn and its melancholy cemeteries, the tombs of virgins covered with a carved marble veil and those of notables topped with a stone turban.

Nothing could be more distant from Istanbul than this New England town with its freshly painted eighteenth-century yellow wood houses and their dark green shutters or the empty, snow-swept streets with their strange names. Charles, who was used to eating bouquets of fresh mint and raw lamb brains, sweet gazelle horns and fluffy, sugary puddings of creamed chicken, lamb brochettes and parsley-pungent tabbouleh, now sat down to meat loaf and mashed potatoes and brown Betty at the Faculty Club. He could almost picture this "Betty," *une métisse bien en chair.* . . .

Charles stood at the top of the stairs as passengers who'd just arrived on the train ascended the escalator. A husky man with smudged glasses, gliding up, caught sight of Charles and gave a weary, ironic smile and raised his eyebrows high, higher; Charles saw what he thought was a New World expression compounded of embarrassment and humor, as though to say, "Yes, here we are, after all, and we must greet each other just as everyone always does." Except even the greeting turned out to be awkward. Charles put out a hand to be pumped in the American fashion, whereas Tremble bent down to kiss his cheek *à la française*—only it wasn't French after all, it was a New World one-cheek-only peck, which Charles, going for the second cheek, realized too late: their glasses collided and Tremble's went askew.

As they walked up the hill, Charles offered to take one handle of Tremble's suitcase in order to share the weight, but apparently Canadian he-men of a certain age (even such a downtrodden example from Toronto) couldn't be seen admitting physical weakness any more than they could be observed wearing a silk foulard or a cologne other than one based on bracing lemons or virile limes.

"So here we are!" Tremble exclaimed.

"Yes," Charles hastened to interject, "but you'll see that the part around the university is much more beautiful."

"Clean air!" Tremble said, winded, with that trace of faint contempt residents of big cities adopt to praise the provinces, the city mouse's pink-eyed, sparse-whiskered disdain for the dowdy country mouse's dull and healthy habitat.

"Hope you don't pass out from the oxygen intake," Charles murmured, his deadpan delivery making Tremble's glance swerve covertly in his direction: Subject Has Unexpected Wry Sense of Humor, the mental note undoubtedly read.

As they climbed the long hill up toward Benefit, Charles wheezing from an asthma attack provoked by all the flowering trees, Tremble ashen and exhausted, his glasses making his eyes look extinct, like capped wells, the Canadian made a remark about "vigorous Wasp exercise" not quite being his "thing."

"You'd be surprised," Charles replied, testy about Tremble's bid for automatic Jewish complicity, "half of these Jacques or jocks are Jews. See that blond *boeuf* on roller blades? Trevor (if you please) Goldenberg."

Catherine had prepared them tea, which Tremble drank but dubiously, examining the pretty tea service, which had been part of the furnishings of the house, with that same smile, the one that seemed to say, "Nothing in this world is real but woes and grief. How curious that we should be pretending to be people who drink tea." Charles thought such heavy-handed inauthenticity was rather puerile—but perhaps he was misinterpreting the smile.

Well into the conversation Charles realized that Tremble

wasn't taping anything or taking notes—or even asking pertinent questions. When Catherine slipped out of the room in search of more cookies, Charles said, "You know, Catherine is typically French in that she thinks a biography of anyone alive who's not a rock star is slightly absurd."

Tremble had gone sterile behind his glasses; no paramecia were squirming in those stolid petri dishes.

Since one has to be excruciatingly direct with North Americans, Charles added, "I doubt if Catherine would give you a real interview but you might slip in a question or two during the evening."

"And you? What do you tell people when they find out I'm writing your biography?"

"I always say my life is so dull—which it *is*, as you're no doubt discovering to your dismay—that I can't imagine it would make substantial reading ('That winter he deliberated long and hard whether to give Suzy an A or B' or 'His step quickened that morning as he headed toward the archives'). Not just dull but a full treatment is undeserved, unmerited. But I always add that I had so much trouble getting people to cooperate when I was writing biographies that I wouldn't dream of standing in your way."

Tremble nodded as though Charles's words were a tempting but treacherous food, like foie gras, that takes a long time to digest. Or was Tremble silently despising every pompous thing Charles said but suppressing his objections in favor of objectivity? "Yeah, but all the attention must be flattering, huh?" Tremble asked, a half-mocking glance penetrating considerable eyebrow and eyeglass.

Catherine came back in with a bottle of airport whiskey. Charles bit his tongue. An English Cocteau scholar was planning a monograph on Charles's life and works and suddenly Charles thought he'd give each of his two biographers different, conflicting versions of all the same events. There was something entirely despicable about being the subject of a biography. The subject alternately preened and cowered, the most deplorable grandiosity in him responding to the promise of an immortal portrait while his cowardice told him he was about to undergo the worst of all possible fates—to have his fleshly body copied in granite, to have all of his past faults, which he excused because they were redeemed by future aspirations, quarried out of a strong eternal present: nothing but the pitiful facts.

And yet, after all, writing a biography was a métier. Tremble would need to establish a chronology, put together a bibliography, interview friends and colleagues from each period, each intellectual domain, each country. But when Charles gingerly touched on these professional matters, Tremble said, "I've got my own method, the Tremble System. I don't research, I don't take notes, no Xeroxes—I just absorb, absorb, absorb, and then one day I start writing, it all comes out."

Charles nodded, frowning seriously out of respect for the Tremble System, though he hazarded that such an approach might be more appropriate to an article than a book, even the slimmest—unless, of course, the writer had a prodigious memory (something he, Charles, was renowned for, though even he'd found that details dropped out after a few weeks unless he took notes, especially during a period of heavy interviewing).

Charles said, "I'm curious how you're going to reconstruct the Beirut years—how pretentious that sounds, to refer to one's own idle, haphazard life as though it represented a meaningful sequence."

Tremble had found a yellow spot on his trouser leg that he started scratching furiously. "You're the biographer—how would you go about it?"

"If I were Canadian and didn't speak Arabic or French?" Charles asked.

"Oh, that's easy, I can always hire translators. I suppose I'll just go there, to Beirut."

"A visit could always provide a certain sense of . . . atmosphere, although our house is rubble and my father's office was leveled and all our friends and family members are dead or have emigrated."

Catherine apparently had decided Tremble was hopeless; she changed the subject to Asia, which she knew interested him. She asked him constant questions about his years as a teacher in Hong Kong and his interlude leading tourists to Tun Huang. Tremble kept pouring himself large tumblers of Scotch; after the third full glass he'd brightened up, undone his tie and taken off his jacket to reveal a very old white shirt stained yellow under the arms.

Catherine expressed her ideas on the Far East, which were idiotic since she knew next to nothing about that part of the world. She, too, was drinking more red wine than usual; her English, sketchy at best, sometimes gave out altogether, but Tremble, fully awake and on his way to enthusiasm, assured her, as all North Americans do, that he knew exactly what she was saying and that her way of saying it was delightful. After every compliment he cast his eyes balefully, like a spavined workhorse, toward Charles, as though these compliments might be annoying the Master. Charles had spent his life siding with women and children against authoritarian men; he'd been the Artful Dodger, yet now he was being treated as the witless tyrant.

For Catherine it was all a game; she even said, "I hope Charles isn't *vexé* that we speak on other subjects, not only his *life*." She laughed merrily; she had a Gallic disregard for the American language and American pursuits—such as a biography of a living man, virtually unknown and not even sixty years old. Like many French tourists in the States she liked to collect examples of American madness to exhibit later, colorful snaps of "typical" deformities. She chortled over gay studies, guidelines for politically correct usage on all university publications, student evaluations of, if you please, professors; she smiled with curatorial glee when she learned that a local lesbian powwow had gone unattended since no map of the rural location had been provided lest it favor the seeing over those who were visually challenged and thus be guilty of sightism. She rubbed her hands together over the solemn, heavy-handed way young Americans were systematizing only now the whimsical provocations tossed off so long ago by Barthes, Derrida and that impenetrable, illogical Lacan.

Now she was trying to draw Tremble out in order to isolate another amusing curiosity. "But aren't you afraid that Hong Kong will be destroyed by the Chinese?" she asked.

"No, no!" Tremble shouted, though twenty minutes later he lapsed, as Anglophones always do, into anecdotes, which were so complicated he lost his point, if he'd ever had one other than the desire to show his expertise.

Charles the professional biographer was conscious of a mental clock ticking away. He'd told Tremble that he'd be able to see him just two or three times altogether; he'd explained that whereas he in no way opposed the book he thought it would be fatuous to collaborate on it with too much lip-smacking self-regard.

After the cheese, the dessert, the coffee and the chocolate *truffes* (sent in a CARE package from Brittany), Catherine discovered she had a migraine and went to bed with Elizabeth Taylor (the English comic novelist, not the American activist).

Charles found a dusty half bottle of brandy that belonged to the owner of the house. He'd have to replace it before the proprietor returned. Tremble proceeded to toss the brandy back. He was raving intermittently about Singapore for some reason (Charles hadn't followed every twist and turn in his monologue). He was sitting on a rag rug in front of the small

fire Catherine had lit before retiring. His shirttail had come
out on one side and the earpieces of his glasses had worked
their way up his scalp so that the lenses were tilting down
toward the blue flames emitted by the chemical log.

"She's great, Catherine," Tremble shouted. "What a lovely
lady. What class! I've never been entertained so royally. Her
English is impeccable. And her knowledge of Asia is
encyclopedic."

"Yes," Charles concurred. "Living with such an *érudite* can
be a humbling experience."

"And a looker, too, though that may sound sexist."

"Not to our Old World ears," Charles assured his
biographer.

"You're a lucky man, Charles, though—" He suddenly lowered his voice. "Do you think your wife can hear us?"

"No, her room is on another floor. You were saying?"

"Well, one of my informants," Tremble said conspiratorially,
"has suggested you're not indifferent to the attractions of other
women."

His informant must be that infernal Tom Smith, Charles
thought. He murmured, "An elegant periphrasis for adultery."
He despised Tremble and recognized that the book, in the
unlikely event it would ever be finished, would *soil* a life,
several lives, which seemed all the more precious now that
they were about to be desecrated.

"Of course," Tremble admitted, pouring himself another
brandy and making a cursory effort to serve Charles, who didn't
even have a glass, "in Canada and the States there's a saying
bachelors always use against marriage, 'Why buy a cow when
you can get milk through a fence?' "

"Charming," Charles said, going over to his desk and jotting
it down. "You're helping me improve my English by leaps and
bonds."

"Bounds. It's 'leaps and bounds.' "

"*D'accord*. But tell me, frankly, why you took up this thank-less project?" Charles came back to his stool next to Tremble, who was now soggily propped up on one elbow on the floor.

"You really want to know? The real bottom-line reason?" Charles nodded vigorously.

"Well, maybe I shouldn't tell you, you might be hurt, 'cause I never was especially interested in you and it does sound like a lot of work, I mean what with all these exotic locales, Leb-anon and France, whereas I'm really an Orientalist, but I met a young editor at Doubleday who'd read that *Vogue* profile somebody did on you after *Passports* hit the list and they asked me if I knew someone who could write a bio on you and I said, 'What would the advance be?' and they said, 'Roughly fifty thousand, with twenty-five grand on signing,' and I said, 'Done! I'll do it,' because that was exactly the sum I owed American Express. I'd never even read a word by you till then, though now I'm plowing through that book on, how do you say it, Jew-Hand-Do?"

"How did your bill get to be so high?" Charles was now mentally sneering not only at this grubby hack sprawling on the floor beside him but at his own vanity in wondering, earlier in the day, how he would present himself to a biographer he had ridiculously assumed would be at least an admirer.

"Gee, I don't know if I can tell you." Tremble writhed on the rag rug and—could it be?—looked as though he were actually blushing.

"Have you forgotten where you spent the money?" Charles ventured.

"Not at all. You see, I kind of fell for this one dominatrix, I guess you could say I'm sort of a masochist, and—that's why I think I'm good at understanding and forgiving your sexual excesses, Charles, you know, all the banging you're doing on the side? Anyway, I became a complete slave to Mistress Quickly and she did some amazing things to me, I've still got the scars to show for it, but of course that doesn't come cheap, the old meter was ticking on and on and after twenty-five thousand dollars Amex cut me off."

Tremble launched into a discourse about his estranged wife, who'd been "unbelievably cruel," although Charles couldn't sort out whether cruelty in her case had been a desirable or deplorable attribute.

Suddenly Tremble began to heave with sobs, strange hyena yelps that were so immoderate and convulsive that Charles assumed he must never have wept before in front of another human being, unless that person might be a Venus in Furs. Charles, who was always lamenting that he no longer felt anything, was reminded now of the inconvenience of emotion. Did he really want to go back to these humiliating sounds and writhings? For some reason he remembered the ancient metaphor of the poet as a flute played on by the breath of a god, so seized was Tremble by an outside force, an inspiration that flowed from his eyes and barked out of his mouth. Together perhaps Tremble and Charles could make one whole man.

Charles disliked touching men but he knelt beside Tremble and patted him comfortingly on the shoulder.

Charles thought, Tremble will never finish this biography but if by some chance he does he'll make me pay dearly for this sympathy I'm showing him.

After Charles had helped an excessively grateful Tremble into a taxi bound for the train station, he laughed out loud and said to himself, "Perfect! I can't think of a better biographer for me and my absurd life." But he was trying to convince himself that he found this bizarre coupling of subject and biographer "amusing" (that word Parisians always resorted to in order to cool down their irritability and to aestheticize their indignation).

Until today Charles had thought his life was banal and would make dull reading but suddenly, confronted with this drunk, incurious incompetent, Charles sighed, remembered Lebanon and thought of his family's destiny, at once so idiosyncratic and so emblematic of the comic, tragic last days of the Diaspora. He found a cabalistic symbolism in his need to seduce women other men had forgotten and "put out to pasture" (the cruelty of the English language!) because they were getting "long in the tooth."

As he made himself a chamomile tea in the kitchen, Charles thought how tiresome it would be, though, if his biographer were an intelligent, sensitive man capable of understanding his life from within. If the real materials of his life, expertly ferreted out and felt, were to be forced into the mold of a traditional biography, a form in search of a trajectory, an imperative that produced a destiny—well, that would be truly intolerable. He was an elusive man, a seducer, a diplomat, an artist in reticence, a genius of the vague. No, Tremble was perfect; he'd found his ideal biographer.

An Oracle

After George died, Ray went through a long period of uncertainty. George's disease had lasted fifteen months and during that time Ray had stopped seeing most of his old friends. He'd even quarreled with Betty, his best friend. Although she'd sent him little cards from time to time, including the ones made by a fifty-year-old California hippie whom she represented, he hadn't responded. He'd felt all the more offended that she'd forgotten how sickening he thought the pastel leaves and soppy sentiments were.

George had been a terrible baby throughout his illness, but then again Ray had always babied him the whole twelve years they'd been together, so the last months had only dramatized what had been inherent from the beginning. Nor had George's crankiness spoiled their good times together. Of course they'd lived through their daily horrors (their dentist, an old friend, had refused to pull George's rotten tooth; George's mother had decided to "blame herself" for George's cowardice in the face of pain), but they still had had fun. Ray leased a little Mercedes and they drove to the country whenever George was up to it. A friend had given them a three-hundred-dollar Siamese kitten he'd found at a pet show and they'd named her Anna, partly because of Anna and the King of Siam and partly in deference to an ancient nickname for Ray. They both showered her with affection.

Which she reciprocated. Indeed, the more they chased away their friends, the more they relished her obvious liking for them. When they'd lie in bed watching television at night, they'd take turns stroking Anna. If she purred, they'd say, "At least *she* likes us." After George became feeble and emaciated, he would ignore his mother and father and would play with Anna if he had the strength and berate Ray for something or other.

George would become very angry at Ray for not calling to find out the results of his own blood test. "You're just being irresponsible," George would say, "to yourself." But Ray knew that the test would tell him nothing—or tell him that yes, he'd been exposed to the virus, but nothing more. And besides, there was no preventive treatment. Anyway, he owed all his devotion to George; he didn't want to think for a second about his own potential illness.

Every moment of George's last four months had been absorbing. They quarreled a lot, especially about little dumb things, as though they needed the nagging and gibbering of everyday pettiness to drown out the roar of eternity. George, who'd never cared about anything except the day after tomorrow, suddenly became retrospective in a sour way.

They quarreled about whether Ray had ever needed George, which was absurd, since in the past Ray had been deeply reliant on George's energy and contacts. Betty had repeatedly warned Ray against living forever in George's shadow. What she hadn't known was how much he, Ray, had always babied George at home—nursed him through hangovers, depressions, business worries, even attacks of self-hatred after he'd been rejected by a trick.

George, of course, was the famous one. Starting in the early 1970s he'd been called in by one major corporation after another to give each an image, and George had designed everything from the letterhead to the company jet. He'd think up a color scheme, a logo, a typeface, an overall look; he'd redo the layouts of the annual report. He'd work with an advertising creative director on the product presentation and the campaign slogans. He'd demand control over even the tiniest details, down to the lettering on the business cards of the sales force. Since he was six-foot-three, rangy and athletic, had a deep voice and had fathered a son during an early marriage, the executives he dealt with never suspected him of being gay, nor was George a crusader of any sort. He liked winning and he didn't want to start any game with an unfair handicap. George also had a temper, a drive to push his ideas through, and he wasn't handsome—three more things that counted as straight among straights.

He'd also had the heterosexual audacity to charge enormous fees. His job as corporate image maker was something he'd more or less invented. He'd realized that most American corporations were paralyzed by pettiness, rivalry and fear, and only an outsider could make things happen. George was able to bring about more changes in a month than some cringing and vicious vice-president could effect in a year, if ever. George made sure he reported directly to the president or chairman, although as soon as he came "onstream" he solicited everyone else's "input."

On summer weekends George and Ray had flown in a seaplane to Fire Island, where they'd rented a big house on the ocean side complete with swimming pool. Around that pool

they'd spent twelve summers with just a phone, a little acid
and thirty hunky men. They had, or Ray had, pounds of Po-
laroids to prove it. Here was the White Party and the house
flying a thousand white balloons and Skipper in the foreground
with his famous smile, the smile that earned him a hundred
and fifty dollars an hour. Dead now of his own—not hand,
but leap: he'd leapt from his penthouse on angel dust. And
here was the Star Wars Party with George as Darth Vader
and his arm around little Tommy as R2D2, the cute kid who
wanted to be a DJ but never made it, though he did amazing
disco tapes he sold to friends in editions of fifty.

And here was George as Darleen. Older guys hated George's
dabbling in drag, since they associated it with the sissy 1950s.
And the younger kids simply didn't get it; they'd heard of it,
although it didn't seem funny to them. But for George and
Ray's generation, the Stonewall generation, drag was something they'd come to late, after they'd worked their way through
every other disguise. For George, such a sexy big man with a
low voice and brash ways, the character he'd invented, Darleen, had provided a release—not a complete contrast, but a
slight transposition. For one thing, she was a slut, but an
intimidating one who, when horny, yanked much smaller men
to her hairy chest without a second's hesitation. For another,
she had a vulgar but on-target way of talking over George's
current corporation and reducing it to its simplest profile; it
was Darleen in a drugged state who'd mumbled forth the slogans now selling seven of the biggest American products.

And Darleen had introduced a certain variety into Ray and
George's sex life, for she liked to be passive in bed, whereas
George was tirelessly active. No one would have believed it,
not even their closest friends, but Ray had fucked Darleen,
whereas he could never have fucked George. After sex they'd
weep from laughter, the two of them, Ray sweaty and gold

with his white tan line, and George, foundered, skinny legs in black net stockings and the lashes coming unglued on his, yes, his left eye.

When George died, Ray thought of burying him in his drag, but the two people he happened to mention it to (although fairly far-out numbers themselves) drew back in horror. "You've got to be kidding," one of them had said, as though Ray were now committable for sure. Ray had wanted to say, "Shouldn't we die as we lived? Why put George in a dark suit he never wore in life?"

But he didn't say anything, and George was buried as his parents wished. His father had been a cop, now retired, his mother a practical nurse, and in the last twenty years they'd made a lot of money in real estate. They liked fixing up old houses, as did George. Ray had a superstition that George had succumbed to the illness only because he'd worked so hard on his own loft. George was a perfectionist and he trusted no one else to do a job correctly. Every little chore, and most especially the lacquering of the loft walls, was something he'd done by himself, again and again to get everything right.

Now he was dead and Ray had to go on with his own life, but he scarcely knew how or why to pick up the threads. The threads were bare, worn thin, so that he could see right through what should have been the thick stuff of everyday comings and goings, could see pale blue vistas. "You must look out for yourself," George had always said. But what self?

Ray still went to the gym three times a week as he'd done for almost twenty years. He never questioned anything here and resented even the smallest changes, such as the installation of a fruit-juice bar or a computerized billing system always on the blink.

And then Ray had Anna to feed and play with. Since she'd

been George's only other real companion toward the end, she felt comfortable and familiar. They'd lie in bed together and purr, and that was nice but it wasn't a sign pointing to a new life, only a burned offering to his past, itself burned and still smoking.

He thought he was too young to have had to renounce so much. He'd always known that he'd have to end in renunciation, but he didn't like being rushed. He thought of George's long femur bones slowly emerging in the expensive coffin.

And of course he had his job. He did public relations for a major chemical company with headquarters on Sixth Avenue. It was a gig George had found him; George had done a total facelifting for Amalgamated Anodynes. Nearly everything about the company was reprehensible. It had a subsidiary in South Africa. Its biggest plant was in South Carolina, precisely because there the right-to-work laws, as they were called in the best Orwellian manner, had banned most of the unions. A.A. had produced a fabric for children's wear that had turned out to be flammable; Ray had even had to draft for the president's signature some very high-level waffling as a statement to the press. And Amalgamated Anodynes had a lousy record with women and minorities, although a creepy Uncle Tom headed the company's equal-hiring-practices commission.

Worst of all was Ray's boss, Helen, the token female vice-president. Helen was by turns solicitous and treacherous, servile to superiors and tyrannical to her staff, an old-fashioned schemer who knew more about office politics than her job.

Following a run-in with Helen a few days after the funeral (which, of course, he hadn't been able to mention), he'd locked himself in the toilet and cried and cried, surprised there was so much mucus in his head. Where was it stored normally, in which secret cavity? He was also surprised by how lonely he felt. Lonely, or maybe spaced. George had always been barking at him, scolding or praising him; now the silence was oddly vacant, as though someone had pushed past a last gate and entered into the limitless acreage of space and night.

In order to cry he had to say to himself, "I'm giving in to total self-pity," because otherwise he was so stoic these post-mortem days that he'd never have let himself be ambushed by despair. Why did he keep this job? Was it to please George, who always wanted him to go legit, who'd never approved of his "beatnik jobs"? George had used "beatnik," "hippie" and "punk" interchangeably to dramatize the very carelessness of his contempt.

Ray had grown up on a farm in northern Ohio near Findlay and still had in his possession a second prize for his cow from the state fair; he'd sewn it and his Future Farmers of America badge to his letter jacket. What big-city sentimentalists never understood about the rural existence they so admired was that it was dull and lonely, unnaturally lonely, but it left lots of time for reading.

He'd read and read and won a first prize in the Bellefontaine spelling bee and another as the captain of the Carey debating team against Sandusky on the hot subject of "free trade." His grades were so good he received a scholarship to Oberlin, where, in his second year, he'd switched his major from agronomy to philosophy.

From there he'd gone on to the University of Chicago, where he'd joined the Committee on Social Thought and eventually written a thesis on Durkheim's concept of "anomie." His father, who wore bib overalls and had huge, fleshy ears and read nothing but the Bible, but that daily, would shake his head slowly and stare at the ground whenever the subject of his son's education came up. His mother, however, encouraged him. She was the school librarian, a thin woman with moist blue eyes and hands red from poor circulation, who drank coffee all day and read everything, everything. She'd been proud of him.

But she too had had her doubts when, after he received his doctorate, he'd drifted to Toronto and joined an urban gay commune, grown his blond hair to his shoulders and done little else besides holding down part-time jobs and writing articles analyzing and lamenting the lesbian-gay male split. In the doctrinaire fashion of those days, he'd angrily denounced all gay men and assumed a female name for himself, Anna. The name wasn't intended as a drag name (although later George had insisted he use it as one), but simply as a statement of his position against gender distinctions. Only his friends in the commune could call him Anna with a straight face.

Unlike most of the other early gay liberationists, Ray had actually had sex with other men. His affairs were shy, poetic and decidedly unfancy in bed. Despite his political beliefs, he insisted on being on top, which he admitted was a "phallocratic" hang-up, although nothing felt to him more natural than lavishing love on a subdued man, similarly smooth-skinned, slender and ponytailed.

Then one summer he'd met Jeff, a New Yorker and a contributor to the *Body Politic* who was every bit as ideological as Ray but much more muscular and amusing. When Jeff's Toronto vacation came to an end, Ray moved to New York to be with him. He justified the move to the other communards by pointing out that New York was a literary center. "So is Toronto!" they'd objected, for they were also Canadian patriots.

Ray had inchoate literary aspirations. For years he'd dutifully kept a journal. When he reread it after living in New York awhile, he found: the voluminous self-analysis neither true nor false; the recorded ideas a good deal sharper than those he was currently entertaining; and the descriptions of nature accurate and mildly, solidly of value.

When he looked for a job as a writer in New York, all he

could find, given his lack of credentials (his Ph.D. in philosophy counted as a drawback) was a position on *Conquistador!*—a sleazy tits-and-ass magazine for which he penned the picture captions in the centerfold ("Lovely Linda is a stewardess and flies, natch, for Aer Lingus"). The indignities (plus low pay) of that job he tried to compensate for by reading manuscripts in the evening for Grove Press and evaluating them artistically and commercially. Since he'd read little except the classics in school, his standards were impossibly high, and since his acquaintanceship till now had included only Ohio farmers, Chicago intellectuals and Toronto gay liberationists, his grasp of the potential market for any particular book was skewed.

He drifted from job to job, ghosted several chapters of a U.S. history college textbook for a tottering publishing house, worked as a bartender in a black-glass, red-velvet singles bar, taught one semester at a snooty Episcopalian boys' school in Brooklyn Heights, spent one winter as a stock boy at a chic Lucite boutique some friends owned, fled another winter to Key West, where he wore short shorts and served rum-and-coconut "conch-outs" around the pool of a gay guest house (he saw the coconut shells as shrunken skulls). He was hired because he'd long since joined a gym, acquired a beefy but defined body, traded in his ponytail and severe manner for a ready laugh and a crewcut ("Wear a Jantzen and a smile," as the old swimsuit slogan had put it). Naturally he no longer insisted on being called Anna. He'd also moved bumpily from one affairlet to another and had been embarrassed that most of them had ended in squabbles over money or fidelity.

Into this confusion, so rife with opportunities he was unable to see how little hope it held out, George had entered. They were both guests at someone's house in New York, and when they helped out washing up, their hands met under the suds. When he later tried to pinpoint what had made this relationship

take and stick he thought it could be seen as a barter—George's
forcefulness for Ray's beauty, say. George was homely if sexy,
yet he didn't sense his own appeal and he dwelled on all his
imperfections. Ray on the other hand was "pretty" in the special sense that word acquired in the mid-1970s to mean massive
shoulders, shaggy mustache, permanent tan, swelling chest.
He was also pretty in the more usual sense, for his full lips
seemed to be traced in light where a slightly raised welt outlined them, his deepset blue eyes contained an implosion of
gold particles falling into the black holes of his pupils, his jaw
had comic-book strength and his teeth were so long and white
they looked dangerous. And now that he was in his twenties
one could discern brown-gold hair on his chest spreading wings
over his lungs like that goddess who spreads her arms to protect
the pharaoh from all harm.

Ray didn't take his own beauty too seriously, though he
maintained it as one might conserve a small inheritance for
the sake of security. His spell in the gay commune had made
him suspicious of all "objectification of the body" and "com-
modification of sex," but his years in New York had taught
him the importance of precisely these two operations. He was
a bit of a star on the deck during tea dance on Fire Island, for
his years of training had in point of fact turned him into a
physical commodity—but one he was too ironic, too human,
to sell to the highest bidder. That George was not at all an
obvious candidate, that he was too skinny, too pockmarked, a
diligent but unsuccessful dresser, made him all the more appealing to Ray.

George had a ravenous appetite to win, even in the most
trivial contests, and that made him both infuriating and appealing. Ray had always been accommodating—too accommodating, he now saw, in view of how little he'd accomplished.
He deplored the way George cussed out every incompetent and
sent back the wine and at every moment demanded satisfaction.

And yet George's life was royally satisfying. He drove his Chrysler station wagon to a rented mansion in Water Mill on weekends, he was doing the work he most enjoyed and making a minor fortune and now, to put the final *u* on "parvenu," he had . . . Ray.

Until now, Ray had never thought of himself as primarily decorative, but George saw him obviously as a sort of superior home entertainment center—stylish, electric. Ray didn't like to stare into this reflection, he who'd won the Bellefontaine spelling bee and written one hundred and twenty closely reasoned pages on anomie. He saw that without noticing it he'd drifted into the joking, irresponsible, anguished half-world of the gay sophisticate who always knows what Sondheim has up his sleeve, who might delay his first spring visit to the island until he's worked on those forearms two more weeks, who feels confident Europe is as extinct as a dead star and all the heat and life for the planet must radiate from New York, who has heard most of his favorite songs from his chronological adolescence resurface fifteen years later in their disco versions, at once a reassurance about human continuity and a dismaying gauge of time's flight.

Lovers are attracted by opposites and then struggle to turn them into twins. Ray worked to mollify George's drive to win and George wanted Ray to turn into a winner. "Work hard and play hard" was George's motto, whereas Ray, without admitting it, wanted lots less work than play and wished both to be not hard but easy. Nevertheless, George, true to form, won. He nudged Ray into a series of well-paying jobs that ended him up at Amalgamated Anodynes. "You must look out for yourself," George was always saying. He said it over and over: "Look out for yourself." Ray would sit on his lap and say, "Why should I deprive you of a job you do so well?"

The one thing they'd agreed on from the first was not to be monogamous. Ray's ideological horror of marriage as a model and George's unreflecting appetite for pleasure neatly converged. What wasn't decided so easily was the terms under which they were to be unfaithful. George, who had a funny face, skinny body and enormous penis, was always a hit at the baths; Ray, whose penis was of average dimensions ("a gay eight," meaning six inches), was more likely to attract another man for a lifetime than a night. Ray already had love, George's, but in order to get sex he had to seem to be offering love. When George would see some other beauty, as dark as Ray was fair, melting amorously around Ray, George would break glass, bellow, come crashing through doors, wounded bull in the china shop of Ray's delicate romantic lust. Of course Ray envied George his simpler, franker asset and wished he could score more efficiently, with fewer complications.

And now, a year after George's death, here he was learning all the ways in which he had accommodated George and was still doing so, even though George had broken camp. Ray saw how in their tiny group he'd been billed as the looker with the brain, exactly like the starlet whom the studio hypes wearing a mortarboard and specs above her adorable snub nose and bikini—yet he wasn't in Hollywood but New York City and he realized that he'd fallen way behind, hadn't read a book in ages or had a new, strenuous thought.

He still had the big showboat body that George had doted on and that Ray was vigorously maintaining in two-hour workouts at the gym, even though personally (as in "If I may speak *personally* about my own life") he found the results caricatural and the waste of time ludicrous. And yet he was afraid to let go, stop pumping iron and deflate, sag, shrink, because if he was no longer the greatest brain he was at least a body—Some Body in the most concrete, painful sense. He looked around and realized he was still impersonating George's lover. He was even still using the same deodorant George had liked; George had had such an insinuating way of sticking his big, cratered nose into the most intimate aspects of Ray's habits. He'd made Ray switch from Jockey to boxer shorts, from cotton to cashmere stockings, from Pepsi to Coke, from ballpoint to fountain pen; like all people who make their living from publicity, George had believed that products and brand names determine destiny. Ray was still walking around like a doll George had dressed and wound up before taking off.

In the corner bookstore he picked up a remaindered large-format paperback called *The Death Rituals of Rural Greece*, by Loring M. Danforth. He liked the way the widows resented their husbands' deaths and said, "He wasn't very kind to me when he left me." That was closer to the truth than this twilit grief one was supposed to assume. He liked the funeral laments, especially the one in which a mother asks her dead daughter how Death, called Haros, received her. The daughter replies, "I hold him on my knees. He rests against my chest. If he is hungry, he eats from my body, and if he is thirsty, he drinks from my two eyes."

When he had a midtown lunch with Betty she told him he was having an identity crisis precipitated by George's death. "But your real problem," she said, warming unbecomingly to her subject, "is that you're still seeking an authority, the answer. If you don't watch out, you'll find yourself saddled with another dominating lover; it's your passive Aquarian nature."

Ray could scarcely believe how much his fur was being rubbed the wrong way, although he felt certain that prize had to go to Betty's insinuation that he was well rid of George. That night in an old linen jacket he took out of storage he found a joint of Acapulco gold George had rolled him—how long ago? two years—and he smoked it and cried and ordered in Chinese food and sat in bed and watched TV and played with Anna, who kept wandering over to the lit candle on the floor to sniff the flame. When she felt the heat her eyes would slit shut and she'd thrust her chin up, like a dowager who's smelled something rude.

Even though George had been a baby, he'd fought death with a winner's determination but he'd lost anyway. Ray thought that he himself wouldn't resist it for long. If and when the disease surfaced (for it seemed to him like a creature submerged underwater for an eerily long time but bound eventually to come gasping up for air)—when the disease surfaced he wouldn't much mind. In a way dying would be easier than figuring out a new way of living.

Betty must have taken it on herself to contact Ralph Brooks and suggest he ask Ray to Greece. Otherwise Ray couldn't imagine why Ralph should have written him a belated condolence letter that ended with a very warm and specific invitation.

Ray was flattered. After all, Brooks was the celebrated painter. Betty would say that Ray accepted *because* Brooks was the celebrated painter. Not that she ever accused Ray of social climbing. No, she just thought his "passivity" made him seek out authorities, no matter who or of what. Oddly enough, Betty's nagging, grating Brooklyn accent reassured him, because it was a voice that stylized suffering, domesticated it. Oy, Ray thought when he was with Betty. She wasn't even Jewish, but she was from Brooklyn, and if he used her accent he could actually say it to himself or to Anna: "Oy."

Ray welcomed the trip to Greece precisely because it didn't fit in. George had never been to Greece; Ralph had never met George; Ray himself scarcely knew Ralph. They'd become friendly at the gym and worked out a dozen times together and Ralph had always asked him his bright, general questions that didn't seem to anticipate anything so concrete as an answer. Ralph, who'd worked out for years, had a big bearish body that was going to flab—exactly what envious, lazy people always say happens to weightlifters in middle age. His shoulders, chest and biceps were still powerful, but his belly was as big as a bus driver's. Ralph said he hated the ruin of his looks, but he seemed so relaxed and sure of himself that this self-loathing struck Ray as an attitude he might once have held but had since outgrown without renouncing.

Then again Ray would so gladly have traded in his own prettiness for Ralph's success that perhaps he couldn't quite believe in Ralph's complaints. As for the three weeks in Crete (he found the town, Xania, on the map), it would be all new—new place, new language, no ghosts. He even liked going to the country where people expressed their grief over dying so honestly, so passionately. In that book he liked the way a mother, when she exhumed her daughter's body after three years of burial, said, "Look what I put in and look what I took out! I put in a partridge, and I took out bones."

Betty agreed to take care of Anna. "You must look out for yourself," George had said, and now he was trying.

Ralph had rented a floor of a Venetian palace on a hill over-looking the harbor; at least Ralph called it a "palace" in that hyperbolic way of his. The town had been badly bombed during the war, and empty lots and grass-growing ruins pocked even the most crowded blocks like shocking lapses in an otherwise good memory.

Nothing in town was taller than three stories except two minarets left over from the centuries of Turkish rule and allowed to stand more through indifference than ecumenicism. At first Ray looked for the blazing whitewash and strong geo-metrical shapes he'd seen in trendy postcards from the Greek islands, but in Xania everything was crumbling brick, faded paint, mud or pebble alleyways, cement and rusting cement armatures sticking up out of unfinished upper stories, shabby exteriors and immaculate interiors, dusty carved-wood second stories overhanging the street in the Turkish fashion. Along the harbor a chrome-and-plastic disco, booming music and revolving lights as though it had just landed, made chic racket beside shadowy, abandoned arsenals where the Venetians had housed their warships. One of them had a stone balcony high above the harbor and two doors shaped like Gothic flames opening up onto a roofless void and a framed picture of the night sky—the half-waned moon.

Ralph and Ray ate fried squid and a feta cheese salad at a rickety table alongside the brackish-smelling harbor. The table could never quite find its footing. They were waited on by a Buddha-faced boy who smiled with mild amusement every time his few words in English were understood. He couldn't have been more than nine, but the boy already had a whole kit of skilled frowns, tongue clicks and body gestures, and his grandfather's way of wiping his forehead with a single swipe of a folded fresh handkerchief as though he were ironing something. Ray found it hard to imagine having accumulated so many mannerisms before the dawn of sex, of the sexual need to please, of the staginess sex encourages.

Ralph, who was shoe-leather brown and so calm he let big gaps of comfortable silence open up in the conversation, was much fatter—all the olive oil and rosé and sticky desserts, no doubt. A cool wind was blowing up off the Aegean and Ray was glad he'd worn a long-sleeved shirt. Ralph had helped him unpack and had clucked over each article of clothing, all of which he found too stylish and outré for Xania. In fact Ralph seemed starved for company and gossip and far less vague than in New York. There he seemed always to be escaping sensory overload through benign nullity, the Andy Warhol strategy of saying "Oh, great" to everything. Here he took a minute, gossipy interest in the details of everyday life. Ray thought, We each need just the right weight of pettiness to serve as ballast. George's death had tossed all the sandbags overboard and Ray had been floating higher and higher toward extinction.

Ralph was especially interested in the "locals," as he called the young men. "Now this is the Black Adonis," he said of one tall, fair-skinned twenty-year-old strolling past with two younger boys. "He's in a different shirt every night. And would you look at that razor cut! Pure Frankie Avalon. . . . Oh, my dear, what fun to have another old-timer from the States with me, no need to explain my references for once."

Ralph had a nickname for every second young man who walked past in the slow, defiant, sharp-eyed parade beside the harbor. "This is the tailend of the *volta*, as we call the evening *passeggiata*," Ralph said, typically substituting one incomprehensible word for another. "There's absolutely nothing to do in this town except cruise. In the hot weather they all stop working at two in the afternoon. Now here comes the Little Tiger—notice the feline tattoo?—a very bad character. He stole my Walkman when I invited him in for a nightcap; Little Tiger, go to the rear of the class. He's bad because he's from the next town and he thinks he can get away with it. Stick with the locals; nothing like the high moral power of spying and gossip to make boys behave."

Ray had always heard of dirty old American men who'd gone to Greece for the summer "phallic cure," but he'd assumed gay liberation had somehow ended the practice, unshackled both predator and prey. Nevertheless, before they'd left the restaurant two more Americans, both in their sixties, had stopped by their table to recount their most recent adventures. Ray, used to fending off older men, was a bit put out that no one, not even Ralph, was flirting with him. In fact, the assumption, which he resented, was that he too was an old-timer who'd come here "for the boys" and would be willing to pay for it.

"Aren't there any Greeks who do it for free?" Ray asked, not getting the smiles he'd anticipated.

"A few frightful poofs do, I suppose," Ralph drawled, looking offended by the notion. "But why settle for free frights when for ten bucks you can have anyone in town, absolutely anyone including the mayor and his wife, not to mention the odd god on the hoof?"

For a few days Ray held out. Betty, morbidly enough, had made a tape of all the crazy messages George had left on her answering machine during his last year. She'd given Ray the tape just before he'd left and now he sat in his bedroom, wearing gaudy drawstring shorts, and while looking at the harbor lights listened to George's voice.

Ray remembered a remark someone had once made: "Many people believe in God without loving him, but I love him without believing in him." Ray didn't know why the remark popped into his head just now. Did he love George without believing he existed? Ray described himself as a "mystical atheist." Maybe that was a complicated way of saying he believed George still loved him, or would if God would let him speak.

In his New York gay world, which was as carefully screened from men under twenty-five as from those over sixty, Ray counted as young. That is, some old flame whom Ray had known fifteen years ago—a guy with a mustache gone gray and fanning squint lines but a still-massive chest and thunder thighs under all that good tailoring—would spot Ray at a black-tie gay-rights dinner or health-crisis benefit and come up to him murmuring, "Lookin' good, kid," and would pinch his bottom. It was all continuing and Ray knew that despite the way his body had acquired a certain thickness, as though the original Greek statue had been copied by a Roman, he still looked youthful to his contemporaries.

In the first two weeks after George's death Ray had picked up three different men on the street and dragged them home. Ray had clung to their warm bodies, their air-breathing chests and blood-beating hearts, clung like a vampire to warm himself through transfusions of desire. He and Anna would sniff at these bewildered young men as though nothing could be less likely than a scabbed knee, furred buttocks, an uncollared collarbone or the glamorous confusion of a cast-aside white shirt and silk rep tie. What they, the pickups, wanted, heart-to-heart postcoital chat, appealed to him not at all; all he wanted was to lie facedown beside tonight's faceup partner and slide on top of him just enough to be literally heart-to-heart. Their carnality had seemed very fragile.

After this brief, irresponsible flaring up of lust, which had followed the sexless year of George's dying, Ray had gone back to celibacy. He thought it very likely that he was carrying death inside him, that it was ticking inside him like a time bomb but one he couldn't find because it had been secreted by an unknown terrorist. Even if it was located it couldn't be defused. Nor did he know when it might explode. He didn't want to expose anyone to contagion.

He wrote his will as he knew everyone should. That was the adult thing to do. But the paltry list of his possessions reminded him of how little he'd accumulated or accomplished; it was like the shame of moving day, of seeing one's cigarette-burned upholstery and scarred bureau on the curb under a hot, contemptuous sun. His relatively youthful looks had led him to go on believing in his youthful expectations; his life, he would have said as a philosophy student, was all becoming and no being. All in the future until this death sentence (never pronounced, daily remanded) had been handed down.

Occasionally he jerked off with poppers and dirty magazines. Although he found slaves and masters ludicrous and pathetic, his fantasies had not kept pace with the fashions and were mired somewhere in 1972, best simulated by the stories and photos in *Drummer*. He would read a hot tale about a violent encounter between two real pigs, sniff his amyl, even mutter a few words ("Give your boy that daddy-dick") and then find himself, head aching, stomach sticky, heart sinking, erection melting, alone, posthumous. Anna wrinkled her nose and squinted at the fumes. He hoped his executor, who was his lawyer, would be able to bury him next to George as instructed, since he only slept really well when George was beside him. Once in a Philadelphia museum he'd seen the skeletons of a prehistoric man and woman, buried together (he couldn't remember how they'd come to die at the same time). He was lying on his back, she on her side, her hand placed delicately on his chest.

The days in Crete were big, cloudless hot days, heroic days, noisy with the rasp of insects. They were heroic days as though the sun were a lionhearted hero. . . . Oh, but hadn't he just read in his beach book, *The Odyssey*, the words of the dead, lionhearted Achilles: "Do not speak to me soothingly about death, glorious Odysseus; I should prefer, as a slave, to serve another man, even if he had no property and little to live on, than to rule over all these dead who have done with life." He'd cried on the white-sand beach beside the lapis-lazuli water and looked through his tears, amazed, at a herd of sheep trotting toward him. He stood and waded and waved, smiling, at the old shepherd in black pants with a carved stick in his hand, which itself looked carved; Ray, expensively muscular in his Valentino swim trunks, thought he was probably not much younger than this ancient peasant and suddenly his grief struck him as a costly gewgaw, beyond the means of the grievously hungry and hardworking world. Or maybe it was precisely his grief that joined him to this peasant. Every night he was dreaming about George, and in that book about the Greek death rituals he'd read the words of an old woman: "At death the soul emerges in its entirety, like a man. It has the shape of a man, only it's invisible. It has a mouth and hands and eats real food just like we do. When you see someone in your dreams, it's the soul you see. People in your dreams eat, don't they? The souls of the dead eat too." Ray couldn't remember if George ate in his dreams.

Ralph and Ray rented motor scooters and drove up a narrow road through chasms, past abandoned medieval churches and new cement-block houses, high into the mountains. They chugged slowly up to and away from a goat stretching to reach the lower branches of a tree. They saw a young Orthodox priest in a black soutane out strolling, preceded by a full black beard he seemed to be carrying in front of him as one might carry a salver. He remembered that Orthodox priests can marry and he vaguely thought of that as the reason this one seemed so virile.

The summer drought had dwindled the stream to a brook within its still-green bed. At a certain turn in the road the air turned cool, as though the frozen core of the mountain had tired of holding its breath. In the shepherds' village where they stopped for lunch a smiling boy was found to speak English with them. He said he'd lived in New Zealand for a year with his aunt and uncle; that was why he knew English. Laughing, he offered them steaks and salads, but it turned out the only food available in the village was a runny sour cheese and bread and olives.

Every day, despite the climate's invitation to languor, Ray did his complete workout, causing the heavy old wardrobe in his room to creak and throw open its door when he did pushups. Some days, especially around three, a wind would suddenly blow up and he and Ralph would run around battening down the twenty-three windows. At dusk on Sundays a naval band marched all the way around the harbor to the fortress opposite the lighthouse and played the national anthem ("which was written by a German," Ralph couldn't resist throwing in) while the blue-and-white flag was lowered.

Although the days were cheerful—scooter rides to a deserted beach, vegetable and fish marketing, desultory house hunting out beyond the town walls on which the Venetian lion had been emblazoned—the nights were menacing. He and Ralph would dress carefully for the *volta*, Ralph in a dark blue shirt and ironed slacks, Ray in a floating gown of a Japanese designer shirt and enormous one-size-drowns-all lime-green shorts, neon-orange cotton socks, black Adidas and white sunglasses slatted like Venetian blinds angled down ("Perfect for the Saudi matron on the go," he said).

At least that's how he got himself up the first few nights until he sensed Ralph's embarrassment, the crowd's smiling contempt and his own . . . what.

Desire?

Every night it was the same. The sun set, neon lights outlined the eaves and arches of the cafés, and an army of strollers, mostly young and male, sauntered slowly along the horseshoe-shaped stone walk beside the harbor. Sometimes it stank of pizza or what was called Kantaki Fried Chicken or of the sea urchins old fishermen had cleaned on the wharf earlier in the day. The walk could be stretched out to twenty minutes if one lingered in conversation with friends, stopped to buy nuts from one vendor and to look at the jewelry sold by Dutch hippies. A drink at an outdoor café—ouzo and hors d'oeuvres (*mezes*) —could while away another forty minutes.

The full hour was always devoted to boy watching. Ray looked, too, at the wonderful black hair, muscular bodies, red cheeks under deep tans, flamboyant mustaches, big noses, transparent arrogance, equally transparent self-doubt, black eyebrows yearning to meet above the nose and often succeeding. "Of course they need reassurance," Ralph said. "What actor doesn't?" These guys had loud voices, carnivorous teeth, strutting walks, big asses, broad shoulders. Ralph explained they were more like American teenage boys than other European youths; they were equally big and loud and physical and sloppy and unveiled in their curiosity and hostility.

One of the sixty-year-old Americans, a classics professor in the States, was an amateur photographer of considerable refinement. He'd persuaded, it seemed, dozens of locals to pose nude for him. He paid them something. He was discreet. He flattered them as best he could in the modern language he'd pieced together out of his complete knowledge of ancient Greek. "Sometimes," he said, "they say a whole long improbable sentence in English—picked up from an American song or movie, no doubt."

Among the locals his ministrations to vanity made him popular, his scholarship made him impressive and his hobby risible, but since he always seemed to be laughing at himself in his ancient, elegant prep-school way, his laughter softened theirs. His photographic sessions he dismissed airily but pursued gravely.

Homer (for that was his name, absurdly, "Stranger than epic," as he said) took a polite but real interest in Ray—but strictly in Ray's mind. Ray, who expected, invited and resented other men's sexual attraction to him, found Homer's sex-free attentiveness unsettling. And appealing. Maybe because Homer was a professor and had a professor's way of listening—which meant he winced slightly when he disagreed and cleaned his glasses when he deeply disagreed—Ray felt returned, if only for an instant, to his school days. To the days before he'd ever known George. To the days when he'd been not a New York know-it-all, but a midwestern intellectual, someone who took nothing on authority and didn't even suspect there were such things as fashions in ideas.

This repatriation cheered him. Ralph had made a spaghetti dinner at home ("Enough with the swordfish and feta, already") and invited Homer. Ray and Homer's conversation about the categorical imperative, the wager, the cave, the excluded middle astonished Ralph. "You girls are real bluestockings," he told them, "which is OK for a hen party, but remember men don't make passes at girls who wear glasses." Ralph even seemed disconcerted by their intelligence, if that's what all this highbrow name-dropping had revealed.

After the wine and the laughter Ray thought it only natural to go on to the bar with his friends, the gay bar where they met with "true love" every night, as Ralph said. On the way along the harbor, Ray told Homer all about his sexual qualms. "I just don't think I should expose anyone else to this disease in case I've got it or in case I'm contagious. And I'm not disciplined enough to stick to safe sex."

Homer nodded and made the same noncommittal but polite murmur as when earlier they'd discussed the *Nicomachean Ethics*. Then, as though shaking himself awake, he asked, "What *is* safe sex, exactly?"

"Strictly safe is masturbation, no exchange of body fluids. Or if you fuck you can use a rubber. But I'm not worried about myself. The only one in danger where fucking and sucking is involved is the guy who gets the come."

Silence full of blinking in the dark, blinking with lashes growing longer, darker with mascara, by the second. "But, darling," Homer finally confided, hilariously woman-to-woman, "then the Greeks are *always* safe. They're the men; we're the girls."

"Call me square," Ray said, "but that's old-fashioned role-playing—and I've never, never paid—"

Homer interrupted him with a soft old hand on his arm. "Give it a try. After all, it's your only option."

The alley leading to the bar was too narrow for cars but

wide enough to accommodate four noisy adolescents walking shoulder to shoulder; one of them stepped drunkenly down into the grass-sprouting ruins and pissed against a jagged wall. The kid had a foolish grin and he seemed to have forgotten how to aim, shake, button up. The others started barking and mewing. Ray found the situation and the hoarse voices exciting. Had these guys come from the bar? Were they gay?

The bar was a low room, a basement grotto, one would have said, except it was on the ground floor. There were several dimly lit alcoves just off the room in which shadowy couples were smoking and drinking. The waiters or "hostesses" were two transvestites: Dmitri, who was chubby and brunette and kept a slightly deformed hand always just out of sight, flickering it behind his back or under a tray or into a pocket; and Adriana, who was slender, with straight, shoulder-length blond hair and who responded to open jeers with a zonked-out grin that never varied, as though she were drugged on her own powerful fantasy of herself, which made her immune. Both were in jeans and T-shirts; Adriana had two small, hormone-induced breasts, but his arms were still muscular and his hips boyishly narrow. Dmitri, the brunette, had less beauty and more vitality, a clown's vitality; he was the stand-up or run-past comic. He did pratfalls with his tray, twinkled past on point, sat on laps or wriggled deliciously against sailors, always keeping his hand in motion, out of focus. The bar was called Fire Island.

At first this gay bar seemed to Ray an unexpected trove of sexy young guys until Homer explained that, technically, they (Ralph, Ray and Homer) were the only gays, along with the two hostesses, of course. Everyone else was, well, a gigolo, although that was too coarse a word for it. "Greek men really do prefer male company. All their bars are like this one," Homer said with that ornithological pride old-timer expatriates exhibit to the newcomer. "The women don't go out much. And the men think it's normal to get money for sex—just remember the dowries they receive. And then they're terribly poor, the sailors, five bucks a week, that's all they get. So, you take all these horny nineteen-year-olds away from their villages for the first time in their lives. Here they are, bored, lonely, with too much time on their hands, no unmarried Greek girls in sight . . ."

"Where are the girls?" Ray asked, embarrassed he hadn't noticed their absence till now.

"Their mothers quite sensibly keep them under lock and key. I myself feel an infinite reverence for the intact maidenhead. Of course you know these scandalous mothers teach their daughters to take it up the ass if they must put out; anything to stay intact. Although why am I complaining? That's my philosophy exactly."

"So the sailors are alone and horny . . ."

"And naturally they want to party. That's how they think of it. You buy them drinks and you're a real sport. You ask them home. It's a party. The only problem is how to wean them away from their *parea*."

"Come again?"

"*Parea*. That's their group, their friends, oh, a very useful word. If you want to pick someone up, point to him, then yourself. Say, 'You, me, *parea*?' "

"And what do they call us, the faggots?"

Homer smiled and lowered his voice: "*Poosti*."

"So we're *poosti* on *parea* . . . Don't rain on my *parea*."

"Yes," Homer said somewhat primly, "but not so loud. You'll scandalize the seafood," nodding toward a *parea* of five sailors, smiling at them with lofty politeness.

After two hours of downing gin and tonic, Ray realized most of the boys weren't drinking at all and were just sitting over empty bottles of beer, bumming cigarettes from one another and hungrily staring at the door as each newcomer entered. Only a few were talking to each other. Sometimes they seemed to be inventing a conversation (involving lots of numbers, as even Ray could decode) and an emotion (usually indignation), but purely as a set piece to show them off to advantage to potential clients. The same tape of "Susanna" kept playing over and over, last year's disco tune, which didn't mean much to him, since it had been popular when George was already sick and they had stopped going out dancing.

He excused himself, pecked Homer on the cheek and squeezed past a suddenly amorous Dmitri, the hefty hostess, who smelled of sweat and Chanel.

Outside the night was airless, fragrant, the sky an enormous black colander held up to the light. Since it hadn't rained in months, dust filled the streets, dulled the store windows examined by veering headlights, rose in lazy devils behind passing shoes. In a bridal store the mannequin of the bride herself was snub-nosed and blond, her hair bristling up under her veil at crazy shocked angles as though she'd stuck her finger in an electric socket. She was flanked by curious white cloth bouquets trailing white silk ribbons. Were they held by her bridesmaids? Ray had seen a woman bringing such a bouquet here on the plane from Athens. In that book he'd read, the exhumations of a dead person's bones three years after death were compared to a wedding. The same songs were sung; the words varied only slightly. Both songs began with the words: "Now I have set out. Now I am about to depart. . . ." Something like that.

On the corner a man was selling round green melons from a cart. Everywhere people seemed awake and watching—from a trellised balcony, from a waiting cab, from a rooftop café. In such a hot country people stayed up to enjoy the cool of the night. Kids, calling to one another, sped by on bicycles. In the square in front of the cathedral a whole line of taxis waited, five drivers standing in a circle and disputing—what? Soccer? Politics?

Ray turned onto a deserted street lined with shops displaying lace trimmings and bolts of fabric and spools of thread. An old man with yellowing hair, worn-down shoes and no socks had fallen asleep with his feet up on his desk in an open-air stand that sold ex-votos in tin—a bent arm, an ear, an open eye, a soldier in World War I uniform and helmet—and also tin icons, the metal snipped away to frame crude tinted reproductions of the Virgin's face. He also had long and short candles and something (incense?) wrapped in red paper cylinders, stacked high like rolled coins from the bank.

Cars with bad mufflers blatted and farted through town or throbbed beside a lit cigarette kiosk in front of the dim covered market. The cars were always full of teenage boys, but when they'd get out to buy cigarettes or to go into a bar to pick up a paper, he'd see they were fat or thin, usually big handsome guys with black mustaches or the first faint charcoal sketches of mustaches.

It struck Ray that it had been years since he'd seen guys this young. Expensive, childless Manhattan had banned them. Ray imagined that he was back in Findlay, Ohio, on a Saturday night, the dark silent streets suddenly glaring and noisy with a gang in two hot-rods. He forgot for a moment that he was forty; he felt he was sixteen, afraid of the hoods who'd driven in from Sandusky or even from as far away as Toledo. He was afraid and curious and contemptuous and excited as he darted along under the old trees, hoping he was invisible.

He crossed the street to avoid two strolling straight couples, and now he did feel forty. And queer. And foreign. He wouldn't even know if they were gossiping about him. Worse, he knew he didn't exist for them, he was invisible.

As he headed up the gently winding street toward the town zoo, he passed a lone young guy coming down toward him, who stared at him hard, harder and longer even than the other Cretan men normally stared. The boy spat through his teeth as they passed. And then he stopped. Ray heard him stop behind him. *If I turn around will he punch me?*

When Ray finally turned around the young man was standing there staring at him. *"Ya,"* he said, that short form of *yassou,* the all-purpose greeting. Ray could see he was handsome with regular features, an upper lip pulled back to show white teeth made whiter by his mustache and a black beard that he was letting grow. He had on jeans and a denim jacket, and the jacket sleeves were tight enough to reveal well-muscled upper arms, not the netted cantaloupes Ray had for biceps, but longer, grooved haunches, the tightly muscled arms that the ancient Cretan youths had in those wall paintings at absurdly overrestored Knossos: murderously slim-waisted matadors.

He was either very tan or very swarthy. His hair was long and pushed back behind his ears. His slightly unshaved face (the look of the New York model who wears two days' growth of beard as an accessory to his white silk pajamas), his obviously American jeans jacket and his long hair were the three things that made him look fractionally different from all the other young men in this city of young men.

He kept staring, but then when Ray looked away for an instant, he slipped into a side street. Ray wondered if he'd be jumped when he followed him. As he turned the corner, the boy was standing there and asked aggressively, "What you want?" and his faint smile suggested he already knew and that Ray's desire was disgusting and entirely practicable.

Ray said, "You," with the sort of airiness that could ruin a life, but that word apparently was not one of the boy's dozen English words. He frowned angrily.

"Sex," Ray said, and this time the boy nodded.

"But money!" he threatened, rubbing his thumb and fore-finger together. Ray nodded with a face-saving smirk he regretted but couldn't wipe away. "I fuck you!" the boy added. This time as Ray nodded his smile vanished, a little bit in awe at the mention of this intimacy, once so common, now so rare, so gravely admonished, so fearfully practiced in his plagued city.

"*Profilatikos.* You buy. Here." He pointed to the lit cigarette kiosk on the corner.

"No! *You* buy," Ray said, the facetious smile back in place but genuine alarm in his heart.

"You," the boy insisted, stepping into the shadows of a building.

Now all of his teenage qualms did come rushing back. He felt his fear of and fascination with the prophylactics dispenser he'd glimpsed once in a Kentucky filling-station toilet during a family trip through the Smokies. Or he remembered the time when he'd helped his mother turn back the covers for a married couple who were visiting them, and he'd seen under the pillow the raised circle of the rolled rubber in its foil wrapper. The very width of that circumference had excited him.

He said the word to the impassive middle-aged woman in the kiosk. She lowered her head on an angle, dropped her eyes, said, *"Ne,"* which means "yes" but sounds to English speakers like "no." A second later she'd fished up a box that read, in English, "Love Party," above a photo of a woman in provocative panties, one nyloned knee resting on the edge of a double bed.

Why rubbers? Ray wondered. Has he heard of our deadly new disease way out here at the end of the world, in a country where there are only two recorded cases, both of whom were visitors to New York? No, he must have in mind the old, curable maladies. Or maybe he just wants to dramatize our roles. I don't mind. Rubbers are terribly 1958 Saturday night at the drive-in. Maybe he needs a membrane intact to suggest his own virtual virginity.

A moment later, Ray was pursuing the boy through deserted

night streets under big trees, big laurels so dry their gray-green leaves had started curling laterally. Distant motorbikes were test-drilling the night. The turn-of-the-century mansions lining those blocks were dilapidated, shuttered and unlit behind rusting wrought-iron balconies, although trimmed hedges proved at least some of them were inhabited. The smells of garbage on a hot night alternated with the smell of jasmine, at first sniff slightly sweet, then ruttishly sweet. The boy wouldn't walk beside Ray, although Ray thought it must look much odder, this strange parade. They turned right off the boulevard and walked up, up a hill through residential streets. The boy's Keds shone almost phosphorescently white in the dark. Ray was calculating how much money he had in his wallet, while in his heart, his suddenly adolescent heart, he was exulting: "George, I've escaped you, I've gotten away from you."

In one sense he knew he was a slightly sissified middle-aged New York muscle queen somewhat out of her depth. In another sense he was the teenage debating-team captain in love again with Juan, son of a migrant Mexican worker who'd been brought to northern Ohio to pick fruit. The first confused conversation with Juan, the visit to the workers' compound, the smell of cooking chili, the sight of candles burning even by day before the tin shrine of the Virgin . . . The one thing certain was that whatever was going on in Crete came before or after George and precluded George.

As they walked along, the boy clicked a key chain, vestigial worry beads. Cats were everywhere, gliding in and out of shadows, daintily pawing black plastic garbage bags, slithering through gaps in fences, sitting on top of parked cars. Twice the boy stopped and scented the path—and now he looked like an Indian brave. Or so Ray thought, smiling at his own way of leafing through his boyhood anthology of erotic fantasies.

They reached what looked like a schoolyard, dark and empty

because it was summer and night, but otherwise like any schoolyard in Ohio—broken concrete playing area, an orange metal basketball hoop dripping rust stains onto the wood backboard, peeling benches, a toilet with separate entrances for boys and girls, a high fence surrounding the whole. The boy scrambled over the fence in two quick steps up and a graceful pivot at the top. Ray followed fearfully, awkwardly ("Here, teach, lemme give you a hand"). The boy gave Ray his hand and produced his first real smile, as dazzling as a camel boy's (a new page in the erotic anthology flipped open). His skin was surprisingly warm and plush and there were no calluses on his palm. Homer had told Ray that if parents could afford the luxury they preferred to shield their kids as long as possible from work. The boys, their adolescence extended well into their twenties, sat idly around the harbor at night, trying to pick up foreign girls (the sport was called *kemaki*, "harpooning").

When they ducked into the toilet, in the second that Ray's eyes took to adjust to the deeper dark, he walked by mistake right into the boy. They both gasped, the boy laughed, maybe a bit insultingly, his teeth lit up the room. Ray started to draw away but his hand had brushed against what could only be a big erection, "big" because of normal size; according to gay logic the boy's youth, the night, the danger, the fact he would be getting some money later on, all these things made it "big." Ray noticed the boy had already opened his fly. Out of eagerness?

Ray wanted him to be eager.

And then Ray, a famous beauty in his own right, a perennial hot number, hard to please, easily spooked by a maladroit cruiser, pursued throughout his twenty years of gay celebrity by hundreds of equally beautiful men, that elite corps of flight attendants, junior executives and models—this Ray (he was trembling as he knelt) knelt before what could only be white

Jockey shorts, yep, that's what they were, luminous under undone fly buttons, tugged the jeans down a notch, pulled down the elastic waist of the underpants and tasted with gratitude the hot, slightly sour penis. He whose conscience years of political struggle had raised now sank into the delicious guilt of Anglo fag servicing Mexican worker, of cowboy face-fucked by Indian brave, of lost tourist waylaid by wily camel boy. He inhaled the smell of sweat and urine with heady, calm pleasure. He felt like an alien being recharged by spaceship transfusion.

His mouth had been dry with fear. Now the penis striking his palate drew forth a flow of water. His knees already ached where he knelt on the wet cement floor. He took the boy's limp, hanging hand and laced his fingers into his. He looked up to catch the glance, but his eyes were shut and his face blank, which made him look much younger and almost absurdly unintimidating. At a certain point Ray pressed the unopened rubber into the boy's hand. Like a child peeping through a keyhole, Ray continued to kneel to watch the boy breaking open the packet and methodically unrolling the rubber down the length of his penis. He got it going the wrong way, lubricated side in, and had to start over. Then the boy gripped him from behind and Ray felt the invasion, so complex psychologically, so familiar but still painful or pleasurable to accommodate, he couldn't tell which, he'd never known which. The boy breathed on his shoulder; he smelled of Kantaki Fried Chicken.

When Ray paid the boy, who aristocratically palmed the money without bothering to see how much it was, Ray used one of the few Greek words he'd picked up (this one at the laundry), *avrio*, the word for "tomorrow." The boy nodded, or rather did what Greeks do instead of nodding, he clicked a *tsk* between his teeth and jerked his head down, lowering his eyelids. He pointed to this spot, to the ground in front of them.

Then he flashed ten and two fingers. "You like?" he asked, pointing to his own chest.

"Yes, of course," Ray whispered, thinking: These men . . .

He told the whole story at breakfast the next morning to Ralph, who was courteous enough to appear envious. After their yogurt and honey and the French roast coffee Ralph was at such pains to secure, they moved into Ralph's studio with its one small window looking down to the sea and the lighthouse. The studio had little in it besides a rocking chair, an old battered desk, a small kitchen table freighted with tubes of acrylics, a big, heavy wood easel and a rack for finished paintings. On the wall was a watercolor, poppies brilliant in a silky field of green and tan grasses. "Well, it's the only solution. For you," Ralph said.

Oh, he's turned his envy into pity, Ray thought, pity for me, the ticking time bomb, the young widow, but my solution doesn't seem all that much of a hardship.

As Ray napped in the hot, airless late afternoon he could feel a small painful spot inside him where the boy had battered into him and he smiled to feel that pain again. "Oy," he said to himself in Betty's accent.

That night the boy was there exactly on time. His hair was cleaner and shinier and he'd shaved (not the mustache, of course). But he was wearing the same jeans jacket, although the T-shirt looked clean. They went through exactly the same routine, for Ray didn't want to scare him off. He wanted to build up a fixed routine, the same place, the same acts, the same price. Tonight the only innovation was that Ray pulled the kid's jeans and underpants all the way down below his knees and discovered that his testicles hadn't descended and that his ass was hairy with nice friendly fuzz. Nor did he have a tan line; his skin was naturally just this dark.

After sex the kid hopped over the fence and disappeared into the night and Ray walked home, downhill all the way through the silent, cat-quick, jasmine-scented streets. He felt sad and lyric and philosophical and happy as he'd felt as a teenager; since these encounters with the boy—strictly sexual—seemed a strangely insufficient pretext for so much emotion, he also felt something of a charlatan. Objective correlative. That was the term. T. S. Eliot would have said that his emotion lacked an objective correlative.

The next night he asked him his name, which he discovered was Marco. "You must remember," Homer said during the *volta* the following evening, "the Italians ruled Crete for hundreds of years. Maybe he has some Italian blood." And again Ray had to describe his "find," for that's how the connoisseurs judged Marco. "Not the usual harbor trash," Homer said, and he announced that he was going to start harpooning in the zoological gardens again, which he'd assumed had long since been fished out. Ray refused to divulge where he met Marco every night. He wanted one secret at least, his dowry, the smallest secret he could keep and give to Marco, and again he thought of that book and the way they'd compared marriage to death, or rather marriage to the exhumation of bones.

Once he asked Marco where he lived, but Marco only waved vaguely in the direction of the shantytown inland and to the west of the harbor. *"Spiti mou, to limani,"* Ray announced, which he thought meant "My house is on the harbor," but Marco only lifted an indifferent eyebrow, the counterpart to the Frenchman's weary *"Eh alors?"* when smothered by Americans' doggy effusiveness. That night, Ray broadened his area of conquest and explored Marco's taut brown stomach up to his chest. By now there were several white rubbers on the wet cement floor like jellyfish washed up on the bleak shingle.

———

By day, Ray would go swimming or motorbiking to old churches or ruined monasteries or hidden beaches, but all day long and during the endless evenings, he'd daydream about Marco. He bought a phrase book and pieced together Greek words for that night's rendezvous.

Once Marco asked Ray if he should bring along a friend, and Ray agreed because he thought Marco wanted him to. But the friend was a portly sailor ("Greeks go off early," Ralph had said, as though they were a temperamental triple-cream cheese, a Brillat-Savarin, say). Ray sucked them both at the same time, doing one then the other, back and forth, but his only pleasure was in imagining reporting it to the other Americans tomorrow. The boys seemed embarrassed and talked loudly to each other and joked a lot and Marco kept losing his erection and he sounded nasty and used the word *putana*, which surely meant "whore" in Greek as well as Italian.

Ray paid them both and was tempted to mutter *putana* while doing so, but that might queer the deal, so he swallowed his resentment (yes, swallowed that, too) and drew Marco aside and said, *"Metavrio,"* which meant "the day after tomorrow" (*meta* as in metaphysics, "beyond physics"). The delay was meant as some sort of punishment. He also indicated he wanted to see Marco alone from now on. Marco registered the compliment but not the punishment and smiled and asked, "You like?" pointing to himself, asked it loud and clear so the other guy could hear.

"Yes," Ray said, "I like."

As he walked home, Ray took a stroll through the zoological gardens, where there was also an outdoor movie theater. Inside people sat on folding chairs and watched the huge screen on which a streetlamp had disobligingly cast the shadow of a leafy branch. Tonight he sat outside but he could hear the end of *Querelle*, of all things, dubbed into Greek and offered to the extended Cretan family, who chuckled over the perversities of northern Europe. In the closing sequence, Jeanne Moreau laughed and laughed a shattering laugh and the caged egrets dozing beside Ray awakened and started to chatter and call. Then the houselights came up, the families streamed out, for a moment the park was bright and vivid with crunched gravel and laughs and shouts, then car doors slammed and motorbikes snarled, the lights were dimmed and finally, conclusively, everything was quiet. Ray sat in the dark, listening to the awakened birds paddling the water, a leaf spray of shadows across his face like an old-fashioned figured veil. The jasmine gave off a shocking body odor, as though a pure girl had turned out to be a slut.

Ray regretted his spiteful decision to skip a day with Marco. The depth to which he felt Marco's absence, and his anxiety lest Marco not show up at their next appointment, made Ray aware of how much he liked Marco and needed him. Liked him? There was nothing to like, nothing but a mindless, greedy Cretan teen who was, moreover, heterosexual. Or worse, a complete mystery, a stranger, a minor tradesman with whom he was only on fucking terms.

Then Ray told himself he liked his own sense of gratitude to Marco, the silence imposed on them by the lack of a common language, liked the metered doses of sex fixed by fee and divergent appetites. He liked the high seriousness of the work they did together every night. He also liked stealing bits of affection from his co-worker, whose mustache was coming in as black and shiny as his eyebrows and whose chest (as Ray's hand had just discovered) was sprouting its first hair, this young man who would never love anyone, not even his wife, as much as Ray loved him.

One weekend Ralph went off on a yacht with a Greek collector of his paintings; they were sailing over to Thera and wouldn't be back till Monday. "Feel free to bring your child husband to the palace while I'm away," Ralph said as he pecked Ray on both cheeks in the French manner. And indeed that night Ray did say to Marco, *"Spiti mou,"* showed him the house keys and led him through town, walking a few paces ahead just as on that first night Marco had preceded Ray. On the street of ribbon shops someone hailed Marco (*"Yassou"*) and talked to him, and Ray, smiling at his own quick grasp of things, didn't look back but turned the corner and waited there, in the dark. After all, it was a little town. And only last week a shepherd had discovered his son was getting fucked and had killed him, which Homer said most of the locals had considered fair enough.

Marco in his white Keds and Levi's jacket came treading stealthily around the corner; he winked his approval and Ray felt his own pleasure spread over his whole body like the heat of the sun.

Marco was obviously impressed by the palace—impressed by its grandeur and, Ray imagined, proud that foreigners had furnished it with old Cretan furniture and folk embroideries.

Impressed? Nonsense, Ray thought, catching himself. Purest sentimental rubbish on my part. No doubt he'd prefer lavender Formica with embedded gold glitter.

Ray, who liked Marco and wanted to show that he did, felt a new intimacy between them as he led him into his bedroom. He gently pushed him back on the bed and knelt to untie the Keds and take them off, then the smelly socks. Then he made Marco wriggle out of his jeans; he started to pull the T-shirt over his head but Marco stopped him, though he, too, was gentle. Every one of Marco's concessions meant so much more to Ray than all the sexual extravagances of New York in the old preplague days—the slings and drugs and filthy raps.

Ray undressed himself. He wondered what Marco thought of him, of this naked adult male body which he'd never seen before. How old does he think I am? Does he admire my muscles? Or does my role as *poosti* on *parea* keep him from seeing me?

Ray worried that the whole routine—nakedness, a bed, privacy—might be getting a little too queer for Marco, so he was quick to kneel and start sucking him, back to the tried and true. But Ray, carried away in spite of himself, couldn't resist adding a refinement. He licked the inside of Marco's thighs and Marco jumped, as he did a moment later when Ray's tongue explored his navel. Strange that his cock seems to be the least sensitive part of his body, Ray thought.

When the time for the rubber arrived, Ray thought that surely tonight might make some difference, and indeed for the first time Marco gasped at the moment of his climax. Ray said, "You like?" and Marco nodded vigorously and smiled, and a young male intimacy really had come alive between them, glued as they were together, their naked bodies sweaty.

Almost instantly Marco stood and dashed into the bathroom, pulled off the rubber, and washed while standing at the sink. Ray leaned against the door and watched him.

In this bright light the boy looked startlingly young and Ray realized, yes, he was young enough to be his son. But his other feeling was less easy to account for. It was of the oddness that a body so simple, with so few features, should have provoked so much emotion in him, Ray. Clothes with their colors and cuts seemed more adequate to what he was feeling—more, far more, than the occasion warranted. No objective correlative. Ray took Marco up to the roof to see the panorama of the sea, the harbor, the far-flung villages, a car burrowing up the mountain with its headlights like a luminous insect. But now that the transaction was over, the tension between them had been cut.

The next night Marco came directly to the palace and Ray persuaded him to take off his T-shirt, too, so that now there was no membrane except the rubber between them. Before they got to the fucking part, Ray paused in his exertions and crept up beside Marco and rested his head on Marco's thumping chest. Marco's hand awkwardly grazed Ray's hair. Ray could smell the rank, disingenuous odor of Marco's underarm sweat—not old sweat or nervous sweat but the frank smell of a young summer body that had just walked halfway across town.

On the third and last night they'd have alone in the palace, Marco came up the steps hanging his head, not giving his hearty greeting: *"Ti kanes? Kala?"* He simply walked right into the bedroom, threw his clothes off, fell back on the bed and with a sneering smile parodied the moans and squirmings of sex.

"What's wrong?" Ray asked. Marco turned moodily on his side and Ray was grateful for this glimpse into the boy's discontent. When he sat down beside Marco he could smell beer on his breath and cigarette smoke in his hair, though Marco didn't smoke. At last, after a few words and much miming, Marco was able to indicate that he had a friend who was leaving the next morning for Athens to begin his compulsory military service and the guy was waiting for him in a bar down beside the harbor.

Ray pulled Marco to his feet, gave him double the usual thousand drachmas, helped him dress, set tomorrow's date back in the schoolyard and urged him to hurry off to his friend. He had a half thought that Marco understood more English than he was letting on. For the first time Marco seemed to be looking at Ray not as a member of another race, sex, class, age, but as a friend.

Friend? Ray laughed at his own naïveté. The boy's a hooker, he told himself. Don't get all moony over your beautiful budding friendship with the hooker.

After Marco had run down the steps, the thuds rattling the whole house, Ray was alone. Definitely alone. He walked to

the balcony and looked down at the harbor, most of its lights
extinguished, the last waiters hosing down the boardwalk. He
put on his headphones and listened to George's telephone messages to Betty. "Hi, doll, this is Darleen, now a stylishly an-
orexic 135 pounds. The Duchess of Windsor was wrong. You
can be too thin." Oh yes, four months before the end. "Hi,
doll, I know you're there with the machine on watching *The
Guiding Light*. Can you believe that bitch Vanessa? Hi!" And
a sudden happy duet of overlapping voices, since just then
Betty picked up and confessed she had indeed been pigging
out on the soaps and a pound of chocolates.

Ray snapped it off. "You must look out for yourself," George
had said, and just now the best way seemed to be to forget
George, at least for a while, to forget the atmosphere of dread,
the midnight visits to the hospital, the horrifying outbreak of
disease after disease—fungus in the throat, a bug in the brain,
bleeding in the gut, herpes ringing the ass, every inch of the
dwindling body explored by fiber optics, brain scanner, X rays,
the final agonies buried under blankets of morphine.

Ray received a call from Helen, his boss, and her tinny,
crackling tirade sounded as remote as the final, angry emission
from a dead star. He had no desire to leave Xania. With Homer
as his translator he looked at a house for sale in the Turkish
quarter and had a nearly plausible daydream of converting it
into a guest house that he and Marco would run.

He started writing a story about Marco—his first story in
fifteen years. He wondered if he could support himself by his
pen. He talked to an Irish guy who made a meager living by
teaching English at the prison nearby in their rehabilitation
program. If he sold George's half-million-dollar loft (George's
sole possession and only legacy) he could afford to live in Greece

several years without working. He could even finance that guest house.

When he'd first arrived in Crete he'd had the vague feeling that this holiday was merely a detour and that when he rejoined his path George would be waiting for him. George or thoughts of George or the life George had custom-built for him, he wasn't quite sure which he meant. And yet now there was a real possibility that he might escape, start something new or transpose his old boyhood goals and values into a new key, the Dorian mode, say. Everything here seemed to be conspiring to reorient him, repatriate him, even the way he'd become in Greece the pursuer rather than the pursued.

One hot, sticky afternoon as he sat in a café with a milky ouzo and a dozing cat for company, a blond foreigner—a man about twenty-five, in shorts and shirtless, barefoot—came walking along beside the harbor playing a soprano recorder. A chubby girl in a muumuu and with microscopic freckles dusted over her well-padded cheeks was following this ringleted Pan and staring at him devotedly.

Ray hated the guy's evident self-love and the way his head drooped to one side, and he hated the complicity of the woman, hated even more that a grown-up man should still be pushing such an overripe version of the eternal boy. He really did look overripe. Even his lips, puckered for the recorder, looked too pulpy. Ray realized that he himself had played the boy for years and years. To be sure not when he'd chronologically been a boy, for then he'd been too studious for such posturing. But later, in his twenties and thirties. He saw that all those years of self-absorption had confused him. He had always been looking around to discover if older men were noticing him and he'd been distressed if they were or weren't. He hadn't read or written anything because he hadn't had the calm to submit to other people's thoughts or to summon his own. George had urged him to buy more and more clothes, always in the latest youthful style, and he'd fussed over Ray's workout, dentistry, haircut, even the state of his fingernails. When they'd dozed in the sun on Fire Island, hour after hour George would stroke Ray's oiled back or legs. Ray had been the sultan's favorite. Now he'd changed. Now he was like a straight man. He was the one who admired someone else. He wooed, he paid. At the same time he was the kneeling handmaiden to the Cretan youth, who was the slim-waisted matador. This funny complication suited him.

A journalist came down from Athens to Xania to interview Ralph for an Athens art magazine or maybe it was a paper. Since he was gay, spoke English and was congenial, Ralph invited him to stay on for the weekend. The day before Ray was due to fly back to New York, he asked the journalist to translate a letter for him into Greek, something he could give Marco along with the gold necklace he'd bought him, the sort of sleazy bauble all the kids here were wearing. Delighted to be part of the adventure and impressed by the ardor of the letter, the journalist readily accepted the commission. Ralph arranged to be away for a couple of hours on Ray's last night and insisted he bring Marco up to the palace for a farewell between sheets. Covering his friendliness with queenliness, Ralph said, "How else can you hold on to your nickname, La Grande Horizontale?"

In the palace bedroom that night, just as Marco was about to untie his laces and get down to work, Ray handed him the package and the letter. Before opening the package, Marco read the letter. It said: "I've asked a visitor from Athens to translate this for me because I have to tell you several things. Tomorrow I'm going back to New York, but I hope to sell my belongings there quickly. I'll be back in Xania within a month. I've already found a house I'd like to buy on Theotocopoulos

Street. Perhaps you and I could live there someday or fix it up and run it as a guest house.

"I don't know what you feel for me if anything. For my part, I feel something very deep for you. Nor is it just sexual; the only reason we have so much sex is because we can't speak to each other. But don't worry. When I come back I'll study Greek and, if you like, I'll teach you English.

"Here's a present. If you don't like it you can exchange it."

After Marco finished reading the letter (he was sitting on the edge of the bed and Ray had snapped on the overhead light), he hung his head for a full minute. Ray had no idea what he'd say, but the very silence, the full stop, awed him. Then Marco looked at Ray and said in English, in a very quiet voice, "I know you love me and I love you. But Xania is no good for you. Too small. Do not rest here. You must go."

Although Ray felt so dizzy he sank into a chair, he summoned up the wit to ask, "And you? Will you leave Xania one day?"—for he was already imagining their life together in New York.

"Yes, one day." Marco handed the unopened package back to Ray. "I won't see you again. You must look out for yourself." And then he stood, left the room, thudded down the front steps, causing the whole house to rattle, and let himself out the front door.

Ray felt blown back in a wind tunnel of grief and joy. He felt his hair streaming, his face pressed back, the fabric of his pants fluttering. In pop-song phrases he thought this guy had walked out on him, done him wrong, broken his heart—a heart he was happy to feel thumping again with sharp, wounded life. He was blown back onto the bed and he smiled and cried as he'd never yet allowed himself to cry over George, who'd just spoken to him once again through the least likely oracle.

Reprise

A novel I'd written, which had flopped in America, was about to come out in France, and I was racing around vainly trying to assure its success in translation. French critics seldom give nasty reviews to books, but they often ignore a novel altogether, especially one by a foreign writer, even one who like me lives in Paris.

In the midst of these professional duties I suddenly received a phone call. A stifled baritone voice with a midwestern accent asked if I was Eddie. No one had called me Eddie since my childhood. "It's Jim Grady. Your mother gave me your number."

I hadn't seen him in almost forty years, not since I was fourteen and he twenty, but I could still taste the Luckies and Budweiser on his lips, feel his powerful arms closing around me, remember the deliberate way he'd folded his trousers on the crease rather than throwing them on the floor in romantic haste as I had done.

I met Jim through our parents. My mother was dating his father, an arrangement she'd been falling back on intermittently for years although she mildly despised him. She went out with him when there was no one better around. She was in her fifties, fat, highly sexed, hardworking, by turns bitter and wildly optimistic (now I'm all those things, so I feel no hesitation in describing her in those terms, especially since she was to change for the better in old age). My father and she had divorced seven years earlier, and she'd gone to work partly out of necessity but partly to make something of herself. Her Texas relations expected great things from her and their ambitions had shaped hers. Before the divorce she'd studied psychology, and now she worked in the public schools of suburban Chicago, traveling from one to another, systematically testing all the slow learners, problem cases and "exceptional" children ("exceptional" meant either unusually intelligent or retarded). She put great stock in making an attractive, even stunning, appearance at those smelly cinderblock schools and rose early in the morning to apply her makeup, struggle into her girdle and don dresses or suits that followed the fashions better than the contours of her stubby body.

In the gray, frozen dawns of Chicago winters she would drive her new Buick to remote schools, where the assistant principal would install her in an empty classroom and bring her one child after another. Shy, dirty, suspicious kids would eye her warily, wag their legs together in a lackluster parody of sex, fall into dumb trances or microscopically assay the hard, black riches they'd mined from their nostrils, but nothing could dim my mother's glittering determination to be cheerful.

She never merely went through the motions or let depression muffle her performance. She always had the highly colored, fatuously alert look of someone who is listening to compliments. Perhaps she looked that way because she was continually reciting her own praises to herself as a sort of protective mantra.

Most people, I suspect, are given a part in which the dialogue keeps running out, a supporting role for which the lazy playwright has scribbled in "Improvise background chatter" or "Crowd noises off." But my mother's lines had been fully scored for her (no matter that she'd written them herself), and she couldn't rehearse them often enough. Every night she came home, kicked off her very high heels and wriggled out of her orthopedically strong girdle, shrinking and filling out and sighing "Whooee!"—something her Ranger, Texas, mother would exclaim after feeding the chickens or rustling up some grub in the summer heat.

Then my mother would pour herself a stiff bourbon and water, first of the many highballs she'd need to fuel her through the evening. "I saw fifteen patients today: twelve Stanford-Binets, one Wechsler, one House-Tree-Person. I even gave a Rorschach to a beautiful little epileptic with high potential." On my mother's lips "beautiful" meant not a pretty face but a case of grimly classic textbook orthodoxy. "The children loved me. Several of them were afraid of me—I guess they'd never seen such a pretty, stylish lady all smiling and perfumed and bangled. But I put them right at ease. I know how to handle those backward children, they're just putty in my hands."

She thought for a moment, regarding her hands, then became animated. "The assistant principal was so grateful to me for my fine work. I guess she'd never had such an efficient, skilled state psychologist visit her poor little school before. She accompanied me to my automobile, and boy, you should have seen her eyes light up when she realized I was driving a fine Buick." Mother slung her stocking feet over the arm of the upholstered chair. "She grabbed my hand and looked me right in the eye and said, 'Who *are* you?' " This was part of the litany I always hated because it was obviously a lie. " 'Why, whatever do you mean?' I asked her. 'You're no ordinary psychologist,' she said. 'I can see by your fine automobile and your beautiful clothes and your fine mind and lovely manners that you are a real lady.' " It was the phrase "fine automobile" that tipped me off, since only southerners like my mother said that. Chicagoans said "nice car." Anyway I'd never heard any midwesterner praise another in such a gratifying way; only in my mother's scenarios were such heady exchanges a regular feature.

As the night wore on and my sister and I would sit down to do our homework on the cleared dining-room table, as the winter pipes would knock hypnotically and the lingering smell of fried meat would get into our hair and heavy clothes, our mother would pour herself a fourth highball and put on her glasses to grade the tests she'd administered that day or to write up her reports in her round hand, but she'd interrupt her work and ours to say, "Funny, that woman simply couldn't get over how a fine lady like me could be battling the Skokie slush to come out to see those pitiful children."

The note of pity was introduced only after the fourth drink, and it was, I imagine, something she felt less for her patients than for herself as the telephone stubbornly refused to ring.

At that time in my mother's life she had few friends. Going out with other unmarried women struck her as a disgrace and defeat. She was convinced couples looked down on her as a divorcée and those single men who might want to date a chubby, penniless, middle-aged woman with two brats hanging around her neck were, as she'd say, scarce as hen's teeth.

That's where Mr. Grady came in. He was forty-five going on sixty, overweight and utterly passive. He too liked his drinks, although in his case they were Manhattans; he fished the maraschino cherries out with his fingers. He didn't have false teeth, but there was something weak and sunken around his mouth as he mumbled his chemically bright cherries. His hairless hands were liver-spotted, and the nails were flaky, bluish and unusually flat, which my mother, drawing on her

fragmentary medical knowledge, called "spatulate," although
I forget which malady this symptom was supposed to indicate.
His wife had left him for another man, much richer, but she
considerately sent Mr. Grady cash presents from time to
time. He needed them: he lived reasonably well and he didn't
earn much. He worked on the city desk of a major Chicago
daily, but he'd been there for nearly twenty years, and in that
era, before the Newspaper Guild grew strong, American jour-
nalists were badly paid unless they were flashy, opinionated
columnists.

Mr. Grady wrote nothing and had few opinions. He occasionally assigned stories to reporters, but most of the time he
filled out columns that ran short with curious scraps of information. These items were called, for some reason, "boilerplate"
and were composed weeks, even months, in advance. For all
I know they were bought ready-made from some Central
Bureau of Timeless Information. Although Mr. Grady seldom
said anything interesting and was much given to dithering over
the practical details of his daily life, his work furnished him
with the odd bit of startling knowledge.

"Did you realize that Gandhi ate meat just once in his life
and nearly died of it?" he'd ask. "Did you know there is more
electric wire in the Radio City Music Hall organ than in the
entire city of Plattsburgh?"

He was capable of going inert, like a worm that poses as a
stick to escape a bird's detection (I have my own stock of
boilerplate). When mother would hector him for not demand-
ing a raise or for not acting like a man, his face would sink
into his jowls, his chin into his chest, his chest into his belly,
and the whole would settle lifelessly onto his elephantine legs.
His eyes behind their thick glasses would refuse all contact.
He could remain nearly indefinitely in that state until my
mother's irritation would blow over and she would make a
move to head off for Miller's Steak House, a family restaurant

with a menu of sizzling T-bones, butter and rolls, French-fried onions and hot-fudge sundaes, which would contribute to Mr. Grady's early death by cardiac arrest.

In September 1954 the Kabuki Theater came from Tokyo to Chicago for the first time, and my mother and Mr. Grady bought tickets for themselves and me and Mr. Grady's son Jim, whom we had never met (my sister didn't want to go—she thought it sounded "weird," and the prospect of meeting an eligible young man upset her).

The minute I saw Jim Grady I became sick with desire—sick because I knew from my mother's psychology textbooks, which I'd secretly consulted, just how pathological my longings were. I had looked up "homosexuality" and read through the frightening, damning diagnosis and prognosis so many times with an erection that finally, through Pavlovian conditioning, fear instantly triggered excitement, guilt automatically entailed salivating love or lust or both.

Jim was tall and tan and blond with hair clipped soldier-short and a powerful upper lip that wouldn't stay shaved and always showed a reddish-gold stubble. His small, complicated eyes rapidly changed expression, veering from manly im-penetrability to teenage shiftiness. He trudged rather than walked, as though he were shod with horseshoes instead of trim oxford lace-ups. He wore a bow tie, which I usually associated with chipper incompetence, but in Jim's case seemed more like a tourniquet hastily tied around his large, mobile Adam's apple in a makeshift attempt to choke off its pulsing maleness. If his Adam's apple was craggy, his nose was small and thin and well made, his bleached-out eyebrows so blond they shaded off into his tanned forehead, his ears small and neat and red and peeling on top and on the downy lobes.

He seemed eerily unaware of himself—the reason, no doubt, he left his mouth open whenever he wasn't saying "Yes, ma'am" or "No, ma'am" to my mother's routine questions, although once he smiled at her with the seductive leer of a lunatic, as though he were imitating someone else. He had allergies or a cold that had descended into his larynx and made his monosyllables sound becomingly stifled—or maybe he always talked that way. He could have been a West Point cadet, so virile and impersonal did his tall body appear, except for that open mouth, those squirming eyes, his fits of borrowed charm.

Someone had dressed him up in a hairy alpaca suit jacket and a cheap white shirt that was so small on him that his red hands hung down out of the cuffs like hams glazed with honey, for the backs of his hands were brushed with gold hair. The shirt, which would have been dingy on anyone less tan, was so thin that his dark chest could be seen breathing through it. He wasn't wearing a T-shirt, which in those days was unusual, even provocative.

Mr. Grady was seated at one end, my mother next to him, then Jim, then me. My mother took off her coat and hat and combed her hair in a feathery, peripheral way designed to leave the deep structure of her permanent wave intact. "You certainly got a good tan this summer," she said.

"Thank you, ma'am."

His father, heavily seated, said tonelessly, without lifting his face from his chin or his chin from his chest, "He was working outside all summer on construction, earning money for his first year in med school."

"Oh, really!" my mother exclaimed, suddenly fascinated, since she had a deep reverence for doctors. I too felt a new respect for him as I imagined the white surgical mask covering his full upper lip; "I want you on your hands and knees," I could hear him telling me, "now bend forward. Arch your back, spread your knees still wider." He was pulling on rubber gloves and from my strange, sideways angle I could see him dipping his sheathed finger into the cold lubricant. . . .

"Have you chosen a specialty already?" my mother asked as the auditorium lights dimmed.

"Gynecology," Jim said—and I clamped my knees together with a start.

Then the samisens squealed, kotos thunked dully, and drums kept breaking rank to race forward faster and faster until they fell into silence. A pink spotlight picked out a heavily armored and mascaraed warrior frozen in midflight on the runway, but only the scattered Japanese members of the audience knew to applaud him. The program placed a Roman numeral IV beside the actor's name, which lent him a regal importance. Soon Number Four was stomping the stage and declaiming something in an angry gargle, but we hadn't paid for the earphones that would have given us the crucial simultaneous translation, since my mother said she always preferred the gestalt to the mere details. "On the Rorschach I always score a very high W," she had coyly told the uncomprehending and uninterested Mr. Grady earlier over supper. I knew from her frequent elucidations that a high W meant she saw each inkblot as a whole rather than as separate parts, and that this grasp of the gestalt revealed her global intelligence, which she regarded as an attribute of capital importance.

A mincing, tittering maiden with a homely, powdered white face and an impractical hobble skirt (only later did I read that the performer was a man and the fifth member of his improbable dynasty) suddenly metamorphosed into a sinister white fox. With suicidal daring I pressed my leg against Jim's. First I put my shoe against his, sole planted squarely against sole. Then, having staked out this beachhead, I slowly cantilevered my calf muscles against his, at first just slightly grazing him. I even withdrew for a moment, proof of how completely careless and unintended my movements were, before I sat forward, resting my elbows on my knees in total absorption, leaning attentively into the exotic squealing and cavorting onstage— an intensification of attention that of course forced me to press my slender calf against his massive one, my knobby knee against his square, majestic one.

As two lovers rejoiced or despaired (one couldn't be sure which), Jim's leg held fast against mine. He didn't move it away. I stole a glance at his profile, but it told me nothing. I pulsed slightly against his leg. I rubbed my palms together and felt the calluses that months of harp practice had built up on my fingertips.

If I kept up my assaults, would he suddenly and indignantly withdraw—even, later, make a remark to his father, who would feel obliged to tip off my mother about her son the fairy?

I decided to wait for reciprocal signals. I wouldn't let my desire fool me into seeing mutual longing where only mine existed. I was dreading the intermission because I didn't know if I could disguise my tented crotch or the blush bloom that was slowly drifting up my neck and across my face.

I flexed my calf muscles against Jim's and he flexed back. We were football players locked into a tight huddle or two wrestlers each struggling to gain the advantage over the other (an advantage I was only too eager to concede). We were about to pass over the line from accident into intention. Soon he'd be as incriminated as I. Or did he think this dumb show was just a joke, indicative of other intentions, anything but sexual?

I flexed my calf muscles twice and he signaled back twice; we were establishing a Morse code that was undeniable. On-stage, warriors were engaged in choreographed combat, frequently freezing in midlunge, and I wondered where we would live, how I would escape my mother, when I could kiss those full lips for the first time.

A smile, antic with a pleasure so new I scarcely dared to trust it, played across my lips. Alone with my thoughts but surrounded by his body, I could imagine a whole long life with him.

When the intermission came at last, our parents beat a hasty retreat to the bar next door, but neither Jim nor I budged. We had no need of highballs or a Manhattan; we already had them and were already in New York or someplace equally magical. As the auditorium emptied out, Jim looked at me matter-of-factly, his Adam's apple rising and falling, and he said, "How are we ever going to get a moment alone?"

"Do you have a television set?" I asked (they were still fairly rare).

"Of course not. Dad never has a damn cent; he throws his money away with both hands."

"Why don't you come over to our place on Saturday to watch *The Perry Como Show*, then drink a few too many beers and say you're too tight to drive home and ask to stay over. The only extra bed is in my room."

"OK," he said in that stifled voice. He seemed as startled by my efficient deviousness as I was by his compliance. When our by now much-livelier parents returned and the lights went back down, I wedged a hand between our legs and covertly stroked his flexed calf, but he didn't reciprocate and I gave up. We sat there, knee to knee, in a stalemate of lust. I'd been erect so long my penis began to ache, and I could feel a precome stain seeping through my khakis. I turned bitter at the prospect of waiting three whole days till Saturday. I wanted to pull him into the men's room right now.

Once at home, my mother asked me what I thought of Jim, and I said he seemed nice but dumb. When I was alone in bed and able at last to strum my way to release (I thought of myself as the Man with the Blue Guitar), I hit a high note (my chin), higher than I'd ever shot before, and I licked myself clean and floated down into the featherbed luxury of knowing that big tanned body would soon be wrapped around me.

Our apartment was across the street from the beach and I loved to jump the Lake Michigan waves. Now I'm astonished I ever enjoyed doing anything that athletic, but then I thought of it less as sport than as opera, for just as in listening to 78 records I breasted one soaring outburst after another by Lauritz Melchior or Kirsten Flagstad, so was I thrilled by the repeated crises staged by the lake in September—a menacing crescendo that melted anticlimactically away into a creamy glissando, a minor interval that swelled into a major chord, all of it as excited and endless as Wagner's *Ring*, which I'd never bothered to dope out motif by leitmotif, since I too preferred an ecstatic gestalt to tediously detailed knowledge. We were careless in my family, careless and addicted to excitement.

Jim Grady called my mother and invited himself over on Saturday evening to watch *The Perry Como Show* on television. He informed her he was an absolute fanatic about Como, that he considered Como's least glance or tremolo incomparably cool, and that he especially admired his long-sleeved golfer's sweaters with the low-slung yoke necks, three buttons at the waist, coarse spongy weave and bright colors. My mother told me about these odd enthusiasms; she was puzzled by them because she thought that fashion concerned women alone and that even over women its tyranny extended only to clothes, certainly not to ways of moving, smiling or singing. "I wouldn't want to imitate anyone else," she said with her little mirthless laugh of self-congratulation and a disbelieving shake of her head. "I like being me just fine, thank you very much."

"He's not the first young person to swoon over a pop star," I informed her out of my infinite world-weariness.

"Men don't swoon over men, dear," Mother reminded me, peering at me over the tops of her glasses. Now that I unscramble the signals she was emitting, I see how contradictory they were. She said she admired the sensitivity of a great dancer such as Nijinsky, and she'd even given me his biography to make sure I knew the exact perverse composition of that sensitivity: "What a tragic life. Of course he ended up psychotic with paranoid delusions, martyr complex and degenerative ataxia." She'd assure me, with snapping eyes and carnivorous smile, that she liked men to be men and a boy to be all boy (as who does not), although the hearty heartlessness of making such a declaration to her willowy, cake-baking, harp-playing son thoroughly eluded her. Nor would she have tolerated a real boy's beer brawls, bloody noses or stormy fugues. She wanted an obedient little gentleman who would sit placidly in a dark suit when he wasn't helping his mother until, at the appropriate moment and with no advance fuss, he would marry a plain Christian girl whose unique vocation would be the perpetual adoration of her mother-in-law.

At last, after our dispirited Saturday night supper, Jim Grady arrived, just in time for a slice of my devil's food cake and *The Perry Como Show*. What a coincidence that I'd chosen the Como show at random but that Como really was Jim's hero! My sister skulked off to her room to polish her hockey stick and read through fan-magazine articles on Mercedes McCambridge and Barbara Stanwyck. Jim belted back the six-pack he'd brought along and drew our attention with repulsive connoisseurship to every cool Como mannerism. I now realize that maybe Como was the first singer who'd figured out that the TV lens represented twenty million horny women dateless on Saturday night; he looked searchingly into its glass eye and warbled with the calm certainty of his seductive charm.

As a homosexual, I understood the desire to possess an admired man, but I was almost disgusted by Jim's ambition to imitate him. My mother saw men as nearly faceless extras who surrounded the diva, a woman; I regarded men as the stars; but both she and I were opposed to all forms of masculine self-fabrication, she because she considered it unbecomingly narcissistic, I because it seemed a sacrilegious parody of the innate

superiority of a few godlike men. Perhaps I was just jealous
that Jim was paying more attention to Como than to me.

Emboldened by beer, Jim called my mother by her first name,
which I'm sure she found flattering, since it suggested he saw
her as a woman rather than as a parent. She drank one of her
many highballs with him, sitting beside him on the couch, and
for an instant I coldly appraised my own mother as a potential
rival, but she lost interest in him when he dared to shush her
during a bit of the singer's studied patter. In those days before
the veneration of pop culture, unimaginative highbrows such
as my mother and I swooned over opera, foreign films of any
sort and "problem plays" such as *The Immoralist* and *Tea and
Sympathy*, but in spite of ourselves we were guiltily drawn to
television with a mindless, vegetable-like tropism best named
by the vogue word of the period, "apathy." And yet we certainly
thought it beneath us to *study* mere entertainment.

Jim was so masculine in the way he held a Lucky cupped
between his thumb and middle finger and kept another unlit
behind his ear, he was so inexpressive, so devoid of all gesture,
that when he stood up to go, shook his head like a wet dog
and said, "Damn! I've had one too many for the road," he was
utterly convincing. My mother said, "Do you want me to drive
you home?" Jim laughed insultingly and said, "I think you're
feeling no pain yourself. I'd better stay over, Delilah, if you
have an extra bed."

My mother was much more reluctant to put Jim up than
I'd anticipated. "I don't know, I could put my girdle back
on. . . ." Had she picked up the faint sex signal winking back
and forth between Jim and her son? Perhaps she worried how
it might look to Mr. Grady: drunk son spends night in Delilah's
apartment—and such a son, the human species at its peak
of physical fitness, mouth open, eyes shifting, Adam's apple
working.

At last we were alone, and operatically I shed my clothes in a puddle at my feet, but Jim, undressing methodically, whispered, "You should hang your clothes up or your mother might think we were up to some sort of monkey business." Hot tears sprang to my eyes, but they dried as I looked at the long torso being revealed, with its small, turned waist and the wispy hairs around the tiny brown nipples. His legs were pale because he'd worn jeans on the construction site, but he must have worn them low. For an instant he sat down to pull off his heavy white socks, and his shoulder muscles played under the overhead light with all the demonic action of a Swiss music box, the big kind with its works under glass.

He lay back with a heavy-lidded, cool expression I suspected was patterned on Como's, but I didn't care, I was even pleased he wanted to impress me as I scaled his body, felt his great warm arms around me, tasted the Luckies and Bud on his lips, saw the sharp focus in his eyes fade into a blur. "Hey," he whispered, and he smiled at me as his hands cupped my twenty-six-inch waist and my hot penis planted its flag on the stony land of his perfect body. "Hey," he said, hitching me higher and deeper into his presence.

Soon after that I came down with mononucleosis, the much-discussed "kissing disease" of the time, although I'd kissed almost no one but Jim. I was tired and depressed. I dragged myself with difficulty from couch to bed, but at the same time I was so lonely and frustrated that I looked down from the window at every man or boy walking past and willed him to look up, see me, join me, but the will was weak.

Jim called one afternoon, and we figured out he could come by the next evening when my mother was going somewhere with my sister. I warned him he could catch mono if he kissed me, but I was proud after all he did kiss me long and deep. Until now the people I'd had sex with were boys at camp who pretended to hypnotize each other or married men who cruised the Howard Street Elevated toilets and drove me down to the

beach in station wagons filled with their children's toys. Jim
was the first man who took off his clothes, held me in his
arms, looked me in the eye and said, "Hey."

I was bursting with my secret, all the more so because
mononucleosis had reduced my world to the size of our apartment and the books I was almost too weak to hold (that afternoon it had been Oscar Wilde's *Lady Windermere's Fan*). In
the evening my mother was washing dishes and I was drying,
but I kept sitting down to rest. She said, "Mr. Grady and I
are thinking of getting married." The words just popped out
of my mouth: "Then it will have to be a double wedding." My
brilliant repartee provoked not a laugh but an inquisition,
which had many consequences for me over the years, both good
and bad. The whole story of my homosexual adventures came
out, my father was alerted, I was sent off to boarding school
and a psychiatrist—my entire life changed.

My mother called up Jim Grady and boozily denounced him
as a pervert and child molester, although I'd assured her I'd
been the one to seduce him. I did not see him again until
almost forty years later in Paris. My mother, who'd become
tiny, wise and sober with age, had had several decades to get
used to the idea of my homosexuality (and my sister's, as it
turned out). She had run into Jim Grady twice in the last three
years and warned me he'd become maniacally stingy, so much
so he'd wriggle out of a drinks date if he thought he'd have to
pay.

And yet when he rang me up from London, where he was
attending a medical conference, he didn't object when I proposed to book him into the pricey hotel next door to me on the
Ile Saint-Louis.

He called from his hotel room, and I rushed over. He was
nearly sixty years old, with thin gray hair, glasses with clear
frames he'd mended with black electrician's tape, ancient Cor-
fam shoes, an open mouth, a stifled voice. We shook hands,

but a moment later he pulled me into his arms. He said he knew, from a magazine interview I'd given, that this time I was infected with a virus far more dangerous than mononucleosis, but he kissed me long and deep, and a moment later we were undressed.

Over the next four days I had time to learn all about his life. He hadn't become a gynecologist after all but a sports doctor for a Catholic boys' school, and he spent his days bandaging the bruised and broken bodies of teenage athletes. His best friend was a fat priest nicknamed "the Whale," and they frequently got drunk with one of Jim's soldier friends who'd married a real honey, a great little Chinese gal. Jim owned his own house. He'd always lived alone and seemed never to have had a lover. His father had died from an early heart attack, but Jim felt nothing but scorn for him and his spendthrift ways. Jim himself had a tricky heart, and he was trying to give a shape to his life. He was about to retire.

It was true he'd become a miser. He bought his acrylic shirts and socks in packs of ten. His glasses came from Public Welfare. At home he went to bed at sunset to save on electricity. We spent hours looking for prints that cost less than five dollars as presents for the Whale, the army buddy and the great little Chinese gal. He wouldn't even let me invite him to a good restaurant. We were condemned to splitting the bill and eating at the Maubert Self, a cafeteria, or nibbling on cheese and apples we'd bought at the basement supermarket next to the Métro Saint Paul. He explained his economies to me in detail. Proudly he told me that he was a millionaire several times over and that he was leaving his fortune to the Catholic Church, although he was an atheist.

I took him with me to my literary parties and introduced him as my cousin. He sat stolidly by like an old faithful dog as people said brilliant, cutting things in French, a language he did not know. He sent every hostess who received us a thank-you letter, which in America was once so common it's still known as a "bread-and-butter note" although in France it was always sufficiently rare as to be called a *lettre de château*. The same women who'd ignored him when he sat at their tables were retrospectively impressed by his New World courtliness.

On his trip to Paris I slept with him just that first time in his hotel room; as we kissed, he removed his smudged, taped welfare glasses and revealed his darting young blue eyes. He undressed my sagging body and embraced my thirty-six-inch waist and bared his own body, considerably slimmer but just as much a ruin with its warts and wattles and long white hair. And yet, when he hitched me into his embrace and said, "Hey," I felt fourteen again. "You were a moron to tell your mom everything about us," he said. "You made us lose a lot of time."

And if we had spent a life together, I wondered, would we each be a bit less deformed now?

As his hands stroked my arms and belly and buttocks, everything the years had worn down or undone, I could hear an accelerating drum and see, floating just above the rented bed, our young, feverish bodies rejoicing or lamenting, one couldn't be sure which. The time he'd come over when I had mono, my hot body had ached and shivered beside his. Now each time I touched him I could hear music, as though a jolt had started the clockwork after so many years. We watched the toothed cylinder turn under the glass and strum the long silver notes.

Palace Days

to Maxine Groffsky

They came to Paris from New York as lovers, although they hadn't slept together in a year. Of course they kept sleeping in the same bed, and of course they would never have admitted the shameful secret of their chastity. If other people had known they weren't having sex together, they would have undervalued their love, which was growing at once more detailed and more unified every day, like an epic poem bristling with events and characters all held together through a mysterious system of balanced echoes.

Their poem, however, was more a nursery rhyme, since they had a stuffed bear they named Mr. Peters and they called each other Peters or Pete or Petes and were generally silly to the point of rapture, endlessly shouting their love from room to room. One of them would sing out, "Do you still like me, Peters?" The other would reply, "Petes, I *love* you."

The truth was they were both so insecure that the ordinary discretion between lovers would never have suited them. They were willing to trade in thrice-weekly sex for hourly affirmations of love. "You're going to leave me, I know it," one of them would suddenly announce with mock fear to disguise the real fear. "I'll *never* leave you, Peters," the other one would swear with mock solemnity to take the embarrassing edge off the real solemnity.

There was almost a twenty-year age difference between them, but when they were horsing around in the apartment they scarcely noticed it. The older one, Mark, had always been considered immature back in New York because the things he liked—going out every night, disco dancing, sexual conquests, smoking dope and screaming and sobbing through pop-music concerts—were the things wild, affluent kids had liked in the 1970s. Although Ned, the younger one, liked to drink, he did everything else in moderation and even when drunk he was always the one in the group who remembered where the car was parked or could explain things clearly and politely to an enraged policeman.

Living it up had been a way of making a living for Mark. He was the president of the Bunyonettes, a gay travel agency that arranged all-male tours. Forty gay guys would float down the Nile from Aswan to Luxor, impressing the Egyptians with their muscles and mustaches and shocking them with their pink short shorts and filmy, drawstring *après-piscine* harem pants. Or Mark would charter a small liner that would cruise the Caribbean and surprise the port town of Curaçao, where two hundred fellows, stocky, cheerful and guiltless, would ransack the outdoor clothes market looking for bits of female finery to wear to the Carmen Miranda Ball scheduled for the high seas tomorrow night.

A computerized dating service, a rental agency for Key West and Rio, a caterer that put its waiters in shorts, T-shirts and, to emphasize those powerful calves, orange work boots and sagging knee socks—these were just a few of the satrapies in

Mark's empire. Actually the whole business was run by Manuela, a tough Puerto Rican everyone assumed must be a dyke, though after two rotten marriages she wasn't into anything but money and good times. She did the accounting, hired and fired the staff, organized the trips. Mark was just there to socialize, to "circulate," as his hostessy Virginia mother put it.

When things fell apart in '81 Mark couldn't face it. An old roommate came down with the disease, and Mark wrote on his desk calendar nearly every week "Visit Jason," but he never got over to St. Vincent's until it was too late. At the bars, discos and gay restaurants between rounds of rusty nails, he'd look up to see the starved, yellow face of an old playmate. The short hair and mustache made him ashamed for some reason, as though God had contrived a rebuke of their past fashions. Of course the worst rebuke to the fashion-conscious is to be no longer in style, and these eyes ringed in dark and these sallow cheeks looked like daguerreotypes of what they'd represented in full living color just a year ago.

Of course Mark went through the motions. He was a sort of community leader. Although he knew plague talk was bad for business, that no one wanted to take a cruise on a death ship, he quickly put aside such mercenary thoughts. He organized safe-sex jerk-off parties, thought up themes for benefits, signed petitions for money and against bigotry, but his heart wasn't in it. He was a good-time Charlie and the times had soured.

And he felt guilty.

He wondered if he'd set a bad example. So often he'd trusted excess. He'd tripped out on acid every night in Water Island that summer of 1978, tempering the speediness with rusty nails and Valium. He cheerfully visited his cheerful doctor almost once a week all though the 1970s for clap in the throat, dick or bum, for anal warts, for two different kinds of hepatitis, for the syph (a night of fever and shakes after the first massive dose of antibiotics). He saw every ailment as a badge of courage in the good fight against puritanism.

He knew he was charismatic owing to his Virginia drawl, his shiny straight hair, his blue eyes under scribbled-in, black-black brows, and especially owing to his way of respecting men for their successes while never losing sight of their vulnerability, which for most of them constituted their sexuality. "OK, Harold, we know you're the world's greatest ichthyologist but that doesn't mean your ass ain't as cute as a twelve-year-old's and how about parking it here"—he pointed to his knee—"right here."

Without doing much Mark attracted a whole solar system of playmates around him every evening. Like a stage Irishman in London, he'd always played the Rebel Gentleman among the Yankees, for whom southernness meant gallantry, borderline intelligence and a bibulous conviviality. He feared that he'd misled all those guys who, imitating him, had worn madras, sniffed ethyl and voted Republican—and had had sex with hundreds and hundreds of partners. All those hot athletic men came now to haunt him with their skin hung like a wet shirt on a hanger.

Mark began to change. His doctor, no longer so cheerful, ordered Mark to stop smoking: "You have chronic bronchitis and it can only get worse. Go to Smokenders; they have a foolproof program." Mark had a charming way of hanging his head like a kid, pawing the floor and saying loudly with that winning southern accent, "Aw, Doc, give a fella a break," but the doctor, pudgy and owly after his own recent double withdrawal from nicotine and cocaine, stood firm.

Mark went to the Smokender sessions dutifully, switched to a vile mentholated brand, wrapped each pack in a paper sleeve, sat through gruesome movies of lungs, saved all his butts in one big Mason jar and compiled lists of minor, personal, nongruesome reasons for quitting.

It worked. He stopped smoking, gained twenty pounds and went almost overnight from a young guy in his early thirties to a middle-aged man deep into his forties. He watched his father's jowly face overwhelm his own sharp features. He had no desire to touch a cigarette. But he felt that stopping smoking had turned him from a hot number into a slow-burning cipher. Without the nicotine to counteract the effects of alcohol, he became drunk more easily. One night he was so high he couldn't get his newly fat body up the ladder to his loft bed. He slept on his couch and woke with such a feeling of drenched, panicked shame that he never again took another drink. He warned himself that if he started again he'd have to join Alcoholics Anonymous, and that dire prospect kept him sober. Of course his AA friends screeched at him he was just on a "dry drunk," but that suited him fine as long as he stayed sober. Sometimes he did envy them. The party was still going on for them, if dry this time, whereas he was slowly withdrawing.

After he sobered up a previously unsuspected sweet tooth grew in and he became still stouter. He gnashed at Godiva chocolates and Lanciani brownies with fury, wolfing his curse.

Ned was his only consolation. Ned was sweet and adaptable without being a pushover. If people ignored him at a dinner party or failed to remember his name after he'd been introduced several times, he complained loudly. He was handsome without the loss of individuality that good looks usually imply. He had teeth that weren't perfect and a queer way of cocking his head to one side which, when coupled with a confused smile, gave him a goofy, dazzled air. On bad days he was certain that people were making fun of him, and then Mark would call him Paranoid Petey. His sweetness touched Mark—every feeling that was struck inside Ned vibrated somewhere inside Mark.

They'd been introduced formally (well, not so formally as

all that) by a mutual friend who'd said to Mark, rubbing his hands like a matchmaker, "Have I got a boy for you." That had been in late '81 when the official line had been "Limit the number of your partners. Know their names." Ned was a very cute name to know, and if less was better, then just one would surely be best.

There was an old-fashioned sweetness about their love from the very beginning. At their first encounter over drinks Ned had been cooking a roast lamb and had asked Mark how to test it for the right degree of pinkness. Mark didn't have the foggiest and they both laughed at their shared ineptitude. Two nights later Mark had been entertaining three friends from Venice and had invited Ned to help out, since Ned had studied a year in Florence and sort of spoke Italian, as did Mark. Ned dressed perfectly, smiled often and kept Mark company while he washed up.

As a southerner, Mark took social life very seriously. He couldn't endure New York insolence—the spiteful attacks called "teasing," the shameless social climbing (heads poking up like periscopes over the sea of faces), the charged pairings of conspirators who ignored the melee around them. Mark believed in keeping one conversation (frivolous, decorous) going among the eight dinner guests. He believed in dressing carefully for every occasion, even schlepping to the deli. He was for stoicism rather than bellyaching, for quips rather than teasing, for light opinions rather than heavy information, dull kindness rather than rapier wit—all the values, in short, his Episcopalian mother (poor, imperious) had imparted to his (rich and humble) Baptist father.

Although Ned wasn't a southerner he was a little Boston aristocrat who shared Mark's patriarchal values. Ned automatically called older men "sir," opened doors for ladies, instantly identified himself on the phone by name and said "Good evening" when he got into a taxi. He also had fresh, clear emotions. If someone told him a sad story (and more and more of the stories these days were sad), Ned cried quickly and copiously. He never worried about being consistent. He wasn't the kind of stuffed shirt who decides you're only hurting beggars by giving them handouts; if the beggar looked pitiful, Ned would brush away tears and empty his pockets. He was a volunteer for lots of charities.

Ned especially liked Joshua, Mark's best friend, who was well into his fifties, an English professor and a well-known critic of contemporary poetry. When Joshua was recovering from cataract surgery Ned worked for him, reading him his mail, taking dictation, preparing meals, telling him what the characters were doing on TV.

In fact, for a while Ned saw a lot more of Joshua than Mark did. Mark had to settle for daily phone calls.

Joshua was a master of the art of the telephone call. Like Madame de Sévigné, who could plunge headlong into a story in the first line of a letter, Joshua would sometimes start off by singing the latest pop song or quoting the latest advertising jingle. Sometimes he'd pretend to be someone else. Mark would have an ancient sex pervert on the line wanting to join the Bunyonette Orgy Club, or a little kid saying, "I'm twelve years old and I read your profile in *Christopher Street*, the gay magazine. . . ."

Or Joshua would start by quoting a really juicy academic absurdity he'd gone truffling after in a learned journal. Or he'd quote from Wallace Stevens's "The Auroras of Autumn" or discuss brim width at his hatmaker's, Gélot, in Paris. For such an unworldly man he was terribly *mondain*.

If he was munching something he'd give the recipe. An eavesdropper might have been startled by his instructions for grated zucchini: "First you peel and rape six courgettes. . . ."

In their drinking days Joshua and Mark would eat a T-bone and green beans at Duff's on Christopher Street, down a bottle of wine and then head over to the Riv on Sheridan Square, where they'd sip sweet, dangerous stingers. In the warm weather the glass walls would open up and they'd be seated almost in the midst of all the grit and clowning, the sudden updraft through the subway grate, the mammoth black men in shorts on skates, their wrists circled by glowing fluorescent bracelets, the susurrus and scent of queens from the provinces mixed in with the sweat and grunts of the local machos. When they were quite drunk Mark and Joshua would speak to each other in their version of Italian, because they'd spent many summers together in Venice and liked to imagine they were Italians, even Italian housewives who addressed one another with feigned affection as *carissima*. Then Mark and Joshua would pour themselves into separate taxis, wave and head in opposite directions home. There they'd call each other once more, just to say good night. No one could ever have fitted into such a closed corporation of a friendship, but Ned did.

Mark and Joshua had met fifteen years ago at the ballet. At first they had had nothing else in common (later their friendship itself was what they shared). For Mark the ballet was prowess, gymnastics as a foreglimpse of paradise, a way of seeing perfect men powering long-legged, long-necked women through the crosslit air. For Joshua it was Utopia. As he said, "All these physically deformed, argumentative New York intellectuals in the audience couldn't accept any vision of society except something nonverbal and sublimely athletic." They went at least twice a week to the State Theater and called all the performers by their first names, although they didn't know them. Mark thought of Balanchine as by definition a European—a Russian who had lived in Paris—and he ascribed Balanchine's clarity and hardness to his cosmopolitan background.

As things became grimmer, Mark was summoned more and more frequently to bedsides and graves. Ned kept him happy, not through any services he performed, since they were equally sloppy and incompetent in the kitchen and Ned never hid his depressions except from what they both called "company." No, what Ned offered was sweetness. They'd hug each other in the loft bed and say, "I love you, Petes."

"Aren't we cozy here, Peters?" That was their word for happy: "cozy."

And then they moved to Paris, not for any special reason but because Mark knew that if he didn't make an effort he'd end up in St. Thomas, get totally lazy, still fatter, and start drinking again. Mark had heard about this really neat cooking school in Paris where the chefs worked under mirrors all morning while everyone looked up and took notes, then the class ate the results. American apprentices did all the chopping and translated the instructions into English. The Paris trip sounded appealing to Ned, who'd once studied Italian and art history at an American brat school in Florence and had never stopped daydreaming about "Europe," a unity that existed more in the American imagination than in any actual Frenchman's or Englishman's mind.

What they didn't say, Mark and Ned, was that they hoped the party would go on in Europe as it had before in the States. It amused Mark to call Europe the "New World," since it was all new to him. And just as Europeans had once gone to America in search of sex, in the same spirit he'd come to the New World.

They found a pretty house on the rue de Verneuil, just a few blocks from Saint-Germain-des-Prés. The street was lined with the gray, unbroken façades of severe eighteenth-century town houses, but if you punched out the right code and pushed through the teal-blue lacquered doors you crossed a courtyard filled with planters and reached their white wood house with the green shutters and the small rooms that an inspired maniac had painted floor to ceiling with *faux marbre*, faux malachite and putti swirling in gray and pink clouds. Despite this hectic decor, the house was charming and quieter than a cottage down a village lane, where invariably there are animals, birds, people and cars. Here there was only silence filtered through the crepitation of rain in the courtyard. Mark amused his French friends when he referred unwittingly to the stately *hôtels particuliers* in his neighborhood as *palais*; he was used to Italy, where even the meanest apartment block counted as a *palazzo*.

He and Ned made big fires in the fireplaces, thoroughly enjoyed the comedy of half learning French and took trains nearly everywhere, to Stockholm and Barcelona, Rome and Amsterdam. Mark told himself he was scouting picturesque locales for the Bunyonettes, and from time to time he took notes on prices, quality of service, sights to see and nearest gay bars.

He even enrolled in the cooking school and bought all the *batterie de cuisine* that the school had for sale. But though he took down the instructions for lobster bisque, rabbit in its own blood and lemon crêpes, he never even unpacked the crêpe pan.

They both cruised. Without discussing it they had an agreement not to bring anyone home. They'd also tacitly consented to continue sleeping in the same bed. Every night they headed out to the back-room bars where indeed the party was still in full swing. People were shorter and more perfumed and kissed more than in the old days in New York, but what the French called *touche-pipi* went on without restraint. One couldn't say the gay community in Paris was irresponsible, since no such community existed, at least not as far as Mark could figure out. They'd stumble home at two or three in the morning, shower and crawl innocently into their big bed with the old, eyeletted linen. Back home people had warned them to say they were from Canada or England, but the French weren't scared of the disease and besides appeared to like Americans.

The French thought Americans were at once uncultured and wildly up-to-date and kind, although the kindness was sometimes taken as proof of stupidity. Some kid assured Mark, *"Ned est toujours gentil—et pas du tout bête!"* as though good humor were usually cretinous.

Here Mark was, dashing about from the Alliance Française to the cooking school, checking out the discos and saunas, renting cars for jaunts to châteaux and running up thousand-dollar phone bills calling all his friends in New York to praise Paris and to assure them the French were "real shy and sweet" under that stylish Gallic disdain. He felt rejuvenated and even lost three kilos, though he had ten more to go. Joshua filled him in on the latest doings of Mr. B. and Jerry, that is, the choreographers George Balanchine and Jerome Robbins.

Although Ned was twenty-eight he looked twenty and picked up Parisian styles so quickly that soon he'd become the choicest Kiki in town, hair military short on the sides and gelled high on top, jeans rolled and military boots huge. He and Mark would wander separately about in the rain for hours memorizing street names. Often they'd help lost compatriots for a moment, then vanish into the attractive mystery of being half-Gallicized Americans. Mark overheard Ned pretending to confuse "assist" for "attend" and "actual" for "present," and kept teasing him ("You big phony") with a happy smile on his face. The happiness was that of children who laugh to see themselves in a distorting mirror.

But they couldn't get a real social life off the ground. In New York Mark had had his regulars stopping in unannounced for cocktails. There'd always been pretty men hanging out for the coke or the good times or to meet one another. In Paris people seemed to think it was sufficient to check in once a month to keep a friendship alive. And if they liked Mark and Ned and submitted with a laugh and a blush to their nosy questions in English, in French they were disdainful toward

the other French guys. Everyone, moreover, thought it strange
Mark and Ned knew only gays; French people kept referring
contemptuously to the "ghetto."

So now social life was something Mark surrendered as well,
along with booze and cigarettes and drugs. Soon he'd have to
give up sex, no doubt, but not yet, not yet. Like the French
boys he knew he said he was being "prudent" and "cautious,"
but the prudence amounted to nothing more than approaching
only those boys who appealed to him, the caution to vowing
not to go this far tomorrow night.

Even so, Mark had much less sex, since in Paris no one
knew who he was and he didn't get any free rides. In New
York people admired money more than here, or rather they
confused wealth with sexiness.

Ned had no such restraints imposed on him. He had that
foolish grin, crazy American accent and never worked, so he
was as attractive as he was available. He met someone named
Luc.

"Is he cute, Petes?"

"Peters, he's just a flirt."

"Petey, I know you're going to leave me." Mark whispered
to their stuffed bear, "Mr. Peters, he's going to dump fat old
us for this garlic-smelling, lap-swimming, four-foot-tall, fire-
ball do-nothing."

"Luc hates garlic and he has more energy than both of us.
He's some sort of weird French nurse running around to old
ladies at six in the morning giving them shots."

The more Mark heard about Luc the more he worried. Ned
found every banal remark Luc made *génial* or *géant*. He was so
enamored he was even slipping into scrappy French around
Mark, who had to lay down a new rule: "Look, Petes, no Frog
in the house. I'm serious." Ned tried to downplay his ardor,
but since Mark was his only real friend in Paris and certainly
his best buddy in the whole world, he couldn't resist talking

to him about his obsession. He attempted to disguise it as a series of complaints: "Luc is such an egomaniac he invites three of his friends over to watch him take a bath"; "I know you never thought I'd like opera but I'm humming it because Luc plays that damn caterwauling all day"; "He's so absurdly macho he always insists on running the show sexually, not that I exactly mind."

Mark realized then how fragile their love was. Since he and Ned didn't have sex, they were dependent on outsiders. The least threatening kind of adventure was one-time-only tricks, and in the old days New York would have turned up an inexhaustible supply of them. But the statistics were closing in on them and they'd die if they kept up this pace. Luc was right for Ned, but what if Ned moved out? Mark would have preferred a less possessive lover for Ned.

He thought they might already be harboring this lazy seed, this death plant. Ned and Mark both believed that if they slept enough their immunities would resist the virus; they were always sinking into deep, swooning naps to the sound of the rain in the courtyard, which was like the sound of newspaper burning.

Out of deference to Mark, Ned saw less of Luc, but this very gift caused Ned to resent Mark and made the already troubled Luc crack. He sold his nursing practice, sublet his apartment and headed off to Brazil to be a Club Med GO (*Gentil Organisateur*).

To compensate for this loss Ned enrolled in a History of French Art course at the Louvre, but in June, after a year in Paris, they both realized they were as rootless as when they'd arrived. Ned was on a nodding, beer-buying basis with dozens of men in the bars, on a lovemaking basis with a few, but with none could he go to a movie or share a secret. Mark knew only a few guys from his gym.

They made plans to spend the end of the summer with

Joshua in Venice. They joined Joshua in the rambling apartment he rented in a palace on the Grand Canal. Despite the flame-shaped windows, the colored marble façades and the turbaned heads that served as door knockers, Venice still felt very familiarly luxurious.

Joshua looked as burnished as the city. He was tan and slim from his daily bastings at the Cipriani pool, where the rich clients were so old Gore Vidal had dubbed the place Lourdes. Joshua worked every afternoon at his desk under the painted allegory of the ceiling. He listened to the soft lapping of the little *rio* under his windows. In the evening they'd wear white shirts and linen suits over that day's burn and saunter forth into Campo Santo Stefano, which Joshua liked because it was dominated by the statue of a nineteenth-century Dante scholar. Their conversation, however, was anything but scholarly; it was all laughter, boys and gossip. Mark thought he was making such a mistake living in Paris and depriving himself of Joshua's good humor, always subtle no matter how exhilarating it became. This friendship was the brightest jewel in Mark's diadem.

And then Ned flew home to Boston for a visit with his parents. Just before he left he said to Mark, "I hope I'm not making a mistake. I've never left you alone before. Peters, you're going to leave me, I know you are, you're bored with me." That very night Mark was cruising in jeans along that dark patch between the Piazzetta and Harry's that looks out across the lagoon toward the illuminated façade of San Giorgio Maggiore. He saw a man with a dazzling smile leaning against the railing. Mark said, "Hello," and the man said, "You must be American."

"How did you know?"

"It's completely obvious—in a nice way."

Mark, wary of a put-down, said, "Actually I'm an American who lives in Paris. And right now I'm staying with some friends

in an extraordinary palace where Henry James lived and John
Singer Sargent painted—it's a real American hangout. Wanna
see it?"

"Sure."

On the way through the echoing streets they went past the
ugliest church in town, San Moise. "Exactly who was Saint
Moses?" Mark asked.

His new friend introduced himself as Hajo and said he was
German. He mentioned he had become very careful given the
health crisis, and Mark, who identified himself as a sort of
gay leader, lied and said he, too, had long been circumspect.
Mark felt very self-conscious about his weight and told himself
there was no reason this blond, slender Hajo in the cashmere
blazer would want someone like him. Of course, Mark had to
admit to himself, he *had* picked up a cute Spanish kid the night
before at the very same cruising spot.

They lit the courtyard, walked past the abandoned *felze* (the
shuttered cover for the gondola on rainy days) and mounted
the outdoor stone stairs to the *piano nobile*, went on up the
inner stairs to Joshua's floor, closed the painted wood doors to
the library and made drinks for themselves. The transistor
played some old string concerto and the wake of the passing
vaporetti slapped the steps of the water gate below.

But no sooner did Mark toast Hajo under that artificial
paradise of scholarly muses bearing tomes of Petrarch and
Aretino than Hajo put his drink down on the stone floor and
kissed Mark, and Mark wondered if you could get high off the
liquor in someone else's mouth, then he wondered how many
more times in his life a handsome stranger would kiss him like
this with real desire, then he wondered how much longer he'd
be alive, then he wondered what this guy's angle was, why
me? It even occurred to him Hajo was a gigolo whom Joshua
had hired to cheer him up.

They went to bed and tried to eat each other alive, so hungry were they both for affection. Up close Mark could see Hajo must be more or less forty himself, and that made him feel good. Everyone assumed Mark went for nothing but kids. But it just happened that way. Twinkies were available, adaptable, ready to pack a bag and take off. Another grown-up came with a complete set of friends, habits, hesitations.

Hajo seemed to like Mark's body. Over the next few days Mark started giving Hajo a tour of his favorite paintings in Venice. Although Mark got the names and centuries all turned around, Hajo began to call him Professor Bear.

Wounded, Mark said, "Like Jerry Lewis, the Nutty Professor?"

"No, Mark, but because you know so much and you look like a lovable bear, so Professor Bear, but maybe 'professor' is a better word in German I think?"

"Maybe. Nobody wants to be a professor in America."

Whereas Ned had given Mark back his childhood, the silliness and sweetness of lazy days in Charlottesville so long ago, Hajo represented middle age, but not the dimness that term suggested in English, rather the ripeness implied by the French phrase, *la fleur de l'âge*.

Hajo was staying at the Gritti Palace in a corner room people called the Elizabeth Taylor suite, because she'd slept there once years ago with Richard Burton. Like most Germans' his English was fluent, but more unusually he was equally at ease in French and Italian. His clothes were beautiful, not the dark undertaker's suits Frenchmen affected on the theory that sobriety is discreet and discretion is elegant, but, rather, bright Armani jackets over jeans, antique silk ties with handmade check shirts, high boots so intricately laced they suggested perversion. For someone so dandified Hajo was winningly reluctant to talk about clothes; he even blushed when Mark snooped into his closet and said, "Wow."

For years Mark had been the one to plan the evening, order

the food, pay the bill, light cigarettes, ask questions, but now he felt himself the focus of attentions more refined than those he'd ever paid anyone. Hajo was especially gallant to Joshua, who was instantly seduced.

Hajo was a film producer and he'd come to Venice for the festival. Unlike everyone else, who stayed at the Excelsior on the Lido to be near the screenings and hoopla, Hajo preferred to live in town at one remove.

As Mark grew to know him, he discovered so many complexities in Hajo that he despaired of ever explaining his new friend to the folks back home. Not that Hajo was full of inner conflicts. No, he was all of a piece, but that piece had strange new contours. Hajo was both a socialist and a socialite—his politics the residue of 1968, a year Americans could scarcely single out but that had marked every European who'd been young at the time, whereas his taste for *mondanités* was something he'd come to more recently and hoped to contain, like a dangerous but exciting drug habit. His picture was frequently in the paper for having escorted a starlet or skied with a prince, and yet he insisted that at Gstaad he preferred to go to bed early with a book and be flown by helicopter to the top of virgin trails ("That way you see all the wild animals on the way down instead of the usual Muffies and Babs").

He was really a bit like the European movie business itself, Mark came to realize. There was the Berlin Film Festival in freezing February with all those dirty, long-haired hippies in their fifties scuttling through the snow to look at movies from a leftist or lesbian perspective; and then in May there was the Cannes Festival with stars in ermine and chauffeured Mercedes and bathing beauties granting bikini sessions to photographers on the beach. Hajo embodied the contradictions but did so by finding unsuspected kindness and softness in steely international hostesses as well as a queer glamour in dour ex-Maoists who'd traded in revolutionary politics for beer and bitterness. He seemed to like everyone. As soon as Mark mentioned a name Hajo smiled his huge smile and said, "She's great! A fabulous woman!" or "Isn't he sympathetic? Please give him my very best."

Among his Parisian acquaintances Mark had grown accustomed to a low level of constant grumbling, but with Hajo everything was upbeat. He liked most movies, he was curious about most new political or artistic developments and he thought nothing of hopping on a plane to see a new ballet in Marseille or a fashion show in Milan. For several summers he'd rented a house in East Hampton, and he prided himself on his knowledge of America. His only hypocrisy consisted of pretending he'd been trying to reach someone for hours by phone. When that person answered even on the first try Hajo invariably sang out "Finally!"

The America of old movies he also liked—westerns, Minnelli musicals, the films noirs of the 1950s, Hitchcock—but he felt the more recent super-budget sci-fi kiddy crap was endangering the entire industry. A photo of a cowboy would make him grow misty-eyed but he could also say quite casually, "You're lucky you live in Europe, Mark. The quality of life in America is so low. The clothes, the crime, especially the food."

Unlike Mark's Parisian acquaintances, who all seemed to despise their jobs, Hajo loved his work. Like an American, Hajo bragged about how much he worked, even exaggerated how long and arduous were his hours, and he quite gratuitously attributed grueling efforts to indolent Mark. ("Poor Mark, you spend every moment studying the tourism allure—do you say that? allure?—of Venice.") As far as Mark could see, Hajo's work was much like his own, mainly a matter of kissing babies and cutting ribbons, of "circulating."

Unlike an American businessman, Hajo revered art. In Berlin he shuffled into the ugly modern opera house with all the fat ladies in galoshes to listen to the upsetting stridencies of *Lulu.* His big house in Grünewald was filled with the newest German expressionist paintings and Hajo had once even been asked by the reigning genius of the moment to find him wild hare's blood to be sprinkled over a legless, hacked-to-pieces Steinway; Hajo had guiltily confessed to Mark in bed one night that he'd been so busy that week he'd settled for plain rabbit's blood from the butcher ("I pray this lie is never revealed— even the title is *Hasenblut!*"). Mark learned that Hajo had been faithful to his previous lover for ten years until last June when the lover had left him for a "phony" Austrian baron ("It's even against the law in Austria to use titles; you can be fined for putting 'baron' on your *carte de visite*").

When Mark returned to Paris, Ned was already there; he'd enrolled at the Sorbonne. Mark couldn't help talking about Hajo all the time. Besides, Hajo phoned twice a day and sent by express mail unbearable tapes he'd concocted out of all the most recent dissonant music, a quartet by Henze, water dripping and gurgling by Cage. Ned would come home from school and catch Mark doing sit-ups to Stockhausen blips and bleeps. Now it was Ned's turn to apostrophize their stuffed bear: "Mr. Peters, he's going to leave boring old us for this arty-farty Kraut who's as old as he is, why it's obscene, sex between two people of the same age!"

Because Ned loved Mark, he accepted Hajo. "It could have been worse," Ned told the bear. "It could have been a gold-digging twenty-year-old Parisian, who would have driven poor aging us out of our home, Mr. Peters." Later, over dinner, Ned said, "I'm happy for you. And I want you to be faithful to him—it's better for your health."

"What about yours?"

"I think it's odd"—this back to the bear—"that he broke up my affair with Luc and then started up with A-hole or is it Hajo?"

Love had taken Mark by surprise. He spent hours selecting postcards and sent six or seven a day to Berlin. He bought a book on German history and read it until he was thoroughly confused. He hung around the German bookstore next to his gym and even contemplated buying a beginning German course on cassettes for French speakers before he came to his senses. He dieted and exercised, hoping to impress Hajo on his first visit to Berlin three weeks hence.

He'd never been faithful to anyone before. In fact, he'd preached against fidelity, which he'd considered as barbaric as female circumcision. Now he liked it because it meant he was consecrating all his energy and desire to one person, just as he was the sole object of Hajo's love. He was less fearful than before of competition. He trusted Hajo—so much so that he wondered if he'd ever really trusted anyone before.

When he arrived in Berlin in the new clothes he'd bought for the occasion with the new pigskin bag from Hermès and the big illustrated book on Jean-Michel Frank under his arm (Frank was Hajo's favorite designer), Hajo kissed him on the lips and hurried him into the waiting car. As they sat side by side Hajo kept interrupting himself or Mark in order to pull back an inch, look at Mark and say, "Good to see you!"

Mark was so in love he kept losing his erection. He suffered two days over these fits of impotence until, scarlet-faced, he blurted out to Hajo, "Look, don't think I'm always such a dud, it's just you're so great and—"

"But, Mark," Hajo said, "I don't even notice. Don't be so complicated, Herr Professor Bear."

In bed Hajo was slender and hairless to the point of puerility and he slept with his head on Mark's chest. But in public places, dressed in his double-breasted jacket, outsize raincoat and high-laced boots, Hajo could be unsmilingly severe with headwaiters or ushers or drivers. In bed his face softened and he seemed to be sleepily nuzzling Mark, but out on the tense, shoddily modern Ku'damm he looked pale and lined and determined.

In the same way he seemed to like Mark's strength, his physical bulk, as a kid might like his father's, but over dinner at the Paris Bar Hajo himself would turn paternal and counsel Mark on everything from health insurance to diet. "Don't eat pork at night!" he said, scandalized. "It's bad enough at lunch, but never at night. You might as well eat a *sausage!*"

Like many people in the theater and movies, Hajo cultivated superstitions about food. He wouldn't drink anything, not even water, with meals for fear the liquids might dilute his digestive juices. He ate nothing but fruit till noon, nothing but vegetables after six, and he never combined the two, but a month later it was all cheese and potatoes and spinach pasta. For cold sores he had drops of homeopathic potions and something he called "salvia" and he told Mark he'd never in all his forty years had a shot of penicillin.

What most astonished Mark was how little Hajo knew about gay life. For years Hajo had lived with a woman, then with one man for ten years, and in all that time he had been to a gay bar only twice and to a sauna only once. None of Hajo's friends were gay, although all of his straight friends knew Hajo was "homosexual," as they said without the slightest shade of condescension or embarrassment.

"Just my luck," Mark said, "to find the only Berliner who doesn't drink beer, doesn't eat sausage, has never been to a cabaret and never worn a garter belt."

Hajo's house was his hobby. It was filled with French furniture from the 1920s and '30s and German paintings from the 1980s. A Turkish woman came twice a week to clean, but everything was already so scrubbed and gleaming she had little to do except iron Hajo's shirts (he'd sent her for ironing lessons with a friend's maid, a Spanish woman who had once been in service to the Spanish ambassador to Vienna).

To Mark the house gave off the feeling of silk and barbed wire—the silk was the faded Kilims, the polished pearwood and pale upholstery, and the wire was the brutal paintings, those burned and anguished figures, abandoned Icarus wings and scrawled words. The cold winter light cast a haze over the plants, which were huddled in the conservatory like people waiting for the train. The expensive furnace burned noiselessly.

For all his pride in his house, Hajo liked excitable, bohemian film people given to what Mark thought were strange political resentments against Reagan, nuclear weapons and U.S. intervention in Central America. Mark knew from his mother never to discuss religion or politics, which led Hajo's Greens to assume Mark was as ecological and leftist as they were.

At two or three in the morning the drunk guests would roar off through the dark, silent suburbs, Hajo would open the French doors to let in the cold night, he and Mark would empty ashtrays and load the dishwasher and suddenly their peace was restored, like the birdsong spring brings back to the garden. "How ya doin'?" Mark would say.

"Fine," Hajo would reply as their intimacy emerged from hiding. Despite the sudden noise and laughter of these visits from friends, Hajo struck Mark as a solitary, someone who preferred a night alone in which to read the world press for movie news, to repolish his Puiforcat silverware, to watch videos of movies about to be released or to study the paintings reproduced in the art magazine *Wolkenkratzer*.

In bed they were passionate but cautious—ardent in their kisses but afraid to exchange those fluids that had once been the gush of life but that now seemed the liquid drained off a fatal infection. In Mark's dreams Berlin itself—this pocket of glitz and libertinage surrounded by the gray hostility of East Germany—became an emblem of their endangered, quarantined happiness.

On the last night of his visit Mark stretched sleepily and said, "You know I've never been faithful to anyone before."

"No?"

"And I like it!" He smiled into the dark. "There's even a Spanish kid I met in Venice just before, uh, well, a kid who's been writing me, but I was proud to write to him and say I was faithful to a guy in Berlin and, well," he mumbled into the ominous, breathless silence on the pillow beside him, "I've never burned a bridge before or turned down even the remotest sexual possibility, it's all so new. . . ."

Hajo didn't say a word.

At last Mark asked, "Is there anything wrong?"

Hajo said, "Do you mean you make love with many men now, during *die Pest?*"

"No one since I met you."

"But before? In Paris and Venice?"

Now it was Mark's turn to say nothing. Hajo went into the kitchen and came back five minutes later with something in his hand that smelled of a summer roadside.

"What are you drinking?"

"Chamomile. Mark, you lied to me. You said you were a gay leader. You said you are health-conscious since a long time. Now I understand you were with a Spanish the night before you met me—that was why your nipples were too sore to touch then but never now."

It occurred to Mark that "health-consciousness" had become a new word for jealousy.

Hajo took more and more precautions when they made love. When Mark compared their lovemaking with his own heavy sex scenes of the 1970s (losing consciousness in leather harness, the smell of poppers, his legs coated in grease), he had to admit how tame a porno movie of Hajo and him would look. Yet Mark no longer felt like a sex star and he even pretended to be shocked when he heard about things he used to do at least once a week. With Hajo he felt like a conductor awakening the blare of brass with a raised hand, hushing the massed strings simply by closing his eyes. But the moment it was over, Hajo wouldn't stew in their juices, not even for a second; he dashed off to wash with a special surgical soap. At dinner he wouldn't taste anything from Mark's spoon; from even the merest brush of lips he'd draw back, as though Mark were carved out of burning ice.

Even if Mark conceded Hajo was perfectly within his medical rights, he couldn't help bridling at the thought he was being faithful to someone afraid to kiss him.

When Mark flew back to Paris, Ned announced Luc had returned from Brazil. Apparently Luc had drunk too much one night in Belém, tried to jump-start a car and had been shot in the leg by the irate and equally drunk owner of the car. Luc was in a Paris hospital. Bits of his hipbone were being transplanted into the damaged femur. Nothing, naturally, was more romantic than nursing a sunburned young lover in pain, and they'd already had sex while a sympathetic male nurse stood guard.

In the delicate cantilevering of Mark and Ned's love, the precarious downward thrust of forces required a solid underpinning, which they had now—Ned had Luc and Mark had Hajo. But of course no one had anyone for sure, and Mark feared one day he'd lose both Hajo and Ned. Then that calculation shamed him and he sought to imagine himself splendidly alone. He realized he'd picked up the superstition that so long as someone or other was his lover he'd continue to live; to love and to live were near rhymes.

One night Mark said he wanted to read late in the guest bedroom; the next night he wasn't feeling well; by the third he and Ned had definitely stopped sleeping in the same bed.

Hajo now insisted that Mark take out a good German health insurance policy, one that would cover hospital and doctor expenses no matter where in the world he fell ill. Mark was grateful to have the policy since he knew many single men had become uninsurable. He was also touched by the attention, the sort he'd usually paid to his younger, dizzier boyfriends. But he also registered the thought that Hajo might be expecting something to go wrong with his health.

That spring Mark and Hajo spent one week out of every month together. Two of Hajo's Berlin friends became ill, one with the pneumonia, the other with the parasite in the brain. In America more and more of Mark's friends were dying or dead, and his profits were way off. When he went home to New York for a week he couldn't stay in his own apartment, since he'd sublet it. He stayed with Joshua and they laughed a lot, but Mark couldn't help but notice that he, Mark, wasn't up on the latest fads and feuds, nor was he a constant in his friends' calculations. Oh, they all liked him and if he came back they'd make room for him soon enough, but as an expatriate he didn't count as an ally, an introduction or even an ear.

On the street there seemed to be fewer gay men, or perhaps they were just less visible; they'd shaved their mustaches, put on some weight and let the holes pierced through their ears grow back. On the Upper West Side there were ten more gourmet shops and two fewer gay bars. Young heterosexuals— loud, rich and confident—swarmed down Central Park West, gaudy in leg warmers and pink jogging shorts over midwinter tans.

George Balanchine had died and the company was performing his ballets perfectly, but now that Mark knew there would be no new dances he saw each work as part of what the French called the *patrimoine*, a sad and pompous word. All of these swans, even the cygnets, had known Mr. B.; his old hands had stretched a leg still higher or relaxed the rigid circle of lifted arms into a softer ellipse. But soon there would be new troops of seventeen-year-olds and the old coolness and precision would slacken, blur. Having lived in Paris, Mark no longer believed in progress. When he looked at the Tinkertoy tackiness of the new buildings at Les Halles, he was grateful Paris had been built in earlier, better centuries.

When he went back to Paris, it didn't feel like home. He could barely understand the muttered conversation of the taxi driver with his Montmartre Titi-Parisian accent. The dollar was losing value every day and anyway Mark had fewer and fewer of them. He and Ned started ironing their own shirts, buying clothes during the sales, eating in, cutting short their calls to America.

They both expected to die. "I just hope I graduate first," Ned said. "I'd love to finish one thing before buying the farm." Mark had an attack of shingles. Before his doctor diagnosed it, Mark looked at the spots across his solar plexus and panicked and said out loud to his reflection in the mirror, "Dear God, I'm not ready to die." The same week, after learning what was wrong with him, he read that shingles in someone under fifty was an accurate "tracer disease," a sure sign of dangerously lowered immunities. The illness made Mark sleep all the time. He felt as though he were suffocating under wet, heavy eiderdowns. The only thing he could do was watch television, but the foreign language made him anxious. He didn't like being ill in a foreign country.

He recovered. In May when he saw Hajo in Berlin they went to the hospital for a blood test. Hajo had insisted on it, although Mark had warned him, "You know how it'll turn out, you'll be negative and I'll be positive and then we'll break up. It's just that simple." Hajo was sure they'd both be negative.

At that point the blood samples still had to be shipped to America to be analyzed. They would have to wait a month for the results. Their doctor also gave them physicals and a multitest, that is, they were each scratched with eight different infections. The idea was that someone with intact immunities would respond to them all or at least five or six. Mark developed only two red bumps, whereas Hajo grew all eight.

The doctor refused to give out the results over the phone. He insisted that Mark return to Berlin for a face-to-face conference. That wasn't really inconvenient since he and Hajo had planned anyway to fly together for a week to Vienna, which neither of them had ever visited.

In the interval Mark seldom thought of the disease. He had decided, almost as though it were a question of personal elegance, to be courageous. He wasn't going to complain or suffer. He was going to be very brave, no matter what happened. That was because he was a gay leader, sort of, and people expected him to set an example. His Virginia ancestors had been courageous. Anyway, even if he sometimes panicked he wasn't all that attached to life. He thought it was fun, but he wouldn't mind giving it up. Of course he had no idea how he'd act when worn down by the long, painful reality. He probably wouldn't have the energy to be courageous.

He begged Ned to take more precautions. Ned said that Luc had swollen glands in his neck and under his arms and night sweats. He also had athlete's foot and bad skin. They hugged their bear and Ned said, "Peters, I guess it's curtains for us." They agreed that if they became ill they'd travel to India and commit suicide beside the Ganges. It was Ned's idea: "We've never been there. It would be an adventure. We should do something absolutely new. Anyway, they know all about death and cremation there—it's their specialty."

Whereas the French were calm and rational in their responses to the epidemic, the Germans, like the English, were being driven to hysteria by their press. In France one could forget the disease for whole days at a stretch, but in reactionary Bavaria, for instance, the minister of health had proposed quarantining even healthy carriers. Mark was afraid their test results wouldn't be kept confidential, no matter what the hospital had said.

The Berlin sun was shining on the gilt Spirit of Victory on top of the Siegessäule the day Mark and Hajo walked through the Tiergarten on their way to the hospital. Beds of red and pink tulips alternated around the statue of Bismarck, who stood with a sword in one hand and a drapery below the other, as though he were a portly, exhausted torero. They'd each dressed carefully and Hajo had taken the day off from work.

At the last moment Hajo decided he didn't want to know the results.

"Don't be silly," Mark said.

"But what good are they?" Hajo asked. "I'm afraid. If I'm positive I'll freak." That was one of his Americanisms: "freak."

"Look," Mark said, "we've always been careful, but I was such a slut before; I'll be positive, you'll be negative, I'm sure of it, but we'll know we must continue to be extra extra careful. If we're both negative we'll be able to fuck each other like bunnies and you'll never be able to leave me, you'll be sealed to me for life, you poor sucker."

Their original doctor had gone off on holiday and had been replaced by a young man who'd just come back from two months in San Francisco, where, he told them in his almost accentless English, he'd learned how to do all the lab work for the blood test. Then he shuffled through their reports, crossed and uncrossed his long legs. He told Hajo he was negative and Mark he was positive. He took another blood sample from Mark just to be sure. The next day he called and confirmed the diagnosis. At the first meeting he said, "We don't really know what 'positive' means, but we're finding that at least a third of the positives are developing the symptoms and that percentage appears to be growing over time. There are even those who say one hundred percent of the carriers will become symptomatic."

"You mean die?" Mark asked.

"But there are new methods every day," the doctor said, embarrassed or maybe vexed, as he stared at Mark's chart again.

That night they ate dinner at the Paris Bar and Mark joked with the two beefy, handsome guys who owned the place and Hajo quizzed them about Vienna, where they were from. But suddenly, Mark thought that it was all over, his affair with Hajo, his grown-up European love. It occurred to him he'd never been loved by anyone quite so thoughtful and kind and mature. Mark looked at his own fat face in the mirror over the banquette and he feared no one would ever love him again. He felt sorry for himself and he went into the toilet, locked the door and sobbed, pulled himself together and returned to their table. But that night in the big lacquered sleigh bed, under the painting of a scorched field still smoldering, Hajo went right to sleep. He was wearing shorts to bed for the first time. In the past he'd always slept bare-assed. His soft, rapid snores sounded like kindling being trimmed by the smallest Braun saw. Mark started to quake silently from thinking their beautiful love was over. He went down the hall and locked himself behind the toilet door to sob out loud, but then Hajo, skinny in his black T-shirt advertising Kurosawa's *Ran* and his baggy boxer shorts, was tapping at the door and saying, "Mark, darling, Mark, come to bed, it will be all right, I love you, nothing's changed," but Mark knew everything had changed, starting with the shorts.

Vienna was hot and airless and deserted. They walked slowly through the museum of natural history and looked at dinosaur bones. The famous horses weren't performing their tricks right now, it was off season, and at the opera *Die Fledermaus* was playing only to Japanese group tours; Mark and Hajo left during the first intermission. The Mozart apartment was supposed to

prove how poor the great composer had been, but Mark reck-
oned it would rent for four thousand bucks a month in Manhattan today.

They lay in the sun in their swimsuits at a public pool on
the outskirts of the city. He made Hajo translate what the
young people on the towel beside them were talking about.
Hajo said that one young man, the one with the hair held back
with red rubber bands, was recounting the plot of a story he
was writing, or maybe it was a dream. Mark said, "Perhaps
he'll be a famous writer," but he thought all of this was like
a dream: the woods in the distance under a color-leaching sun;
this turn-of-the-century brick spa; the virtually naked
strangers all around him, each of whom knew the best bus
routes, the name of the best neighborhood butcher and the
date of the next concert to be given by their favorite local
singing star—a whole life Mark would never fathom. Wherever they went, Mark kept murmuring to himself, "It's over."

Obviously Hajo couldn't do or say anything. It was Mark's
responsibility to break up with him. Maybe the heat as they
swayed in the tram along the brilliant, nearly deserted Ring-
strasse recalled summer days in Charlottesville, yes, that time
he'd led an out-of-town cousin through Monticello. He and
Willie Lee had stood formally, sweating in seersucker jackets,
and watched the lady guide demonstrate "Mr." Jefferson's system of pulleys by which double doors could be opened sym-
metrically. Some little Yankee brats had been cutting up,
refusing to stick with the tour, until the mono-bosomed volunteer had said in perfect Tidewater tones, "Thank you. This
way. Thank you." Those thank-yous had chilled the boys into
obedience.

The formality of that place, sweating inside a jacket, could
be paired with the shadowless heat of Vienna. They stopped
and stared at a Russian war memorial; the inscriptions were

entirely in Russian, not a word of German, and Mark said to himself, "It's over."

But it wasn't. Hajo lay in his arms in the hotel room and said, "You must forgive me. I'm such a coward, and all my German cleanness manias."

"Hell, no," Mark said, "it's a question of dying, not of politeness. Why should you risk your one and only life?" Their intimacy was very deep, maybe because they were both far from home in a hotel with the jaunty name the King of Hungary.

On the television every newscast was about the Austrian wine scandal; vintners were lacing their wine with antifreeze. Mark and Hajo made deep love—physically reserved but emotionally deep. For the first time Mark understood that the precautions they were taking weren't an insult directed against him; he'd always known that, of course, but he hadn't accepted it.

Two days after he returned to Paris he learned that Joshua had been hospitalized for the pneumonia. His doctor had been treating it as though it had been just bronchitis, but Joshua had fainted in his apartment with a high fever and the friend he'd stood up at the ballet had made the police break down his door. That same friend had waited to call Mark until Joshua was better. The pneumonia went away as fast as it had come on, but it foreshadowed, of course, a future that made Mark think of the words in that Yankee hymn, "His terrible swift sword."

He told Ned the news with a smile he couldn't suppress and Ned wept in his arms. They stared at the truth only a few minutes. Soon Ned was hurrying off to his class at the Sorbonne and Mark was ironing a shirt for the evening, but as the iron slid over the damp fabric and awakened wisps of steam, he thought he had too few attachments to the world. Maybe that was why he'd become such a porker, to weight himself down. He felt the circle was tightening around him. In a way he was grateful he'd lost the habit of talking to Joshua twice a day and going to the ballet with him twice a week; if their lives had stayed so intertwined Mark would never have been able to give Joshua up.

Joshua had been—*still was!*—Mark's civilized friend. Mark had forgiven himself his own hell-raising, his own shallowness, because he'd been loved by this serene, subtle man. Joshua's love had vouched for Mark's value, but now Mark felt shabbier. Mark didn't know many French people well, but he doubted if any of them came in Joshua's variety—this sense of fun linked to the most lightly worn erudition, this kindness redeemed by the least malign bitchery. Anyone who lived in a circle as tight, as overbred, as Joshua's needed to complain a bit; at least he always said he felt his blood had been oxygenated after a good complaining session. Who else but Joshua could hold in suspension so many different elements—his Venetian elegance, his scholarliness, his camp humor, his ballet fanaticism, his passion for society (he was the most collegial of creatures). His social being was an achievement, a work of art. His laugh—his great, head-thrown-back, all-out, unthrottled laugh—announced his forbearance and hilarity in the face of experience (he pronounced it "high-larity" and certainly his friends all got high off it).

Mark called his mother in Virginia. She was in her eighties but as starchy as ever. They seldom spoke of personal matters. She'd met Joshua several times. When Mark told her about Joshua's illness and his prospects, she said, "You're too young to be losing your friends. That's more for folks in my league, the golden oldies."

"Yes, ma'am, I guess you're right there. I hope you're taking it easy."

She laughed. "Easy? Why I'm so relaxed I'm downright

trifling." Her voice darkened. "Now if you get sick, you come home to Virginia and I'll nurse you, you hear?"

Mark said, "Yes, ma'am," but he thought he'd rather make a pilgrimage to India. He hadn't come this far, moved north to live among the Yankees and then come on over here to Paris, France, just so he could end up back home in Charlottesville. He didn't want to be pitied by his father's Baptist kin.

As though she were reading his mind, his mother (Miz Ellen, as they called her) said, "I don't want you killin' yourself if you take sick. I'd never forgive you. In my family we fight the good fight."

"Yes, ma'am," he said, but he thought he didn't want to undergo the humiliation of dying among friends, losing his looks and powers, or the loneliness of dying slowly among strangers. He'd kill himself beside the Ganges.

Mark invited Luc and Ned and another friend to a restaurant in the Eiffel Tower for dinner. As they looked down on the river valley and picked out Notre Dame in the distance, Sacré-Coeur on a hill, the pale square of the Place de la Concorde just this side of the dark rectangle of the Tuileries, they watched the early-summer sunlight fade and the blue blaze of streetlamps ignite, laced by swarming yellow headlights. Every moment of beauty had its valedictory side these days for Mark. He took a real pleasure in ordering a good bottle of Chassagne-Montrachet for his guests, and he suffered not the slightest temptation to sip it. He wished he were very thin and lined and dry-looking, an old man with a gray ponytail and bony, Cocteau-like hands, for that look would better correspond to the way he felt.

Luc was still hobbling and he'd lost weight, but his charm was intact if too consciously dispensed in the right doses to the right recipients. They all broke up in a flood of warmth after dinner, but around midnight Ned surprised Mark by coming home in a rage. "Here it is, a nice romantic evening,"

Ned said, "and Luc wanted to go out to a bar. I know he's terribly worried about his health, he's got *champignons* in the throat—what's that in English?"

"Fungus. Thrush."

"Oh. Anyway, he's driven. He's afraid to have sex with other people, but he can't stop prowling, and I just keep getting hurt. He thinks I should be there to keep him from being lonely, but I feel lonelier when I'm beside him, wanted but not really, you know what I mean? He's afraid of missing out on the action and he thinks you and I are it."

In Berlin one night Mark cut his thumb slightly with the vegetable peeler. It was just a nick, but Hajo must have noticed it. In bed, when Mark reached for Hajo's penis in the dark, Hajo said, "Do you mind, not with your thumb, you cut it."

Mark said, "OK, that's it. Let's just be friends. I can't live this way."

Mark realized Hajo was relieved. He'd been too kind to break it off himself, but he was grateful Mark had finally made a move.

Ned flew home to the States to see his parents at the end of August. Mark took the train to Venice.

He'd decided he'd let Joshua set the tone. If Joshua wanted to be frivolous, fine; if he wanted to talk about illness and death, fine. Joshua chose frivolity, which Mark considered gallant.

Once again, if for the last time, they settled into their old habits. They'd be awakened by the spluttering, rumbling, honking, shouting water traffic under their windows. They'd sit in the kitchen, which had been John Singer Sargent's studio a hundred years ago, and look down into the courtyard and nibble on bread rusks and listen for the furious rumbling of yet another pot of brewed espresso. Then Joshua retreated to the cool immensity of the painted library, where he sat beside a window laced with a morning-glory vine and tapped at his typewriter. Joshua listened to the classical music station on his transistor and the thin reproduction of a full-bodied piece for strings floated from room to room over the lustrous floors and under the bands of pink and beige plaster layering the cornices.

Daydreaming on his bed with the door open, dozing in the middle of a day too breezy to be hot, Mark heard the radio and the typewriter, these faint life signals Joshua was emitting. Mark thought that this summer everything was just as it had been the twelve preceding summers. The only thing that was different was that this summer would end the series.

He wanted to know how to enjoy these days without clasping them so tightly he'd stifle the pleasure. But he didn't want to drug himself on the moment either and miss out on what was happening to him. He was losing his best friend, the witness to his life. The skill for enjoying a familiar pleasure about to disappear was hard to acquire. It was sort of like sex. If you were just unconsciously rocking in the groove you missed the kick, but if you kept mentally shouting "Wow!" you shot too soon. Knowing how to appreciate the rhythms of these last casual moments—to cherish them while letting them stay casual—demanded a new way of navigating time.

Maybe that was why these days were so beautiful. Hadn't Joshua quoted the poet he was working on, Wallace Stevens, who'd said, "Death is the mother of beauty"? Joshua had explained that eternal, unchanging beauty would seem insipid and not at all beautiful—"a bore."

The maids, mother and daughter, arrived at noon and began the never-ending task of washing and polishing the *pavimenti*. They preferred working together, since that way they kept each other company. Joshua liked them and he kept giving them little presents—an extra coffeepot, an old typewriter, some picture books devoted to Venetian painters. In fact, Mark noticed that Joshua was silently disposing of most of his belongings; they carried down a sack full of old clothes and left it with the garbage outside the *portone*.

Then they sauntered across Campo Santo Stefano in search of lunch. Joshua looked leaner; there was something gray and slack about his cheeks. He who'd always suffered from writer's block was now working with greater fluency than ever before. Tap, tap, tap—the typewriter pecked its way across the page. At the pool they'd gossip. Sometimes they'd assume new characters, loosely based on their own but exaggerated toward archness. With Hajo, Mark impersonated an adult; with Ned, a child; but he and Joshua styled themselves as fantasy versions of themselves—themselves in their role of bored Venetian housewives (*"carissima!"*) or as catty Milanese queens in the rag trade, an act which would provoke astounded laughs from the two thoroughly American fellows inside them.

The days were sunnier, the nights more ambrosial than ever before. At the Ca' Rezzonico they looked once more at the *pulcinelli* playing obscene leapfrog, but it was downstairs, as they passed a banal Canaletto, that Mark realized these palaces had been here for centuries past and would still be here for centuries to come. Only the people came and went, supernumeraries. He wanted to ask Joshua if this Venetian eternity was a consolation or an insult, but he didn't know how to broach the subject.

Hajo called him every day from Berlin. "I'm so glad you're with Joshua," Hajo said. He told Mark about his friends who were dying; Mark told Hajo about Joshua. When Hajo said that both of his friends who were ill had fooled around for years at the saunas, Mark flared up. "If Joshua had sex ten times in the last five years that would be a lot. It's not a reward for promiscuity, Hajo. It's just bad luck."

Mark knew they'd always be friends, but the sexual tie between them was broken now, that tension that had kept drawing them back to each other. Now Mark wondered if he'd ever sleep with another man. If he met someone new he'd have to say he was positive. In the past he'd sometimes imagined he'd end up with a woman, even father children, but being positive had scotched that little fantasy.

Although he avoided newspapers, he picked up the *Herald Tribune* one day and read that India was planning to require blood-test results before granting visas to tourists. There went the notion of being cremated on a burning ghat.

He missed Ned.

After the regatta, Joshua decided to leave Venice. He stored a summer fan, a box of books, and his beach things—"for next summer," he said with deliberation. He'd given away everything else; this little pile was his sole lien on life. A water taxi pulled into the *rio* under the library windows. The driver, a portly, sunburned man in a starched white uniform who stood and steered with one hand, backed them out into the Grand Canal. A barge went past carrying the stacked bleachers from the regatta viewing stand. They looked up at the new wooden Accademia bridge, then downstream to the white stone lions sipping water at the Guggenheim and beyond at the gold ball above the old customs house agleam even on this cloudy day. As they were pulling away, they took a last look at *their* palace and, smiling shyly at each other, pushed the tears aside.

In Milan Joshua boarded his plane for New York and Mark flew home to Paris. Mark behaved well at the airport, just as though it were a question of keeping up a good front until the company had all left. Maybe because his life had been so charmed (Ned called Mark and himself "the brat brigade"), the hardest thing about grief was just to accept it was happening "live" and not like a commercial on a videotape that could be edited out later.

A few weeks later Mark and Ned went to a Robbins-Balanchine evening at the Paris opera house. They were happy to be back together. They had so little money now, it looked as though they'd be going home soon; if Mark didn't make an effort, his business would surely go under.

The Robbins ballet was new, but the two Balanchines were old friends, *Apollo* and the Stravinsky Violin Concerto. They were both nicely danced, but the somnolent audience scarcely applauded and Mark felt offended. He'd never been able to make Parisians understand that the lobby of the New York State Theater had been the drawing room of America and that we, yes, we Americans saw in the elaborate *enchaînements* onstage a radiant vision of society.

Hadn't Robbins called his best piece *Dances at a Gathering?* The old hymn said, "We gather together to ask the Lord's blessing." Now there was no Lord left to ask anything of, but in the book on modern poetry Joshua was struggling to finish hadn't he quoted Wallace Stevens, who'd said that if Americans were to have a god now it would have to be art?

The last movement of the Violin Concerto was clearly both Stravinsky's and Balanchine's homage to the square dance, and just as clearly these Parisian dancers had never seen a square dance in their lives; nor had the people in the audience. The idea of a courtship dance held in the midst of a whole smiling world of grown-ups ("Alleman left and do-si-do")— oh, the sweetly unsensual spirit of checked, flouncy dresses and hand-held Stetsons—eluded these bored Parisian per-formers, all state employees eager to wrap it up and head home.

Mark wept at this old mirror, leprous with flaking silver, that was being held up to reflect the straight young features of Balanchine's art. Ned held his hand in the dark and Mark spoiled Ned's silk *pochette* by blowing his nose into it.

Ned whispered, "Are you crying for Joshua?"

Mark nodded. Seeing the beauty he'd known with Joshua so distorted made him feel all the farther from home. His muscles registered the word "home" with a tensing, as though to push himself up out of the chair and head back toward home, to Joshua and the stingers at the Riv and the wild nights of sex and dance, but then he relaxed back into his seat, since he knew that home wasn't there anymore. Ned was the only home he had.

Watermarked

I've written various versions of my youth but I've always left out my first real lover, a man I lived with for five years and whom I met in the spring of my senior year at the University of Michigan. He's been stamped onto every page of my adult life as a watermark, though sometimes faintly; the French would say he's made his appearance *en filigrane*. His name was Randall Worth and I liked to think he was a descendant of the great Worth, one of the first Parisian couturiers of the 1890s, but in fact he was from a long line of Episcopalian ministers in Canada and small midwestern merchants.

In old-fashioned comedies the star always makes a late entrance, as will Randall, just to build up the suspense.

I'd known a few older gay men while I was still in junior high school back in Chicago and from them I'd learned to camp outrageously, as we used to say. At least I could report on it and feebly imitate it, even if I didn't have the guts to do it publicly. Camping meant to make a spectacle of yourself, a loud, hissing, gender-switching, self-dramatizing piece of street theater. You might take over a busy corner with a "girl-friend" and start to denounce him: "You vicious quane, I saw you makin' goo-goo eyes at mah man."

To which the "girlfriend"—a skinny six-footer in ballet slippers, wheat jeans, powder-blue angora sweater and full, glorious makeup composed of every color of an industrial sunset—might reply, a grin on his lips to indicate it was all a contest, though no less likely to tip over into a cat fight, "Girl, why would I ever make a play for that overgrown matron, that lisping, limp-wristed tired old fairy you call your husband? Honey, she's pure gal, you can just hear those estrogens surging when she gets near a real man like my George, why she's the only person I know who wears knee pads to a public toilet. They're attached to her garter belt. If she's butch she could die with the secret. . . ."

And on and on. Because I'd learned this shocking dialect, this role-reversing, value-toppling form of self-display, this mock hostility trembling on the edge of real hostility and un-aware of the distinction, I enjoyed a certain cachet among the five other middle-class gay men I met in a playwriting seminar at the University of Michigan. I taught them how to be gay, how to denounce each other humorously or "read each other's beads," as we said. Up till then the only homosexuals I'd encountered had been either these street-fighting queens in Chicago or wary, self-effacing professors in Ann Arbor who recognized (but would not directly acknowledge) an affinity with me. But in the playwriting seminar everything was funny, even "naughty," and charged with an electrifying energy. We kept egging one another on toward excess.

In class we'd discuss our work while the professor nodded uneasily, his smile fading while we doubled up with incomprehensible laughter or gushed over with extravagant praise. We'd brook no contradictions, for we were affirming our absolute sovereignty as arbiters of taste.

Each one of us would be given one session to present his work, which meant reading it out loud and playing all the parts. Then all of us in the inner queer circle would declare loyally that the play was stunning, a triumph of calculated wit and sophisticated repartee.

Our professor, a soft-spoken old man considered too important to allow to retire, had cobbled together a theory of play construction thirty years ago, one that had reputedly guided some of the leading names of the American theater to their current success. It was a stolid, workmanlike theory that held that every script must pose a MDQ, a Major Dramatic Question (Will Hamlet avenge his father's death?) in the first scene, flirt with possible solutions and doubts in the development (Yes, but can the ghost be trusted?), before terminating with an answer (Hamlet will assassinate his uncle) and, as an added fillip, Hamlet's death, a transposition of the resolution into a higher key that brings the drama to a surprising but inevitable close. Throughout, the action must advance and retreat in a "wavelike motion" as it phrases and revises the MDQ.

The professor had an unwelcome knack for dismissing our most potent verbal effects, our most thrilling *coups de théâtre,* in order to uncover underlying flaws of construction. He might as well have reproached a bitchy, camping Chicago queen after a tirade for having committed a small error in grammar or told a panting diva at the end of an aria that she'd not dotted her eighth notes. Dr. Smith seemed unimpressed with the "vehicle" Tom had written for the Lunts, a sex farce about an aging actress who runs into her first lover, a retired matinee idol, at Baden-Baden. Nor did he much like my Ionesco pastiche about a black maid who destroys the white family she works for, then goes mad.

Dr. Smith's cavils would be forgotten as soon as we queens withdrew to a restaurant for an after-class session. "Darling, your curtains are impeccable! That second-act finale!"

"Oh, you're talking about my play, I thought you were talking about my home decoration."

"I'm serious, it gave me goosebumps, hardly a look suitable to the extreme décolleté I happen to be wearing."

"My pet, is it wise to wear something so diaphanous given your full figure? And is *green* altogether suitable to a *gel* no longer in her first youth?"

"I treasure the advice of an older woman."

We sat upstairs at the Pancake Palace (the Palazzo to us) and camped outrageously, our lips stained blue from the sweet blueberry sauce we'd been pouring over our stacks. Soon we were a bit sick from the endless cups of coffee, the bottled fruit sauces and the ambition to be as bitchy as the dialogue in *All About Eve* or *The Women*.

Of course we were the sons of plumbers or salesmen and their idea of conversation was the unseasonable weather or the fine mileage that little Chevy's been getting; not all of our sweaty determination could turn us into sassy Hollywood smart alecks. We could roll our eyes, do double takes, coo and murmur like pouter pigeons, but still silences would creep into our dialogue and our snappy comebacks would go soggy. If accused of something I'd describe a great arc with my hand, touch my chest and ask, soundlessly, *"Moi?"* exhaling a mouthful of mentholated cigarette smoke. Of course even our most extravagant gestures and whoops were muted as we oscillated between our desire to establish an identity and our fear it would be discovered. The Chicago queens I knew "turned out," as actors said, that is faced the audience and projected their voices; we turned in. Whereas they were itching to radicalize every Elevated car or coffee shop they entered, the minute we left the Palazzo we reassumed the protective coloring of forgettable fraternity boy, silent classmate, invisible passerby.

One member of our group had worked as a sound engineer on the student station and knew how to undermine someone else's monologue by flashing all the hand signals used in radio to indicate just one more minute to go (a forefinger held up), a half minute (the finger crooked), closing moments (a finger turning wildly like a sweeping clock hand) and time to wrap it up (a finger slashing a throat below bulging eyes). He'd start flashing these infuriating signals the instant one of us would launch into a speech.

Another member, Tom, had a rich, unspontaneous laugh and a resonant way of lifting his face upward as though he were a beautiful woman and not a prematurely balding, hairy-shouldered man. He could execute a pout that only half concealed a complicitous smile. He had mastered something we named a "lightning transition," by which we meant he could throw his head back recklessly and emit his trademark laugh to indicate girlish merriment before turning on a dime to wide-eyed solemnity. He'd look at us reproachfully over the tops of his glasses ("Very *Our Miss Brooks*," we'd murmur approvingly, referring to a pert, pretty schoolmarm on a popular television series). He pretended to find one witty because it gave him a pretext for fluttering his long-lashed eyes and pursing his lips forward as though in an isometric exercise for eliminating the marionette lines bracketing the mouth, the whole a hieroglyph for saying, "You're fiendishly clever, you rogue. *Comme tu m'amuses!*" During a reading he would ask us to "leave our personalities at the door."

He wore glasses though they seldom actually mitigated his vision; no, they were a prop he could nibble meditatively, put on slowly while locking our eyes to indicate the reproach "I hope we're returning to business at last." Or he could snap them off like a collapsed fan to suggest exasperation or tap his forehead with them to read "It's coming, it's coming, I'm about to have an insight!"

Whereas all men and most women in Michigan spoke in a monotone, verbally trudging ahead in a straight line, Tom's voice skipped and swooped in virtuoso cascades.

He knew everything about classic Hollywood films, Broadway musicals and Noël Coward comedies, and someone's simplest allusion could trigger the recitation of pages of dialogue. Tom had learned them by heart, but all the rest of human knowledge passed his eager, absorptive intelligence by. His favorite actress was Helen Hayes and he was outraged when Mary McCarthy referred to her as "that brave little body."

The last regular member of the Pancake Palazzo Circle was a small, boneless man with the pallor and wounded smile of the coprophile. We called him, I fear, Graybelly, since his color was as unhealthy as his small frame was bloated. His tiny moist hands seemed fetal, whereas his face was aged or rather ageless; we thought he was forty though he turned out to be thirty. He lived with an even older man in a farmhouse in the country reputed for its orgies and dungeon. Whereas the merest hint of sex would send us into fits of cockatoo shrieks and fierce fannings up imaginary skirts to cool off easily inflamed nether parts, Graybelly had a cool fetishistic way of burrowing into detailed discussions of foreskins, hair distribution and extent of rectal receptivity. We were a tribe of Lady Bracknells, he the solitary Walter Winchell of onanism.

He'd written a play based on Goethe's *The Sorrows of Young Werther*, a choice that seemed all of a piece with his predilection for Wagner and his collection of German pornography which showed wavy-haired Teutons in posing straps stretched over—

and chained to—a mountaintop while an eagle soared overhead in a sky rent by lightning.

We all went to the opening night and it was there I first saw Randall Worth, who played Werther. He was small, shorter than the hefty Charlotte whom Graybelly had cast. He seemed suitably self-destructive although it was rare for so much melancholy to be expressed by so many unfocused smiles. His head was large and his profile old-fashioned. At first I thought he had a sleepwalker's muzzy, wet-eyed seriousness, although later I figured out the fact his contact lenses kept floating free accounted for most of his characterization, the simultaneous vulnerability and unavailability. Graybelly, who was sitting next to me, whispered, "What he needs is ten inches down his throat and a profound colonic irrigation," which seemed an unusual cure for adolescent self-consciousness.

The play was much too long, the monologues interminable, the prevailing punctuation mark an exclamation point. Tom was squinting boredom and hatred over the tops of his glasses toward an oblivious Graybelly enraptured by his own words or rather Goethe's while our impatient sound engineer friend, seated appropriately in the royal box, was desperately slashing his throat and bugging his eyes, all to no avail.

I didn't care about the tragedy onstage or the comedy in the audience. All I could think about was this aristocratic somnambulist onstage, this Sleeping Beauty waiting I hoped for a mere kiss to awaken him rather than ten inches, six more than I could provide. For some reason his suicide was preceded by a long scene in which Werther addressed the portraits of his ancestors; in this staging the portraits were conceived of as two rows of empty gilt frames suspended in midair to create a corridor on a bias brilliantly lit from above.

"Just look at how the tart's dusted her hair with sparkles,

the huzzy," Graybelly murmured, chuckling soundlessly. With a start I realized he was referring to Randall, for as the program revealed that was Werther's name. Graybelly added profession-ally, "Not bad, that cross on the diagonal; got to hand it to Minny," calling Winston, the director, by his *nom des plumes,* as we said.

None of the muggery in the audience could distract me from the vision on the stage. As Randall slowly paced his castle corridor, murmuring to the portraits, I felt he was moving a cool magnet across my brain.

I suppose now, looking back, I'd say I was attracted by Randall's prestige as a beauty; if he would sleep with me then I'd demonstrate to everyone that I must be exceptional. Back then I didn't think it out. I knew that if I cruised at the swimming pool or at the Flame Bar I wasn't likely to attract anyone special. In the shower room I wasn't endowed enough to interest a size queen; at the bar I wasn't sufficiently lively to engage a loner's attention. But if experience had taught me my erotic place, I hadn't learned the lesson. I knew that if to all appearances I was banality itself, in my inner being I was convinced I concealed a rare quality, a frozen asset that could be awakened by—well, this very prince.

Perhaps such a theatrical act seemed plausible since given that I'd first seen Randall on the stage, in my last few months at the university—a time when I longed to change my life but feared the future and masked that fear behind an exuberance about my playwriting class, its sexual ambiguity, its daring exploration of artifice, its enabling recasting of reality into the shifting, insubstantial forms of fantasy.

"Tonight's my twenty-second birthday," I whispered to Graybelly. "I'd love to give the cast party at my place." The playwright was delighted and during the curtain calls he went backstage and handed on the invitation to the eighteen mem-bers of the cast and their various girlfriends and boyfriends.

Everyone came and drank the ethyl alcohol my biologist roommate sneaked out of his laboratory, where it was used to asphyxiate or perhaps preserve rabbits. For days afterward it seemed I kept stumbling over unconscious actors passed out in yet another of the many rooms I shared with five other men.

Everyone came but Randall, who went off walking alone till dawn, rethinking his role.

Perhaps as a recompense for the party, a pleasure for everyone else but a missed chance for me, Graybelly arranged for me to meet Randall over coffee at the student union. "I've told him you want to write a play for him." Maybe Graybelly just wanted another funny anecdote about us for the Palazzo Kids.

I don't remember what we said, but I do recall how awkward the occasion was. That and Randall's extraordinary beauty. The top of his head came just to my shoulder. But he held himself ramrod straight. He had abundant light brown hair with gold highlights which he parted severely on the right side, an arrangement that added to his clean-cut good looks, the looks of a young man in a shirt ad. His full but not overripe lips described a relaxed bow, slightly downturned . . . an Attic smile more sculptural than amiable. Attic also was his long straight nose that dropped without a bump plumb out of his strong, intellectual brow. His deep-set eyes glowed like sunlight dancing at the end of the tunnel on water seen in the afternoon when the late hour renders back the colors that noon had absorbed—you must forgive this fancy description, but this is more than a routine homage to just another cute guy. No, he had leading-man looks, all the more striking then before everyone had a great haircut, designer jeans, a gym body and perfect teeth. In the 1950s we thought beauty was God-given or at least a freak of nature. They say when Brahms first heard the Beethoven Ninth, he fainted, certainly a likelihood before records; by extension, imagine our awe when faced with physical beauty before it became mass-produced.

He blinked uncomfortably and darted his eyes rapidly to one side, a tick provoked by his loose contact lenses. He had long, even very long, white teeth without a single irregularity or stain. Later I found out they'd been so long his dentist had filed them down; he'd even had a *second* row of canines that had to be pulled. A powerful lot of white teeth for just one small guy.

Because he wasn't tall or white-blond or overly muscular or loud or surrounded by a spectacular entourage people didn't notice him at first. You had to be seated opposite him at a table to notice his skin, which was uniform, matte, without the slightest blemish and peculiarly expressive; he changed color with every flicker of emotion. His skin seemed to be a layer of his brain, as the eyes are said to be neural—the feeling part, since it registered every mood. A mental map printed on the skin—quite literally a tactile map, since he had a rare skin sensitivity, you could write your name on his back with your finger and a moment later the letters would rise in painless red welts that would soon enough fade.

Did I mention his hands? His fingers were short and stubby, the nails shell-pink and glowing, the backs unveined and hairless—a baby's hands, and he held them out at the odd, stiff angles a baby presents to the world, as though faulty coordination makes the infant think he's reaching for you whereas he's actually doubling back his chubby hand at the wrist and shoving it toward the ceiling in an unintentional gesture of festive irresponsibility. Randall wasn't limp-wristed or archly gestural; on the contrary, his baby hands, frozen at improbable angles, were the only part of his self-presentation he hadn't entirely polished. I once praised his "baby hands" and he never forgave me the praise.

Oh, and his voice could be a problem, too; in true midwestern fashion it could cut glass when he was excited. Again, not a queen's shrill cry. No, more a young salesman's tenor tirade amplified.

Enough descriptions. I'm trying to throw in a few minor criticisms to suggest I was—or at least am now—objective, but in truth back then I was besotted. In high school I'd had a persistent fantasy about inviting Marilyn Monroe to my prom; in college the idea of going out with Randall seemed every bit as glamorous and unlikely. Yet I told myself I might become a playwright; hadn't Marilyn married Arthur Miller?

I went to a party at Randall's where he drank so much he rushed outdoors, lay down on the ground and flapped his arms to create an angel in the thick new snow. He let me kiss him but he was so drunk that he thrashed in my arms with point-less, driven energy. I was drunk, too.

Soon I became aware that everyone in the Pancake Palazzo Crowd was in love with Randall though they all said bitchy things about him. He and I would have coffee in the student union and I could barely concentrate on what he was saying. If I told him how much I liked him he turned on a smile, as blind as it was blinding. I thought he was indifferent to my homage.

He told me that he was from a good family in Bloomington, Indiana, where his father owned a printing press and his mother was the local gossip columnist. Every night both his parents drank themselves into a rage (mother) or stupor (fa-ther). Randall despised both of them as well as his four younger brothers. He hid himself in his room. He locked his door and prayed they wouldn't break it down.

He had a television set in his room and watched westerns late into the night. He found his penis became erect whenever he saw a bare-chested Indian on the screen, though the only person he trusted enough to kiss was Lynne, a girl in his high school class who wore a heavy leg brace and mocked him and adored him. Her love was as potent and irrational as Elektra's.

Before he met Lynne the only affection he'd ever known had come from the black maid, who liked children so much she kept taking them in, all her great-nieces and grandsons. He was a conscientious but not inspired student. His mind wandered. He played no sports. Lynne offered him not kindness but an ancient Greek passion and a modern American irony, the passion as sharp as steel, the irony as corrosive as rust.

Only at the University of Michigan did he discover he was handsome. Through a mixup at Student Housing he was put in a dormitory room not with another freshman but with a graduate student, a math whiz who promptly fell for him. The mathematician had never been in love before, so he assumed his feelings must be reciprocated. But Randall had not escaped his family only to fall into the hands of a new tyrant. He was ostentatiously indifferent to the mathematician. One afternoon Randall came back to the room to find it full of poisonous smoke. His roommate had sealed the window shut and gone to bed with a block of dry ice; he was inhaling its fatal fumes under a sheet. Randall merely opened the window, threw the ice out and left, never to come back.

He moved in with Tony, a theater major, who was hopelessly in love with someone else—oh, I don't remember all the details. I just remember that the mathematician was sent by Student Health to a mental institution for six months and that Randall renounced love forever when he realized he'd never win over Tony, a skinny, bespectacled guy whose hairless torso resembled an Indian's only if one squinted at him from a distance. Randall had found the one homosexual student on campus who didn't desire him.

Randall's selfish, irresponsible father gave his son the same weekly allowance he himself had received twenty-five years earlier. Randall was too proud to ask for more so he worked thirty hours a week at the library for a dollar an hour and ate so little that he lost his boyish plumpness and became hauntingly pale and thin. Lynne wrote him daily letters denouncing the foolishness of everyone around her at the University of Indiana. She reserved a belligerent, mocking affection for Randall; when she wrote it out every other radioactive word was sealed between asbestos quotation marks.

In his junior year, when I met him, Randall switched his major from history to theater. His inebriated parents didn't even register this troubling change. In his acting class he was discovered by Graybelly, who was visiting all the workshops in search of Werther. It was Graybelly who introduced him around; perhaps as a playwright he wanted to see what kind of havoc so much beauty would wreak on his friends.

Randall also knew other acting majors. Artaud and Brecht were their gods and I had to hear hours and hours of theorizing about "cruelty" and "alienation." Not from the Palazzo Crowd, interested only in repartee in which each line "capped" the preceding one, or in the "build" of an act to a thundering climax, even if the closing thrill depended on nothing more than "shtick." If the Palazzo Boys were, despite their Protestant midwestern origins, given to Yiddish words and were very showbizzy and "commercial" (a positive word, as in the question, "Yes, but is it commercial? Will it run? Will the little old lady from Topeka get it?"), the drama majors, by contrast, were beatnik intellectuals who thought theater should be all at once engagé and avant-garde, Marxist and Freudian, somehow both nonverbal and rhetorical, ritualistic as the mass and revolutionary as a bomb. We Palazzo Queens were willing to appropriate an idea or borrow a word here or there from this tangled discourse in order to intimidate our playwriting teacher or beef up a graduate school application, but only the true drama majors could contemplate selflessly taking their plays into the streets where they might reach the people. They longed for an unspecified sort of spiritual renewal, but they could only imagine instigating it through a populist staging of *Coriolanus* or *The Cenci* ("They'd have better luck with a glitzy production of *Oklahoma!*," Graybelly opined). Randall and I were bedeviled by these issues but we remained, in very different ways, untouched by them. I wanted to be a rich and famous playwright so that my father would not think I'd ruined my life and Randall would love me. Otherwise I found the ideas animating theater talk in Ann Arbor contradictory and certainly irrelevant to my ambition. Like the Palazzo Kids I was concerned primarily with results, even with effects, though I doubted that another well-made Terence Rattigan comedy, even if it was a hit, could provide the frisson my spirit longed for. For me the Palazzo Kids were fascinating not because of the plays they were writing but because of those they were living out as they struggled to invent a style for their homosexuality.

Randall was idolized as a beauty and mocked as an artist; paraphrasing Dorothy Parker, Tom said, "Boy gorgeous is actor lousy" and "He runs the gamut of emotions from A to B." But for Randall acting as an art was only a means to the end of being universally admired. He liked Stanislavsky's theories more than Brecht's because the Russian's doctrine of "sense memory" in *Building a Character* made self-absorption sound productive. Randall might have been a good movie actor since his best moments onstage were those when he spoke calmly and nobly to someone silent, his eyes lit with a sad, angelic wisdom, his golden head inclined slightly downward, his full lips wreathed in a complex smile, one baby hand raised at an improbable angle, as though unscrewing an invisible light bulb.

I wrote a poem for Randall in which I referred to myself as an older man smoking cigars (rather than the Kools I really smoked) and contemplating my younger beloved dancing (the sex of the dancer was carefully veiled). Randall scanned it quickly, ransacking it efficiently for compliments; when he discovered my admiration was vague and general, he folded the sheet of paper neatly and put it into his briefcase.

I complained to Graybelly that I was getting nowhere with Randall, who'd granted me only one drunken kiss in the snow. "She's a snow queen herself," Graybelly advised, "and you've got to rape her. That's what she's begging for. Climb into her window and rape her."

That night I drank lots of Drambuie and wandered through the Arboretum past lovers, homosexual and heterosexual, writhing beneath old trees like exposed root systems come to life. I felt seized by a great, unspecified emotion that was certainly pagan, so imbued was it with a reverence for nature, so musical was the way a single melody or sentiment encompassed so many notes or invocations to the worship of the body, Randall's body. For the moment, fame and riches no longer interested me; now I just wanted to turn and turn with Randall on a narrow white bed.

At last I had worked up my nerve sufficiently to climb into his basement window. He woke with a start.

"Hi, it's me," I said.

"Yeah, I see, but—what time is it?"

"Late. Very late. I just—well, can I sit down on the edge of your bed?"

"OK, but no funny business. You see, I like you tremendously, but not like that." And yet he went over to the sink and brushed his teeth, which surely he wouldn't have bothered to do if he didn't think I'd kiss him, would he?

I kept remembering Graybelly had said Randall needed to be raped, but I was too much in love to do anything except smile nervously. When he came back to his bed he hugged his knees. He was wearing Jockey shorts.

"Do you mind if I kiss you just once?" I asked. "Come on,

it won't kill you, just once. I know we're just friends, but you can't imagine how long I've thought about this moment."

"What do you mean?"

"Come on, you know, just sitting next to you, all alone, you're so . . . gorgeous."

"Really? Do you really think so?"

"Of course. For me you're perfect."

"I'm too short, for one thing."

"No, you're compact and—may I?—your skin is flawless." At that point I began to kiss his shoulder and to put an arm around his waist. I had no desire to go any further, nor did I that night, though I knew Graybelly and my other Palazzo Pals would laugh at my timorousness.

Holding him was like holding some improbable gardenia, something at once noble and sensual—which must be the definition of "romantic." I'd thought about him so long that he'd become nearly mythic for me, so that it was his actual presence that was the improbability, like the host which is at one and the same time Our Lord's body and a nearly tasteless wafer consumed in Holy Apostles Church in Akron, Ohio, say, on a Sunday morning in the spring of 1962. The insertion of a myth into a precise moment and place is both miraculous and fairly humorous. I tasted the comic tang of kissing Randall.

He didn't ever clearly reject my suit that last spring in Ann Arbor. Perhaps he sensed that my devotion was deep and would last. I tried to spend as much time with him as possible, but I noticed that he'd see me only by day, never at night. I asked him endless questions about his childhood and learned that he lived only nominally in the present. Most of his daily energy went toward staring into the flickering images of his erotic fantasies and blocking out the sound of breakage. Randall lived a tidy, Spartan life, rushing from an acting rehearsal to a workshop on movement and speech and then directly on to the library, where he returned borrowed books to the stacks. I loved his library job since every day at certain hours I would know where to find him, briskly re-alphabetizing the novels of Pearl Buck or inserting the second volume of a government demographic study of Wisconsin between the first and third. He wore white gloves for the job, which gave him the look of a West Point honor guard; surely it was no accident that they contrasted so nicely with his blue crewneck sweater and darker blue trousers.

I allowed myself to imagine that every night he was rehearsing a scene for class. But one day over pancakes Tom said, "You poor big distraught girl, you must be heartsick about Randall's new love."

Does he mean Lynne? I wondered. Or his favorite instructor, a married graduate student from New York who might be gay but who didn't fancy Randall (the instructor had told me so himself between discussions of Ugo Betti and Dürenmatt).

"Which lover?"

"Oh, Mother! *Edith!* You mean you don't know about his *affaire du coeur* with that excessively fetching Cy? How could you have missed him? They're joined at the hip. And though your sweet Randall is modest and sincere, that fetching Cy just fetches and fetches, oh, here he comes fetchalizing now *à droite et à gauche* even as we speak."

Down below on the ground floor of the Pancake Palazzo a taller, cruder version of Randall with a big smile and a booming laugh was making his entrance alongside a girl, the one who'd been the stage manager for *Werther.* I thought, Obviously Randall would prefer a tall slender blond with too much jaw to me.

Randall's favorite graduate student had cast him in a workshop production of a play by that (as he said) 'incorrigibly kitsch but wildly theatrical' Thornton Wilder (a writer I accordingly sneered at but whom I'd intensely admired until this very moment, the only contemporary "man of letters" I knew about and a model for the career I hoped to have). I nursed along my friendship with the director so that I could attend rehearsals and observe Randall. I had to remember to take mental notes in order to have something to say later both to the director and to Randall. Left to my own devices I would have just stared and stared, addled by desire and hurt.

Randall's love for Cy (I'd already promoted it into love) made me wince with pain and toss and turn on my narrow bed when I'd try to sleep. The warm weather had finally come to Ann Arbor. I'd won the school's major literary prize for my Ionesco-inspired play and with some of the money I bought a case of Asti Spumante, which I chilled and served with melon balls inside a hollowed-out watermelon, my idea of casual sophistication. Like all boarding-school boys I was used to Spartan simplicity but prized my little luxuries, which were usually eccentric. I served this sweet but sparkling concoction to all my friends one Saturday afternoon but Randall didn't drop in.

He was just a junior and had one more year to go at the U. of M., but I was being graduated. His plans were to spend the summer in New York with Cy; they'd stay with an older, established actor, a friend of Cy's, and find odd jobs and go to casting calls. I returned to Chicago and drove a panel truck delivering fruit juice and eggs in Des Plaines. I was supposed to go to Harvard in the fall and work toward a doctorate in Chinese, but I was terribly lonely for Randall. I was living with my best high school buddy at his family's home in Evanston. He was learning to drive a city bus. One night I picked up a boy prostitute on Rush Street; two nights later I had my first case of gonorrhea. I lied to the doctor and said a girl had given it to me. A day after I received a penicillin shot I was cured, but I felt dirty and ashamed.

I flew to New York on July 19 in order to surprise Randall on his twentieth birthday. I checked into the YMCA, then headed right over to the address he'd given me. I walked the entire way, a good forty blocks, through a stagnant heat held clasped between the uplifted hands of seemingly empty skyscrapers. Occasionally a subway would rumble by and animate a ghostly dance of old newspapers above a grate. Cars manned by drivers with loud voices sputtered past. The length of lower Park Avenue was almost empty; the traffic lights changed all at the same time like sentinels presenting arms. The last rays of sunlight struck a white fire off the highest windows in towers opulently trimmed in bronze; New York seemed rich above, poor below, truly a stratified society, as we'd learned to say in sociology class.

The squalor of my venereal disease, the cruel tedium of my summer delivery job, the vertigo of being out of school for the first time in my life and on the loose in a strange city—these were all things that made me feel uneasy. Suddenly my university years no longer appeared to me a frustrating prelude to a wonderful life to come but rather a lost golden age. I was sure that Randall must have maintained his verve and momentum even in this soggy, dirty city, a vigorous gentian springing up out of the asphalt.

Randall wasn't there. No one answered the doorbell. When I finally found a phone that worked, no one picked up. Of course it was his birthday and Cy had undoubtedly asked him out to dinner. As a midwesterner, I assumed even the most gala dinner would be over by nine—just an hour to go.

I waited till dawn on the step next door, my heart pounding at the sound of every approaching footfall in that big, abandoned summer city. At six in the morning I started to tremble from the cold and weariness. Whatever small self-assurance I'd had about being a pleasant surprise for Randall had vanished. I'd been demoralized by the Chinese torture of waiting. All night I'd alternately tingled with excitement and then been anesthetized by boredom. Now I was exhausted and empty-headed. I ate a lonely, bitter breakfast in an all-night diner and headed back to my room at the West Side Y. I felt that everyone else here was at home in a city as stony and upright as a cemetery, stele after stele.

I finally got Randall on the phone that afternoon. "Hi. It's *me!*"

"Hi. Where are you?"

"In New York. I came to see you for your birthday."

"My birthday was yesterday."

"I know. I sat on your doorstep—"

"—*stoop*," Randall corrected, using the New York Dutch word.

"Yeah, and, yeah, I sat there for half an hour, then I realized you must be out celebrating, so I made other dinner plans with friends."

"Friends? So how long are you staying?"

"*Forever!*"

"Really? Until you go to Harvard, you mean."

"No. I've given all that up. I'm looking for a job. You know, a play of mine is going to be produced in New York."

"You're kidding . . ."

"No, no, I've got an agent at William Morris who's looking for a producer."

"Too bad there's no part for me."

"But there *is*. I've rewritten it and now there's a juicy—" I caught my breath, realized my voice was pitched too high. I said in what I hoped sounded like a sexy whisper, "What are you doing for dinner?"

"I've got a scene study class at Herbert Berghof's till ten, but we could meet then and grab a bite and you could tell me about the part."

I was too much in love to resent Randall's newfound interest in me; in fact I was grateful for the leverage.

By September I'd landed a job at Time-Life Books and found

a walk-up railroad apartment on MacDougal Street between Bleecker and Houston, once the heart of the Village. The hippie movement was just beginning and the streets were thronged with young people in beads and velvet and rayon polished to look like silk. On a Saturday night cars could scarcely breast their way through the throngs of pedestrians. All the noise and activity, though, were in the streets; the street-level Italian restaurants—serving their heaped platters of spaghetti *vongole*, garlic bread, stuffed breast of veal and sweet, heavy cannoli—were as empty and tranquil as ever as the old waiter with his sparse hair dyed black and his red jacket and black clip-on tie changed the dishes with a mournful sympathy. The cafés, however, with their hissing espresso machines, opera records and wallpaper made of yellowing French newspapers, were crowded.

Two cultures were coexisting uneasily, one young and hip, the other aged but fiercely entrenched and territorial. The hip culture was symbolized by a new shop in which customers could create their own abstract canvases by dribbling acrylics onto squares of white paper spinning in a cylinder. The old Italian ways seemed to be represented by the giant pair of alabaster urns, lit from within, just inside the window of Procacino's Funeral Home.

I brought Randall to my apartment in September when Cy broke up with him and he found himself homeless. Randall had decided not to finish his degree back in Michigan.

Nothing, I suppose, is as powerful for me as the idea of actually living with someone; "living" and "sleeping" are transitive verbs for me, intimate and cherishing ones. Once Randall was in my possession I was happy. I'd rented our tiny three-room railroad apartment furnished from a girl named Sandy who kept threatening to come back to New York but never did. On Sandy's fold-out couch bed with the humped back and broken springs, we tossed and turned, while all around us our old Italian neighbors sang, called to one another from window to window, heated up tomato sauce and cranked laundry across the narrow space between one tenement and the next. In the Midwest we'd lived in seemingly empty spaces where, nevertheless, everyone spied on us; here we saw and heard people on every side but they were profoundly indifferent to us.

The first time we made love I saw my hand marks raise temporary red welts on Randall's extraordinarily sensitive skin. To look at those gray-blue eyes an inch away from my own or to click my teeth against those brilliant white teeth seemed a profanation. We read Cavafy's poems and believed we were his decadent young men consumed by vice, our eyes bistered by desire.

I discovered Randall was subject to deep, annihilating depressions that would last for days. He would go out walking in thin shoes through rain or snow and return at midnight as pale and silent as before. Dejected, he would sit before a cup of tea I'd made him and not even sip it. I felt his unhappiness was a reproach to me. Confident in my powers as a psychologist (hadn't the girls at the office told me I'd really, really helped them?) I told Randall that depression was not an ungovernable act of nature but something one could fight.

"Your trouble," I said, "is that you're too proud to admit that a small slight to your vanity could send you into such a terrible decline, so you prefer to invent some vague cosmic reason for it—the meaninglessness of it all."

Hamlet did not want to be cheered up. I sank to my knees before him at the kitchen table and begged him to feel better. He gave a small wintry smile but I felt he was very remote. It was as though he were looking up at me through a small bathysphere window and I was just a distant, flickering fin.

Our love worked well because Randall was the one man in a thousand who welcomed devotion and who, like a medieval princess, believed in it only after it had been proved by many deeds and long trials. Most men like chasing after—rather than being—the quarry and flee someone too obviously in love; being adored suffocates and gives them too little imaginative scope. Only someone unobtainable leaves enough room for dreams, inspires longing, promotes scheming and implies a rival, whereas a quick and total conquest is the last act and one that abrogates all needs for the preceding drama. But Randall had had enough strife at home and wanted to be cherished.

I so enjoyed serving him and supporting him and listening to him that I forgot my own existence, certainly my own uninteresting face; if I would glance at my own reflection after a long evening spent with him I'd be offended by the reminder that such sustained communion hadn't improved my looks.

I learned what a burden beauty can be. Drunk men at parties would take an instant dislike to Randall. Eventually I figured out their reasoning: I want him—he thinks he's too good for me—the *bastard!*

He didn't want to be liked merely for his looks but needed to maintain them *just in case.* To dress to go down to the corner deli could take an hour and necessitated trying on every garment he owned (he didn't own very many). When he'd meet new people he'd turn on a totally fake smile that struck me as ridiculous but that seldom failed to seduce a newcomer. He worried about being too short and always walked on the inner, supposedly higher side of the sidewalk ("Of course it's higher, so the rain will drain into the gutter"). He knew where every mirror in the neighborhood was and if I thought he was cruising someone I usually surprised him looking at his own reflection. Girls at the Herbert Berghof acting school fell in love with him and spent hours with him discussing his profile, composite, soul. He even slept with one girl who gave him crabs—or so he told me. More likely it was a man.

Not that we ever pretended to be faithful to each other.

Through jokes and the implied morality underpinning apparently casual remarks, we nudged each other toward the promiscuity we longed for, which was integral to our idea of bohemianism. Since he was handsome his affairs were long, romantic seductions that started when an admirer sent him a free drink or whistled at him in the street; the top fashion designer of the day screeched to a halt in his sports car, took Randall's address and messengered him plane tickets to Egypt, which Randall returned with a coolly polite note in his best Palmer-method script. One day I had sex with a brassy young playwright who said, "You make love just like this kid I met yesterday, Randall Worth. What a beauty *he* was!"

I wasn't a beauty. I looked like everyone else, and frequently people greeted me with the wrong name. Because I was so average my sex life was catch as catch can. I let the Village monster, a Frankenstein-monster lookalike, lure me up to his apartment and take pornographic pictures of me. More than once Randall looked at the very men I'd been fucked by the day before and said, "What is that man staring at? How can these *trolls* be so shameless? Does he honestly think we'd want to talk to him?"

I was never envious of Randall. I was proud of him. His beauty seemed heraldic and I felt custodial if elaborately casual toward it, exactly as though I were to introduce a girl with dirty hair and dark glasses to someone as "the Princess Palatine." We made love to each other only rarely. Randall had never been excited by me, since he was drawn to scrawny, dark boys.

I lived day and night beside the hothouse flower of Randall's body and woke to see the faint morning light being absorbed by his porous skin—it was like waking up beside Antinoüs. One night I was still sleeping when Randall entered me, which was a sensation so sweet and soothing—if separated out from the turbulent feelings of guilt when I was awake and being fucked—that I was shocked by this proof that I'd become really and truly gay. Until now I had imagined it was a vice that had something to do with the will. Yes, homosexuality was a disease of the will, yet this deep satisfying pleasure was wholly involuntary.

We weren't snobbish in any of the usual ways. We didn't care about money. Someone—was it Oscar Wilde?—had said that for him the necessities were luxuries, the luxuries necessities, and that became our creed. Randall's necessary luxuries were all the trappings of his acting career. Every day he sent out pictures and résumés to producers mentioned in *Backstage*, the paper for the acting trade. Over endless cups of coffee we would discuss the implications a busy stranger in the profession might draw from one glossy eight-by-ten head shot rather than another. I was earning only a hundred dollars a week. Randall was bringing in another thirty or forty as a filing clerk hired by the hour through a temporary agency. He couldn't take a real job since that would be paramount to admitting he was really an office worker rather than an actor. Accepting a nine-to-five meant one was no longer in the business.

Yet he had a mordant sense of humor about his situation. He made fun of the illusions he and his tribe nourished about themselves. If that friend accepted a real shit job as a dishwasher in a celebrity restaurant, Randall would say, "Well, gee, after all, it's a chance to be seen. Anyway, dishwashing is just a job-job. He's really a Shakespearean leading man and Broadway chorine."

Once every two weeks he'd have to act before his scene study class. The texts were often bits of dialogue from fiction. I'd come home from work to hear Randall whispering something hateful to May, his favorite partner. I'd sit over a cup of instant coffee and a cigarette in the kitchen while they hissed and laughed and sighed in the living room, sitting on our bed retracted into a couch. They were very good and sometimes I couldn't tell whether they were acting or just talking.

May was a twenty-year-old temperamentally unsuited to her age. She was destined to become a motherly forty-year-old leaning over a counter in a diner to console a girlfriend or, giggling, whisper something dirty to a boyfriend. Most of the other Berghof students were anguished about their future and believed that only stardom could redeem their lives of insecurity, humiliation and poverty (an unlikely happy ending in a city where only five hundred actors out of seven thousand actually worked in any given year), but May was thoroughly pleased with her life as it was. She'd guessed Randall and I were gay and winked at it. She liked the theater milieu more than actually being onstage; or rather she saw every moment of her life as theatrical. She'd say, as she headed to Brooklyn for dinner with her parents, "Sorry, hon, I've got my family gig tonight. How do I look? Convincing?"

Whereas most of the actors we knew thought they were right for every role that came along and were willing for the sake of an audition to put on accents, false hair, years or take off pounds or panties, May had such a strong personality she couldn't shed it. She patted boys almost unconsciously on the rump as though they were horseflesh. She never counted calories but was convinced she was beautiful despite a strong overbite and a second chin. She'd receive a compliment with a big, split-level smile and a fluttering of fake eyelashes that hovered between parody and sincerity. If asked to sing she'd grab an imaginary mike, pull down one side of her sweater and kiss her shoulder, then murmur a Kurt Weill ballad in a husky voice at odds with her cracky speaking voice.

Sometimes I'd resent coming home, still in my hated coat and tie, from a job that was difficult only because there was so little to do, to find our minuscule apartment full of May's

smoke and giggles. For her time didn't exist. She had a gig as
a waitress twice a week in a Village restaurant just for lunch;
that was her job-job. Otherwise she was free to shoplift, read
her chart, shop, cruise, rehearse, window-shop, take in a movie
and eat a hoagie.

Like most young actors she was good at imitating other people's gestures and intonations, and if I screwed up my body
into a strange pretzel position in pursuit of an elusive point,
I'd see her frowning slightly as she studied my posture (and
ignored my idea), then worked her own body into the same
puzzle. Only after she'd found the exact combination would
she show by her huge two-tiered smile and raised brows that
she was all ears or at least eyes. "Stop *indicating*," Randall
would grumble affectionately, an actor's way of saying she was
miming attention without actually giving it.

At that time I met a young straight couple who'd just been
graduated from the Northwestern University drama school,
where they had studied with Viola Spolin, a legendary figure
in the Chicago school of improvisation. After two minutes with
this tall, blond, self-assured actor and actress, my heart sank.
I learned they already had an agent, that they were already
cast in a frothy, Broadway-bound sex farce and that they were
agreeing to do only those commercials that were extremely
lucrative or pertinent to the image they were cultivating.
Whereas Randall's scene classes resembled pointless, deeply
disturbing psychoanalytic sessions, these blond victors spent
their days with their lawyer, a tailor, a masseuse, or they were
off to a facial or a voice lesson with the top musical-comedy
coach at a hundred dollars an hour.

I loved listening to Randall and May's shop talk, even though
I suspected now that it was merely abstract and would never
lead to a job. If one of them wept and shook all over in an
emotional scene, the other would launch into a monologue:
"Yes, but can you sustain that eight performances a week,

fifty-two weeks a year? Of course I know your performance must evolve and the only way you can keep it believable is by constantly finding new sense memories and by digging deeper; that's why American actors are so much better than the English, who have loads of technique, sure, but you don't believe in them for a moment. Not that I'm against technique. That's why I do so much voice and movement work and why I'm starting gymnastics; after all my body and voice are the tools of my trade. I try to respect them and not drink or smoke too much or stay up too many nights in a row. I've been rethinking your work on this role. I think your concentration is excellent. I'm not sure you've found everything in the part, though; there are still some colors missing. You've got the basic motivations down, you've done some important character work, but I'm not sure you're respecting the period style. I know, I know, that comes later. . . . Maybe just for now you should figure out some new business for your entrance."

When my play had won a prize at school, my name had been noted in a three-line article in the *New York Times*. A New York playwrights' agent wrote me, asked to see my "property," read it and decided to handle it. She ultimately found a young producer-director whose parents were temporarily rich and could afford for the moment to indulge their son and his expensive hobby. His name was Rhett Goldstein, a compromise between romantic gentile fantasies and solid Jewish realities. He wore country tweeds but was indelibly urban. He was the first person we knew in New York who lived on the Upper East Side in an apartment with new store-bought furniture in a building with a doorman. He had a painting in a gold frame with a little light over it.

He was terribly funny in an unfamiliar New York way. He had a psychoanalyst and his highest word of simultaneous criticism and approbation was "neurotic." His best friend was a neurotic actress who longed to be pitied. She and Rhett would rent wheelchairs, sit in them with little plaid blankets folded nicely over their knees and order in pizza, hoping to draw some sympathy from the delivery boy. Rhett was always perfectly turned out, a tall man with shellacked black hair and broad shoulders who lived on amphetamines lest he gain weight. He went on eating binges, usually rum-raisin ice cream, which he'd confess to proudly: "I don't know why I'm getting so neurotic," he'd say. He shaved above his nose to keep his eyebrows from growing together. He was only four or five years older than we were but seemed much more sophisticated. He'd been to some sort of business school but never spoke of it. He read expensive new bestsellers in hardcover rather than dog-eared paperback classics: Jacqueline Susann rather than Milton. He spoke of "trash" with connoisseurial relish, but he knew the names of celebrities in every domain, thousands and thousands of names, including the most exalted and rarefied. No social situation could have taken him by surprise, although he impressed us by trembling when he lit his cigarette. He often said his nerves were shot and the only cure was to iron his shirts and slacks for an hour. He ironed all his clothes, even his boxer shorts, even his sheets. He had a lot of free time and compulsive ways of filling it.

He did a very funny imitation of my agent. He noticed little things about people; after half an hour with Einstein he would have been capable of saying, "Did you notice the dandruff?" He listened to show tunes and knew all the lyrics which he had to keep himself from lip-synching. At Sardi's or Joe Downey's or Casey's in the Village he could be extremely polite— a bit unsmiling and rigid, a tad imperial—with a new person, but if he didn't like that new person, when the new person went to the toilet Rhett would mime vomiting, a finger down his throat, and even whisper the word "Gag."

Randall was falling in love with Rhett, at least Randall would talk about him all the time, his fascination disguised as mild satire. "Oh, that Rhett is a stitch," Randall would say. "He plays solitaire for hours alone in his apartment, all dressed up in his Paul Stuart suits. Do you think he's gay? I've dropped plenty of beads but he's never picked up a single one."

In March, just before we began rehearsals, Randall moved out of our apartment. I had seen his part in my play (a small one but the "title role" as he pointed out) as my way of winning his love definitively. Far from it. He was worried that people would imagine he'd been cast simply because he was my lover. He wanted people (which people?) to think he'd seen the article in *Backstage*, sent in his head shot and résumé (the very résumé I'd typed, even written, exaggerating his credits) and been summoned to an audition from which he had emerged victorious.

I tried to see things from his point of view but if I'd become Arthur Miller I'd done so to win Marilyn forever—of course she herself had not been dead for long and I should have paid more attention to the end of their story. Randall wasn't even very nice about it; all I wanted was reassuring lies. But with the same aplomb with which he'd thrown his college roommate's dry ice out the window he packed his bag.

Now every square inch in the West Village is expensive if run-down, but then Randall was able to find a room in a boarding house on Eleventh Street between Fifth and Sixth avenues for fifteen dollars a week, breakfast included.

I arranged to feel pity for Randall's things as he packed them one by one in a cardboard suitcase: his one good blue crewneck sweater, the pegged pair of black pants he'd bought for the Martin Luther King march on Washington, the drip-dry white shirt, the black penny loafers, the four pairs of Argyle socks, the three pairs of dingy Jockey shorts with the broken elastic seams. . . . How would he survive without me?

I needn't have worried. No matter what he wore, he always looked splendid given the intaglio sharpness of his features, his long Grecian nose with the small, concealed nostrils, the tender boyishness of his nape, his royally noncommittal smile and the disconcerting way his eyes darted suddenly to one side—yes, of course, a tic he'd developed to recenter his floating lenses, but, to the uninitiated, a sure sign of intriguing inner conflict.

I always wanted to be wonderful—above merely human behavior, unexpectedly kind, uniquely understanding—and with Randall I was once again wonderfully idiotic. All smiles, I walked him to his Eleventh Street boarding house where he'd be living just next door to Mario, a friend of ours who made paper flowers, limped, smiled all the time, laughed at the wicked things other people said but never uttered an unkind word himself.

Mario was a good-hearted nineteenth-century bohemian, a flower-making Mimi, immersed in a mean-spirited twentieth-century bohemia corrupted by the need for more and more money just to survive. Mario survived by listening to everyone and smiling as he continued to make big paper flowers painted Edwardian colors—taupe, puce, bisque. . . . Perhaps he liked Randall so much because he, too, was a throwback to the nineteenth century. Randall was the B.B. (that is, Beautiful Boy), the Shropshire Apollo, Jude the Illustrious. Soon enough the B.B., who'd ruled men's hearts for thousands of years, would be traded in for a new icon, the Butch Clone. Ganymede must give way to the Eagle—the name, oddly enough, of the best-known leather bar of the seventies, where everyone wore mustaches, creaked becomingly and had showboat muscles. Classic beauty was being replaced by body fascism.

During rehearsals Rhett became determined and efficient. Points of sweat broke out on his unsmiling face, which he mopped at with a heavily perfumed white breast-pocket handkerchief. The actors resisted him; they hadn't yet found their actions, worked out their motivations, uncovered the subtext.

As the writer, of course, I felt I knew the answers to all their questions. A natural ham, I wanted to demonstrate to the actors which words they should emphasize and where they should speed up or pause significantly, but Rhett told me one must never, never give a "line reading" to an actor—did I know nothing about building a character?

I soon saw that if I wanted to be wonderful I shouldn't come to the rehearsals at all. I had read the memoirs of a Broadway director who'd declared that rule number one should be to ban the author from the theater. His work was done and all he could do now was meddle. He could find nothing new in his own work. His method was to impose meaning on words; the actor's job was to release a sense of believable life through a sequence of well-chosen actions. The writer was always correcting misreadings of his lines, whereas the actor should be encouraged to ignore the letter for the spirit of passion.

When I objected once to how broadly a scene was being played, Rhett snapped at me, "*Writers!* You guys never realize that we can't pull it out of a hat. The cast is very shaky— they're going through a delicate chrysalis stage. I promise you you're going to be satisfied with the final product. Remember, we're all working for *you* but you've got to allow us our own crazy working methods or else you're going to spook everyone. Your sighs and frowns are making us very neurotic."

My desire to be wonderful outweighed any brutish urge to protect the integrity of my play. In my extreme vanity I was sure my script was so lively and original that it must be actorproof. After all, hadn't my class at the U. of M. been in awe or at least stitches? Everyone, that is, except our professor, who'd detected in the last act a faulty resolution of the MDQ—a criticism I'd mocked upstairs at the Pancake Palazzo but that now came back to haunt me. Graciously I stopped going to rehearsals. Rhett applauded me for being so professional.

I missed Randall. His distinctive body odor of very dry geraniums baking in the sun still clung to the sheets, but there was no small Virgilian boy to wake up to; now I counted sheep alone without a Corydon to tend the flock. At the office I pecked away at captions or roamed the corridors looking for someone to bullshit with, all the while knowing that eight blocks south and four long blocks west the cast was piecing together my play. I ate my TV dinner at home alone, too poor to own a TV. I cruised up and down Greenwich Avenue and Christopher Street, hung out at Julius's bar, drank too much, went home too late, too often alone. It seemed strange that my play was being done and because of it I had lost Randall, my lover and my best friend.

In the second week of rehearsals the blocking had been completed and everyone knew where he or she was supposed to be going. The cast now did a walk-through of the entire play with book in hand; "Let's put it up," Rhett said as though referring to the Big Top.

Like a moron who waits for his own name to be pronounced during an introduction and ignores the other person's, I paid no attention to Rhett's staging and just listened for my own lines. When I complained that everyone was whispering my text or muttering it without any understanding, Rhett covered his face with his hands, then at last asked through them, "You don't want much, do you? An actor is a very fragile thing, a delicate instrument you can easily overwind. They're feeling a bit wobbly right now, like invalids the first day out of bed."
. . . Properly abashed, I again stopped attending rehearsals until Rhett called me up frantically to tell me that the leading man was great in all the scenes where he had to seduce someone or turn violent, but he couldn't remember his lines or even pronounce half the words. Some serious rewrites were going to have to be done rapidly.

"Couldn't we replace him?" I asked.

"Are you *kidding*! He's a name. We're into the last ten days of rehearsal . . . and the posters have already been printed."

"Right." My friends all teased me that I said "right" when I meant "wrong" and "yes" when I meant "no." Apparently the "right" that meant "wrong" was softer and more drawn out and reflective, less certain than the one that retained its primary meaning. Of course, I was such a pushover that only a disinterested connoisseur of my moods would have bothered working out the nuances; my actions were always obliging. I was relentlessly wonderful.

With a pride in my virtuosity I began to hack away at scene after scene, replacing large blocks of dialogue with strong actions for the leading man or sexy moments where he could improvise *ad libido*. . . .

Rhett had received a visit from a famous older director and playwright whose assistant he'd once been. That man had watched a run-through and exclaimed, "It's wild, but it should be wilder. The props should all be outsize—giant mirror, giant comb. When the black butler rapes the white master he should coat himself with tin foil, as though it were medieval armor —he's a *knight*, get it?" Rhett took careful notes and spared no expense nor extra hours of rehearsal in implementing these suggestions.

Snippets began to appear in the papers announcing the upcoming premiere. My picture was taken though never used. An Italian journalist interviewed me about the American race question, but the interview was never published.

The week of previews began. For the first one I sat alone in front of strangers and heard their reactions. The man behind me kept saying to his wife in a running commentary: "So, my God, he's wandering around like a sleepwalker, he really is writing just stream of—oh, shit, he's not going to dig up that tired old trick, is he? The theater of the absurd is over, folks. And has she just switched into *verse*? Look, now they're all talking in unison, I guess it's supposed to be funny, like one of those thundering Verdi choruses, but it isn't funny, it might seem to work on paper, but onstage it's a big dud. Eeek! He just squeaked through that one, but the audience looks thoroughly confused, the parodies are all off-target, and anyway, why should we be parodying grand opera or Racine or Ionesco in a play about race relations, for Christ's sake!"

I sat there, my ears burning scarlet, fascinated by the rapidity and rightness of this guy's commentary; he was young, already balding, wearing corduroys even in the heat, and his wife looked vexed with him or the play. During the intermission—luckily, unluckily—a friend came up to congratulate me and after that the critic behind me was silent. Suddenly I was seized by dread. I recognized that what had seemed snappy and up-to-date in Ann Arbor was leaden and passé in New York. I knew my play was going to flop. I'd read enough reviews to realize that in the case of a new play the writer gets all the notices. Yet I didn't panic. Somehow I felt indifferent to the outcome, perhaps because my Marilyn had already abandoned me, perhaps because I had scarcely participated in the rehearsals, possibly because in my naïveté I still imagined I was in the capable hands of professionals who knew more about the theater than I, a school kid, could ever hope to know. To have a bad case of opening-night jitters would be vulgar and would needlessly tax other people's patience.

Not that I had any sense of solidarity with the cast, whom I scarcely knew. My agent had to tell me to send the leading lady roses; I was so broke they cost twelve of my last twenty dollars. At the final curtain my agent told me to rush backstage and thank the cast effusively; everyone except Randall looked at me as though I were a stranger.

The opening night meant shooting a gold thread of glamour and wealth into my worsted life. Friends and relatives of Rhett's thronged the little theater wearing diamond rings and white-on-white shirts and suits of fabric as sumptuous as Cadillac upholstery (the men) or Bonwit Teller suits, gypsy spit-curls, matching black crocodile bags and flats (the women). They roared at the feeblest jokes, applauded the set changes and gave a standing ovation to Rhett, the leading lady, even me. Finally I realized they were all investors. Randall looked exquisite as Gainsborough's *Blue Boy* come to life, but the wig and makeup actually diminished his delicate beauty or rather provided one that many other young men could have achieved just as easily. I didn't tell Randall that my only fight during the entire rehearsal period had been with Rhett when he wanted to eliminate the scene with the Blue Boy altogether, which was slowing the pace and adding nothing to the play.

Even my midwestern father, a businessman, came to the opening with two of his cronies. "What's it about, pal," he asked me privately, a solemn smile on his thin lips, "the *usual?*" by which he meant homosexuality, which had been the subject of a short story I'd published under a disguised version of my name in order not to humiliate him (we had the same Christian name).

"Yeah, Dad, there's some of the usual, but there's also another theme—"

"I know. Niggers." He threw away a half-smoked cigar and went in with his guests to see the first act. Somehow the season had drifted into early summer and even at seven-thirty it was too warm and sunny to want to enter the dark theater, a former burlesque hall on the far edge of the district (curtain time was an hour earlier than usual because of the newspaper deadlines). As Puerto Rican boys with bare chests played basketball on the street outside, Rhett's diamonded and perfumed guests reluctantly closed ranks around the plump, ill-groomed critic from the *Times*.

Later at Sardi's, the Broadway restaurant, several of Rhett's people told me I was marvelous and the show a big hit, then they talked about their summer plans and about how long it would take to get Hal's yacht from Miami up to the Cape. The cast members were upstairs in a special private room. I was downstairs at my father's table. He was drunk and congenial and said he always knew I was a nigger lover but why not, that leading lady was a looker, and did I know Union Carbide was reorganizing the whole Great Lakes territory.

The *Times* was lukewarm, though it ended on a positive note, assuring the world that I *could* write. The *Herald Tribune* massacred the play and stated that the Negro in America had enough problems without my adding to them. We were living through the height of the civil rights movement and most white Americans felt that the race problem was well on the way to being solved. White critics couldn't understand why I wanted to stir up trouble and portray black anger. Of course it was my own anger as a gay man I was tapping, even though I was unaware of it.

A week after the play opened Randall moved in with Rhett. I was scandalized. And hurt, partly because I'd been attracted to Rhett myself, partly because the closing of my play robbed me of whatever appeal I might have ever exerted over Randall. Mainly, of course, I just felt talentless and lonely. I had no one to eat dinner with. And these two handsome men had found each other and left me behind, plain and unwanted.

I called Rhett. "Hi. So what's new? I guess Randy's moving in with you."

Rhett's voice shot way up and he had to tug it in like a kite. "Well, yeah, for a while at least, although it's awfully small at my place and I may be too neurotic to live with anyone, you know how crazy clean I am, hours and hours of ironing chinos. . . ." The kite took a sudden nosedive to the ground.

"Well, he's very neat and doesn't take up too much room," I said. "Besides, he's always off at his classes or his temporary job. But maybe he'll be able to stop his filing now."

"Stop? Why? I'm not exactly rich—especially not now, after your play. And then I'm too young to *keep* someone."

I thought, *I* kept him as best I could on a hundred dollars a week. But I registered Rhett's reproach about my play, although I didn't want to apologize for it again. "Anyway," I said wonderfully, "I hope you guys are very happy together. I think Randy needs someone like you." If I'd put sentimental gestures aside I would have had to admit that I knew I wasn't in the same league as Randall as a lover, but as a brother I felt his equal—or rather I didn't even think in those terms. I may have chosen Randall originally because he was a prize, but now I loved him because I'd slept beside him two hundred times.

Within a week Randall was back in his boarding house. He called and asked me if I wanted to have a bite with him. There was a new Greek place on the corner of MacDougal and Third Street that served hamburger steaks with chopped onions in them and gravy on top or thin-sliced London broil, same gravy, and a dollop of mashed potatoes. If you were lucky you didn't have to sit at the counter but could find a two-person booth beside the window from which you could watch all the people go past.

"Hi," he said after we'd chatted for half an hour. That was something he said over and over again throughout a conversation as if to make sure the signal was loud and clear, just as it was my habit to say "right," vaguely, softly, to mean "wrong."

"So why'd you move out of Rhett's?"

"He was too neurotic. He didn't want all his straight friends to know I was living with him so when the doorman announced them unexpectedly he locked me in the bathroom and went off with them and he didn't come back for eight hours. I didn't even have anything to read so I just took off my clothes and swallowed a sleeping pill and slept on the floor. What if there had been a fire? And instead of cheering me up and buying me a beer somewhere or just giving me a little squeeze he was sullen and angry with me. At first he said he thought we'd been unfair to you but then he admitted it made him nervous having a live-in lover and his analyst thought he was just acting out—"

"I thought that *too!*" I interrupted.

But Randall didn't want the focus to stray away from him to Rhett's neuroses. "Hi," he said.

And for the first time ever he extended his hand to me, even if it was only under the table. I, too, would have been embarrassed to hold hands with another man in plain view even though it was 1964 in Greenwich Village. We were comfortable holding hands under the table.

Dear Randall, think how many years have passed by, thirty to be exact, and now we live on separate continents and rarely see each other. You and I are both positive and our prospects aren't exactly brilliant. When you discovered just recently that after years of testing negative, you'd goofed up and somehow become infected, you went into a dark, unshakable depression, like the ones you used to sink into in your twenties.

But now you've climbed up out of it again, thanks to the bouncy black humor you've picked up from twelve years in AA and the tender devotion of Saul, your Orthodox Jewish boyfriend, who after a summer in the sun could just about pass for an Indian on the back lot of United Artists. Before you could come to your present equanimity you had to live through your parents' double suicide (your dad's was rapid, bullet in the brain, mom's lingering, binge after binge). You had to take too much acid and even get thrown off Fire Island of all places, but as you once told me, you'd been so disciplined and lonely as a teenager that your late adolescence in your thirties constituted the return of the repressed.

There was a long period there in the 1970s, five or six years, when you didn't make much sense. You needed yellow jackets to go to work and black birds to smooth out your high and, probably, scarlet tanagers to sleep. You thought your lover of those years, Benny, had been converted to devil worship and was going to sacrifice you; all I know is that when you took refuge with me Benny mounted a machine gun on the roof of a neighboring building and threatened to open fire unless I released you. Of course you liked all the excitement, Benny's station wagon with the quadraphonic sound belting out Diana Ross as you headed with eight hunky guys on acid toward the Killington ski slopes. It was only when you lost your job and had a seizure and broke a rib that you knew the seventies had run out. You and your Saul escaped out of the wreckage like Aeneas and Anchises from the fall of Troy—he the Aeneas who bore you, his small, handsome dad, on his strong shoulders.

How you've changed! We lived together for five years until my straight shrink convinced me I'd never "get well" until I left you. The day I moved out you kept playing a record called "Seven Rooms of Gloom" though we only had three. Who would have thought that proper Randall from Bloomington, Indiana, would go on to lead such a racy life? Mine was pretty weird, too, until alcoholism and the death of our whole generation caught up with me.

I sobered up and moved to France twelve years ago, but we spend holidays together every year or two. Remember when we went to Wales in November, of all times, saw Portmeirion in a hailstorm, a fragile make-believe summer resort of fake façades in nougat colors fronting smaller houses? Remember how I was so horny I had sex with the village idiot I picked up at dusk in the public toilet at Caernarvon beside the ruined black castle where the Prince of Wales's investiture always takes place?

The last time we saw each other you came to Paris, just a year ago. We went to Malmaison, Napoleon and Josephine's country house, and you enjoyed everything and wanted to know about everything, you who were so sullen and depressed as a youngster.

The one thing you haven't lost is your beauty, though sometimes your hair color, shifting from ash to straw, seems too much an improvement on nature. To me you're just good old Randy, sometimes too much a motor mouth, sometimes spookily religious (you're always threatening to become a monk), sometimes almost unbearably flippant about all the tragedies we're forced to live through, although I approve of the style and get into trouble with pious friends when I try to emulate it. To me you're just Randy, but when I introduce you to Parisians they often say to me later, "But that's the face that launched a thousand ships!"

I've gotten fat and gray and creak when I stand up, but you've still a thirty-inch waist, lots of ash hair and unspotted baby hands you hold at improbable angles. Politically correct gays don't like it when writers praise physical beauty but they should understand your beauty imposed a scenario on your life. You never had to go after anyone; your looks brought them all to you. Two straight guys you worked with told me later that you were the only man they ever went to bed with, but no wonder, no one could or can resist you. You talk all the time to your intimates but early on you learned to be silent in company and just turn on your klieg-light smile. People would hate you or love you but no one could be indifferent. Sometimes in New York you're at a party where everyone is black or Puerto Rican or, as our parents would have said, "ethnic," and suddenly someone looks at you hard and says "Shit, Randall, you are the *only* fuckin' Wasp!" And though that identification means nothing to you, you've learned to live with the reactions it provokes in other people.

For so many years you were the B.B., but now as the Beautiful Man you take care of lots of lost people, the young drunks in AA or the homeless vagabonds whom you bathe and feed at St. Luke's. You even spend the night with your homeless men once a week, watching out to make sure no one robs or attacks someone else or cracks a rib in a seizure, as you once did after all your black birds and yellow jackets flew away.

Naturally I've left out the most important thing in these vignettes—your decison to leave the theater. Once my play flopped you turned your back on the commercial theater and acted for another two years at the Caffe Cino, the minuscule forcing-shed in the Village for a new, burgeoning performing spirit (I'm sounding like a publicity release). There as Joe Cino hovered in the back and squeezed espresso out of a noisy machine, you and May would stand on the tiny stage, all nine square feet of it, and declaim for the three full tables and four empty ones. I was too snobbish to write for such an amateurish joint after my professional launch in the uptown theater. Now I see what a fool I was. The only good playwrights of the period—Lanford Wilson, Leonard Melfi, Robert Patrick—got their start at the Caffe Cino.

Despite that thrilling interlude in your life, you decided one day you didn't want to stand up before one more audience or submit to one more audition. You were no longer willing to walk down Sixth Avenue wearing a sandwich board just because it was a chance to be seen. You went off, as Americans so blithely do, into another career altogether, a much more respectable one which required you to wear a three-piece suit and beautiful silk rep ties five days a week, a charmingly preppy foil to the antique terror of your beauty.

I wrote play after play, all duds, none optioned, a waste of six years of my life. Now all I have to do is just think of writing the words "Act One, Scene One," and I become as sick as Pavlov's dog. Because of my failure I now pretend I left what

I grandly refer to as the "Theater," sweeping up my skirts in a huff, but the Theater never knew I existed and when recently I was in Newport and met that old cousin of the Windsors who'd written the only positive review my play had received, he had no idea what I was talking about, he the only person who'd vindicated my grandiose ambitions.

By the way, Graybelly became a theater critic in New York and Tom a director of an important regional theater.

What we learned from the theater, improbably enough, was how to be gay. You were in gay plays by those pioneers at the Cino, the first harbingers of the New York Spring that would explode in 1969. As far back as the Pancake Palazzo I was learning that if one wore *enough* pancake one could be a convincing enough Regina in her very own itty-bitty Pitti Palazzo.

But if we've both left the theater, I still see our first apartment on MacDougal as a stage set and I'm at the door now, dull and tired from another idle day at the office, though once I make my entrance and hear May's and your voices "off," I smile, call out, "Hi!," light a Kool and sit down to a cup of instant and listen, smiling, resentful, to your hissing, urgent voices.

Edmund White was born in Cincinnati in 1940. He has taught literature and creative writing at Yale, Johns Hopkins, New York University and Columbia, was a full professor of English at Brown, and served as executive director of the New York Institute for the Humanities. In 1983 he received a Guggenheim fellowship and the award in literature from the American Academy and Institute of Arts and Letters. In 1993 he was made a Chevalier de l'Ordre des Arts et Lettres. For his book *Genet: A Biography* (1994), he was awarded the National Book Critics Circle Award and the Lambda Literary Award. His other books include *Forgetting Elena, Nocturnes for the King of Naples, States of Desire: Travels in Gay America, A Boy's Own Story, Caracole* and *The Beautiful Room Is Empty*. He lives in Paris.

A NOTE ON THE TYPE

The text of this book was set in Fairfield Medium, a typeface designed by the distinguished American artist and engraver Rudolph Ruzicka (1883–1978). Both his original Fairfield and this bolder version display the sober and sane qualities of a master craftsman whose talent has long been dedicated to clarity.

Rudolph Ruzicka was born in Bohemia and came to America in 1894. He designed and illustrated many books and was the creator of a considerable list of individual prints in a variety of techniques.

Composed by PennSet, Bloomsburg, Pennsylvania
Printed and bound by The Haddon Craftsmen,
Scranton, Pennsylvania
Designed by Brooke Zimmer